"Do you have

"I have to go check on the family beach house, a week next Friday," Cameron went on. "Why don't you come along?"

"I'll...I'll have to check my date book." That was a laugh. She *never* had those sorts of plans.

"We can go to Galveston, too," he urged. "Make a day of it."

She said nothing, knowing perfectly well what being alone with Cameron in some isolated beach house would lead to.

But what if...what if she just said yes? Maybe she could just seize the moment and not worry about the consequences. Could it hurt, spending a day and, yes, a night, with a gorgeous, sexy man?

Sure it could. More deeply than anything else in the world. But...

ABOUT THE AUTHOR

"We've got a big, close family," says Judith Linsley, who writes as Marie Beaumont with her sister, Ellen Rienstra. "We've each got three children, live practically next door to each other, and, for the past six years, we've been writing together, too." Judith and Ellen have both lived in Beaumont, Texas, nearly all their lives, so when they started writing contemporary romance novels, it seemed natural to honor their hometown by using its name as their pseudonym.

Judith and Ellen have also written a pictorial history of Beaumont and a historical romance. *Halfway Home* is their second Harlequin Superromance novel.

Books by Marie Beaumont

HARLEQUIN SUPERROMANCE
391—CATHERINE'S SONG

Marie
Beaumont

HALFWAY HOME

Harlequin Books

TORONTO • NEW YORK • LONDON
AMSTERDAM • PARIS • SYDNEY • HAMBURG
STOCKHOLM • ATHENS • TOKYO • MILAN
MADRID • WARSAW • BUDAPEST • AUCKLAND

Published March 1993

ISBN 0-373-70538-7

HALFWAY HOME

CHAPTER ONE

THE GIRL SEATED across the desk from her looked sullen, a little defiant, studiedly unafraid.

But Mickey Mulvaney wasn't fooled. The expression was a mask. Beneath it lurked anger, and beneath that, paralyzing fear. If seven years of working with troubled teenagers hadn't taught her to recognize a smoke screen when she saw one, she would still have known. The girl's expression was the same one she herself had worn each time she'd sat on the other side of a desk like this. And those times had been plenty.

"Come on, Brandy," she said to the sixteen-year-old. "I'll show you around Harbor House."

For a moment Brandy didn't move, and Mickey wasn't sure she was going to. Finally, slowly, Brandy stood up, resistance in every rigid line of her young body.

Pretending not to notice, Mickey led the way out of her office into the large living area of Harbor House, the Houston halfway house for teenage girls where she served as director. "This is where we get together, have meetings, entertain guests," she explained. She indicated the way through a double-wide doorway into a smaller room. "This is the dining room, and that way's the kitchen. Everyone takes turns cooking and cleaning up." She glanced sideways at Brandy.

The girl's sullen expression never changed. A real shame, because in spite of the heavy makeup, the cheap revealing clothing, the multicolored hair, she was pretty. But Mickey was used to the lack of response. She had seen it before.

"All the girls sleep upstairs." She moved into the hall, then started up the narrow staircase, followed by the silent Brandy. They entered one of the two second-story bedrooms. "You'll share this room with Leslie Oliver. She's about your age. I think you'll like her." And Leslie would be good for Brandy, Mickey thought. Leslie was friendly, motherly, might help to bring Brandy out of her self-constructed cage.

For the first time, a faint interest flickered in Brandy's eyes. "Where is she?"

"She's at work. The other two girls, Joni Jefferson and Lisa Parigi, stayed after school. They're trying out for the basketball team. If you have time before you go to work, you can bring up your gear and unpack."

Brandy glanced around the spare, neatly furnished room, her eyes flicking over the two old unmatched desks, the twin beds with their navy-and-red comforters, the chests painted a bright, cheery red to cover the nicks and gouges. Without comment, she turned to go downstairs.

"Brandy."

The girl stopped but didn't look around.

"We all work together here, and we all follow the rules." Mickey kept her tone even, without inflection. "You have to follow them to stay here." Her voice gentled. "We want you to stay."

Brandy hesitated. Then, almost imperceptibly, she nodded and headed down the stairs. For a moment Mickey remained behind, fighting the impulse to go after her, hold her close, give her what comfort she could. But she didn't, because at this point, Brandy would only have pushed her away. She wasn't ready for love and sympathy. For now, she needed a structured environment, and that Mickey could provide. The other would come later.

Brandy's was another damaged soul, only partially healed. Mickey's job was to finish mending it and launch it into the real world. But this looked like a tough one, maybe the toughest she'd ever handled. For a split second the old uncertainty jabbed at her. Even now, at age thirty, after years of counseling that had taught her to deal with her own problems and a graduate degree in social work that entitled her to help others with theirs, she could still have occasional doubts.

But she was good at her job, mostly because she worked at it so hard. She could help Brandy. She *would* help her. She took a deep breath and went downstairs.

Twenty minutes later, with Brandy on her way to her after-school job, Mickey faced the clutter on her desk. As always, untidy stacks of paper took up much of its surface, and all her hard work never seemed to reduce them. Jeanie, the part-time secretary, helped, of course, but the number of forms Mickey had to fill in each week was mind-boggling.

Besides Jeanie, a lot of people helped at Harbor House, including a case manager, a family counselor, three house managers and a housekeeper, not to mention Connie Allen, the consulting psychologist. The girls were encouraged to do much of the cooking and cleaning themselves. And there was M.C., of course. He took up most of the slack. But there was never a time when the work was entirely done.

Ignoring the accusing stacks of paperwork, Mickey reached for a lone manila folder, with edges limp and worn from use. Brandy Williford's case file. One of the secrets of dealing with kids in trouble was to stay one step ahead of

them, and that included knowing more about them than
they did about themselves. Mickey had known better than
to ask Brandy questions; that would only have antagonized
her. This file would at least tell Mickey where to begin.

Before she could dive into it, the front door opened and
someone came in, whistling an off-key approximation of
"Seventy-Six Trombones." Mickey grinned. "Wipe your
feet," she called.

Instantly, the whistling was accompanied by a vigorous
stamping in four-four time. A few seconds later a short, wiry
man with a weathered face and a shock of white hair appeared in the doorway to her office. Melchior Caedmon
Mulvaney, better known as M.C.—even to his daughter
Mickey—stood poised on the balls of his feet, exuding raw
energy and smiling the faintly larcenous smile that always
meant he was pleased with himself.

"Hello, M.C." Mickey put down the folder. "You just
missed our newest guest."

"As a matter of fact, I didn't," he countered. "I caught
her outside on the walk and introduced myself."

Mickey remembered the girl's total lack of response.
"Was she impressed?"

He thought a moment. "She might have been a little...
reserved. But that won't last," he promised, a glint lurking
in eyes as blue as the feathers of a jay. "She'll come
around."

Mickey's grin grew. "I don't doubt it." No one could
withstand M.C. for long. Including herself, she remembered ruefully. After all, he'd literally talked his way back
into her life, when she had needed and wanted no one.

"We're full again," she said unnecessarily. M.C. knew it
as well as she did, but she needed his input on what they
were going to do about it.

"Yep. Good thing I've found a new place for us."

Mickey just stared at him. She should have known. He was always one step ahead of her, of everyone. That was why he dealt so well with the girls at Harbor House. The board of directors had given tentative approval for a larger place, but she hadn't dreamed he was already looking for one.

"You have?" she asked finally. She didn't even ask him the whys or wherefores. M.C. had his ways.

"Yep," he said again. His smile broadened. Like a child, he couldn't hide it when he was really pleased with himself. "The owner's moving to Dallas with his daughter, but he can't quite bring himself to sell. He wants to lease the house on a long-term basis, for a price we can't afford to pass up."

Worth looking into, Mickey thought. "What's it like?"

"Big. Old."

"M.C..."

"All right." He lifted his shoulders in a shrug. "It's worn-out. Structurally sound, but needs a lot of work. That's why I'm here."

That's not the only reason you're here, Mickey reflected, *but I haven't quite figured out the rest of them yet.* "Okay," was all she said, remembering the miracles he had wrought on this house. "Where is it?"

"That's the beauty of it. Over in West Village, not too far from here. The girls won't even have to change schools. It's close to where the express bus goes by, headed to the mall, so they can get to work easier."

"West Village?" She stared at him blankly. "What do you think those people are going to say about having a halfway house in the middle of the neighborhood?"

For a second, but only a second, M.C. looked a little less sure of himself. "Hard to say. It's on Shepherd Drive, right next to where they're turning some of the old houses into a shopping district. I don't think they can keep us out. Houston has no zoning laws, and their deed restrictions are probably too old to cover this situation. We'll have to meet with their neighborhood homeowners' association and explain exactly what we're doing before their imaginations run away with them. That's the best approach."

Certainly the best approach her father could take, Mickey thought, since he was fully capable, as the song went, of selling oceanfront property in Arizona. "I hope it'll work, because right after Brandy was assigned to come here, I got two more referrals this morning that I had to turn down. We need to move, fast."

"Right." M.C. rose and stood for a moment, chewing his lip and thoughtfully slapping his hand on his khaki-clad leg. Mickey watched him fondly. With his trim build and his wise, bright eyes, he was still, at fifty-two, a fine-looking man. In spite of the checkered life he'd led, he had a style, an innate class about him. And the Lord knew the ladies loved him. He flirted outrageously with them. She even had to watch him with some of the society matrons on the advisory board.

Without another word, he turned and walked out. Then he stuck his head back in the doorway. "Sorry, darlin'. I just realized I've got my work cut out for me. Be back by supper."

The house seemed very quiet after he had gone, as though in the wake of a minor tornado. Mickey stared at the wall opposite her desk, where her framed degrees reminded her of her achievements. It was just over four years ago that M.C. had shown up at the door of her Houston apartment and informed her, a little awkwardly, that he was her father. Her father, whom she hadn't seen since she was tiny, in fact barely remembered at all. After years of conditioning by a bitter mother, Mickey had been suspicious and resentful, certainly unwilling to risk her almost nonexistent trust on a man she'd always been taught was an irresponsible alcoholic. But something about his expression, as though he expected her to slam the door in his face, had touched a place deep inside her. Besides, she'd had to admit she was curious about the man who was biologically responsible for her existence. She'd let him in.

That was the last time she had ever seen him hesitant about anything. Once he started talking, she hadn't had a chance. He'd explained that he had retired from the sea, had straightened out his life and hadn't taken a drink for more than three years. Then he'd fixed her with those jay-blue eyes, placed his hand over his heart and announced that he wanted to get to know his only child. She couldn't help laughing.

Without her quite knowing how or why, that had settled it. Just like that, he'd rented an apartment near hers and had become a part of her life.

Nothing of their mutual past, of unanswered questions, of unhealed hurts, was ever discussed or even mentioned, but true to his word, he'd wasted no time in trying to build a real relationship between them. It hadn't been easy, but he'd never wavered, even when Mickey had tried, as she had often, to shut him out. With infinite patience he'd stuck around, undemanding and supportive. Gradually she'd relaxed her ever-present guard a little and allowed herself to take the first tentative steps toward trusting him, particularly since, just as he'd promised, he never touched a drop of alcohol. The frail hope, buried for so long, that she might find someone who wouldn't let her down was resurrected, then began to grow.

As if he were trying to make up for all the lost years, M.C. gave of himself. He earned his certification as a counselor for drug and alcohol abuse and began to help her in her work. Sooner than she would ever have dreamed, she came to depend on him for everything from reaching a difficult kid to painting the house. If she still couldn't ever bring herself to hug him, still stiffened sometimes when he put his arm around her, that was her problem.

Absently, she smoothed the curled edge of the folder, wondering how, in such a short time, M.C. had become so indispensable to her. Actually, it was frightening. She'd learned early not to depend on anyone but herself. Now she wondered how she could ever manage without him.

Ridiculous, she reminded herself. She could make it without M.C. After all, she'd taken care of herself, and her mother, too, until her mother's death. Self-reliance was one of the things she tried to pass on to the girls who came under her wing. But M.C. made things infinitely easier, not to mention a lot more fun. Over time he'd become very dear to her.

How she'd sprung from someone so outgoing, so completely at ease in his dealings with others, was beyond her. It didn't speak much for the heredity factor in personality determination. Actually, the only traits Mickey could see that her father had passed along to her were her small stature, her blue eyes and a strong instinct for survival.

She finally made herself look at the unopened folder. Brandy's file. She opened it and flipped quickly through the assorted material: birth certificate, probation papers, reports from the juvenile court—so much information that the folder bowed out at the sides. She went more slowly through the school transcripts and test scores. Just as she'd suspected, Brandy was an underachiever—bright, but lacking discipline or motivation. It was easy to see almost the exact moment she had begun to use drugs; in one six-week period about a year and a half ago, her grades had fallen from mediocre to disastrous. Only in the past six months had they begun a slow upward trend, and finally, in the previous grading period, had averaged out the highest yet. Mickey made a mental note. That was a starting point.

She continued to flip through dog-eared pages until she came to one headed Psychological Evaluation. This was what she wanted to see. Brandy's official problem might be chemical dependency, but it was only a symptom. Everything else in her file recorded results; the evaluation might provide her with some of the causes, although she had a feeling she knew them already. She picked it up and began to read.

The story was grim . . . and hauntingly familiar. Brandy Williford had been abused, physically and sexually, by her stepfather. When she'd finally told her mother, her stepfather had denied it, and her mother, who was already frightened of him, at first chose not to believe her. By the time her mother was finally made to see the truth and had divorced him, the damage was done. Brandy, her self-image at rock bottom, was headed for trouble, and for the next two years she'd found it with amazing regularity. Alcohol, drugs, shoplifting, casual sex—there was very little she hadn't tried.

Mickey stopped a moment, remembering. Then she pushed her mane of straight black hair away from her face and made herself read on. Brandy had finally been caught, not only with stolen goods but with marijuana, and had been placed in a drug-rehab center. For a time she'd made no progress at all. Then her behavior seemed to turn around. She'd been declared sufficiently rehabilitated to go to Harbor House, to prepare her for her return to the real world.

That was where Mickey came in.

She closed the file and drummed her bitten nails on the desk. From what little she'd seen of Brandy, she was afraid the teenager wasn't really rehabilitated; she just wanted everyone to think she was. A difficult case, but after all, that was Mickey's job. Being sent the worst cases was a back-handed compliment, an unspoken tribute to her skills. There had to be a way to reach Brandy. After all, Mickey reminded herself, someone had found a way to reach *her*.

In the meantime, she had other problems besides Brandy. Until someone "graduated," which took at least six months, even longer under the new guidelines they were expected to comply with, Harbor House was now full. But if M.C. could pull off the West Village deal, they'd soon be moving into a larger place.

She wondered how he would deal with the West Village residents. While the neighborhood didn't house the super-rich, it was still prestigious, reputedly close-knit, and hadn't yet fallen prey to the deterioration that had wasted much of that section of the city.

She put it out of her mind. From experience, she knew she could depend on M.C. She set Brandy's file on one of the few clear places on her desk and pulled down a grant application form from the top of one of the other stacks.

"FOUR O'CLOCK TOMORROW, then. I'll see you there."

Cameron Scott III returned the buff-colored receiver to its cradle, leaned back in his chair and absently loosened his tie. He couldn't keep a slow grin from spreading across his face. Another space as good as leased. Of the original sixteen buildings he'd bought for Phase One, only three remained to be renovated. At this rate, he'd be able to start on

Phase Two of the Village Walk project considerably sooner than projected.

He swiveled the chair to his right and looked at the map that covered almost one whole wall of his spacious, well-decorated office—a street map, blown up to show the part of Houston that residents called "inside the Loop," the area lying inside the giant network of freeways encircling the city. West Village, located near the center of the map, was outlined in red. On either side of Shepherd Drive, the busy thoroughfare that cut through the center of the Village, two blocks had been highlighted with a yellow marker and two more blocks with fluorescent pink. Phases One and Two of the Village Walk. His pet project.

Over the past twenty or so years, increased traffic had made these homes fronting along Shepherd Drive less desirable, less valuable than the ones in the interior of the Village. As the residents had died or moved, these houses were being sold at a reduced price and converted to low-rent apartments or shops. Eventually the deterioration would spread to the quieter streets in the interior. It was happening now in many older parts of Houston, and Cameron didn't want it to happen here. Not in West Village.

Fortunately, he was able to do something to prevent it. Extending a long arm to reach a file cabinet behind him, he pulled out a folder entitled "Village Walk: Projected Profit," and laid it on the highly polished desktop. In spite of Houston's sagging oil economy, he had succeeded as a real estate developer because of good business sense, an almost uncanny feel for which way the market was going to jump and—he was the first to admit it—a lot of luck. All of which put him in a position to indulge himself with the Village Walk project.

That was why he had come up with this plan. He had recruited a group of investors, then, for Phase One, had bought the houses for two blocks along Shepherd, renovated them, and was now in the process of leasing them to merchants. The resulting shops and galleries wouldn't be low-budget, fly-by-night operations like those that had crept into some of the crumbling neighborhoods in Houston. They would be part of a carefully planned shopping district that would produce a profit for himself and his investors, but would also preserve the buildings and the integrity of the neighborhood.

It would work. He would make it work.

So far it was going even better than he'd planned. He'd already talked to the homeowners involved in Phase Two, and all had expressed a willingness to sell if the price was right. Well, almost all. Edward Brock, the elderly owner of the house on the southwest corner of the project, had been hesitant. It wasn't that he really wanted to stay, he had told Cameron; he was getting too old to live alone. In fact, he was planning to move to Dallas, where his children lived. But he loved his home and couldn't quite bring himself to give it up forever.

Cameron understood how he felt, because he himself had grown up in West Village, in the house where his parents still lived. In fact, he'd come back to West Village a few years ago, buying and renovating a house a couple of blocks away from his parents' home, even though at this point in his career he could have lived anywhere in Houston he chose. Since then, he'd talked several young career-oriented families into moving into the Village, including his friends Keith and Penny Rhodes, who had moved into the house across the street from him. West Village was a good neighborhood, a solid neighborhood, the kind of place you'd want to spend your whole life in. But Brock's house fronted on Shepherd, and Cameron was sure he'd eventually decide to move.

Suddenly restless, he raised his arms above his head, stretching to get the kinks out of his back. The pent-up energy inside him clamored for release, and he knew he'd been at his desk too long. He wanted to get back out to the job site. He needed to see concrete results. Or maybe he just needed to run a few miles.

He refiled the folder and pushed back his chair, but before he could leave, the buzzer on his desk sounded. "Cameron? Call on line two. Miss Cunningham." The electronic echo of the intercom didn't quite hide the amusement in Vicky's voice.

"Thanks, Vicky." Cameron chuckled. He heard from Miss Cunningham often, so often that if a day went by without a call from her he felt a little deprived. He picked up the phone with one hand and took out his pen with the other, knowing from experience he might need it.

"Hello, Miss Cunningham," he said with genuine fondness. "How are you?" Jessamine Cunningham, a lady of inherited means, served as perennial president of the West Village Homeowners' Association, and no situation was too trivial to attract her interest. She lived a block off Shepherd, and always knew what was going on all over West Village. She'd taught several generations of West Village schoolchildren because, in her day, schoolteaching was one of the few socially acceptable professions open to genteel unmarried females. Now in her late seventies, Miss Cunningham was an intimidating figure to some, a thorn in the sides of others, but there was no question that she ruled the neighborhood. Cameron, who had known her since he was a small boy, loved, admired and enjoyed her, even when she was chewing him out about something.

"Cameron." The voice was beautifully modulated as always, but she hadn't replied to his polite question, and she never failed to observe the amenities. "There's something I think you should know."

"Yes?" He wondered if it was anything more serious than last time, when the workmen had failed to pick up all the trash and a small brown paper sack had blown into her yard. He began to doodle on his desk pad.

"I was speaking with Mr. Brock earlier today, and he says he has decided what to do about his house." She paused dramatically.

"Good." His pencil slowed. Brock was going to sell. But what was the problem? In spite of Miss Cunningham's complaints about the construction mess, she'd bestowed her approval on the project and had even become a little proprietary about it.

"You may not think so when you hear me out," Miss Cunningham stated in tones of doom. "He plans to lease it to some group for a halfway house. For teenage girls with drug problems." Her voice came dangerously near to rising. "Cameron," she pronounced, "this is *not* good."

"*What?*" The pencil dropped onto the pad. For a moment of total shock, he could hardly comprehend what she was saying. "Why?"

"Because this was to be a controlled area, one where we could feel safe—"

"No." Some part of him realized he had done the unthinkable. He had interrupted Miss Cunningham. But he was too stunned to worry about it. "What I mean is, why is Brock doing this? He knows I want the house."

Miss Cunningham didn't even seem to notice. "He feels that if he leases it, he can always come back to it. If he sells it, he'll lose it forever."

Cameron bit down hard on the word he had been about to say. Even in the stress of the moment, Miss Cunningham would never have forgiven him that one. *Temper, temper,* he reminded himself. But a halfway house! In a commercial shopping district, in the middle of a neighborhood like West Village? It was bad any way you looked at it. For everyone. "Why didn't he tell me?" He tried to keep his voice down. "*I'll* lease it from him."

"I told him so. But he thinks that keeping the place as a residence, such as it is, will change it less than turning it into a restaurant or a shop."

Cameron's mind spun furiously. This could put a real kink in his plans for Phase Two.

"Cameron? Did you hear me?"

"Yes, ma'am." For a second Cameron was back in the third grade, with Miss Cunningham calling him down—for the hundredth time—for gazing out the window during math. "I'm sorry. I was just trying to think."

"Something should be done. These are troubled girls, Cameron. We don't know how they might behave. I thought your project was supposed to prevent things like this from happening." He didn't miss the note of reproach in her voice.

"It is, Miss Cunningham." Cameron set his jaw. "I'll talk to Brock. Surely we can come to some kind of an agreement."

As he hung up the phone, he wondered what in hell he could come up with. At this point, he had no idea. Maybe when he calmed down he'd think of something. He hoped the word wouldn't spread before he could take care of the situation. He didn't need the West Village residents turning against the project. He was on their side, after all; from the beginning, this had been primarily a labor of love.

He took off his glasses and rubbed his eyes. Now it looked as though this project might also become a terrific pain. In the neck, for starters.

MICKEY STARED resentfully at page 7, part B, line 3 of the grant form and wondered how in heaven anyone could be expected to understand, let alone follow, the instructions. No wonder so few people wanted to make their careers in social services. Working with disturbed teenagers was a cinch compared to dealing with the paperwork. Better let Dave, the accountant, handle this part of it. He could work magic with numbers, and what was even more amazing to Mickey, he seemed to enjoy it. To each his own. She tossed the paper back onto the stack.

She was reaching for another when she caught a movement from the corner of her eye. She glanced over. A gargantuan yellow tiger cat stood in the doorway.

"Hi, Rooney," she crooned.

He answered with a sound somewhere between a rasp and a squeak and regarded her from impassive amber eyes, one of which was permanently fixed at half-mast.

"Come on in." She patted the chair beside her invitingly.

He crouched low, bunching his bulky legs tight under him, paused for a moment, then launched himself into the air, clearing the threshold by at least a foot. He executed a perfect four-point landing. It was his usual way of entering a room, and no one had ever figured out why he did it. Mickey had always assumed it was because, at some time in his murky youth, he'd gotten a door slammed on him.

He sauntered over to the desk, jumping to its cluttered top with one smooth, powerful movement. Mickey scratched under his chin and he stretched his neck with pleasure, emitting a rusty purr, one fang protruding, as usual, from under a scar on his lip. When she stopped scratching him, she quickly pulled her hand back to a respectful distance. He glared at her a moment, then, threading his way between stacks of papers, climbed into Mickey's out box, his favorite napping spot. He settled himself comfortably and, giving a huge yawn that exposed a whole arsenal of large, pointed teeth, slowly closed his eyes and went to sleep.

Rooney, the renegade, the roué. He'd been with Mickey ever since he was a young tom, when she'd gotten him off the street, half-starved, scruffy, already hopelessly scarred from fighting. She'd cleaned him up and fed him until he'd become sleek and fat. But with his half-shut eye, protruding tooth and notched left ear, he still retained a strong air of disrepute.

His was a sociable temperament—sometimes unfortunately so. His idea of enough human attention extended considerably beyond what most people were willing to give, and he was happy to make his point with a well-placed nip on the hands or ankles of the unwary. Everyone at Harbor House had learned to pet him carefully, so she brought him to work with her from time to time, where he made himself entirely at home.

He deserved a home. Mickey loved him and he loved her, no strings attached. Until M.C. had come along, Rooney was the only living being who had. She could look at him and see herself—a little scarred, maybe, but unbeaten.

An energetic knock at the front door made her jump. She frowned. Sometimes unexpected visitors were the police, with news that one of the girls was in trouble. But right this minute, everyone seemed to be doing well. Even Brandy. In the few days since her arrival she was at least following the rules, though she still didn't have much to say. Mickey mentally crossed her fingers and went to answer the door.

It stuck, as it always did except in the driest of weather. She jerked at it. On the third yank it swung open to reveal not a police officer but a tall man in a well-cut business suit, an attaché case in one hand. A salesman, she thought, selling office equipment. Then again, maybe not.

"May I help you?" She was still trying to figure him out. Tall, yes, but not exactly slender; his athletic build filled out his suit very nicely. Steel-rimmed glasses. Thick, sun-streaked brown hair, tanned regular features. On the rugged side of handsome, but very attractive. He could have stepped off the cover of *Business Week*. Then she looked up—straight up—and met his gaze. All her speculation ground to a halt.

Through his glasses, gray eyes, as clear as mountain pools and just as cool, probed hers. The question in them did nothing to diminish his quiet self-confidence. He didn't seem arrogant, just sure of himself. Whatever he did, this man had to be good at it. She resisted the urge to step backward and tried to look away. But she couldn't. For a moment they stared at each other without speaking. Finally she was able to jerk her eyes away, but she still felt as if he was standing too close.

"Is Mr. Mulvaney in?" His voice was deep, pleasant-timbred.

Mickey wondered briefly whether he really knew her father or whether his pitch was directed at whoever happened to be the man of the house. "I'm sorry, he won't be in until late this evening. I'm his daughter, Mickey Mulvaney." She smiled politely. "Maybe I can help you."

"My name is Cameron Scott, Ms. Mulvaney." He extended his hand, and she hesitated only a moment before she took it. His grip was firm, surprisingly callused. "I'm a Houston real estate developer, and I'd like to talk to your father about the proposed new location for your halfway house."

CHAPTER TWO

PROPOSED LOCATION. Mickey stiffened. Now she understood. He'd come to tell her he didn't want her halfway house in his neighborhood. If he couldn't change her mind by being polite, he'd resort to threats. Then things would get unpleasant. She'd been through these situations before.

Well, he wasn't going to chase her away. M.C. had shown her the house yesterday, and as usual, he'd been right. In spite of the work it needed, it was perfect for Harbor House—and for her girls. That was the important thing. And she knew there was no legal way this man could keep her out.

Lightning-quick, she dropped his hand, but held his gaze. Strangely, his eyes held none of the hostility she usually ran into in these situations. Only courtesy, friendly but impersonal. Still, she had the uncanny feeling that those gray eyes were seeing right straight through to what she was thinking.

"I'm the director here," she said, still politely.

Surprise flickered across his face, but he masked it quickly. "Maybe I need to talk to you then."

You've got that right. She moved back from the door. "Won't you come in?"

"Thanks." She opened the screen door and he stepped inside. He was even bigger than she'd realized. He made her feel crowded.

"We can talk in my office." She led the way through the living area. From the corner of her eye she could see him looking around. She felt her hackles rise. She was proud of the house. The living room was light and airy, with tall, old-fashioned double-hung windows. She had decorated it herself on a shoestring, had tried to make it warm and inviting, like a real home. But the curtains were of an inexpensive cotton print, the scratched oak floor covered with a cheap area rug, the secondhand furniture slip-covered. She was well aware of what it must look like to someone accustomed to fine, expensive things. Like this man. She glanced up at him and was surprised to see only interest in his gaze. Approval? She must be imagining it.

She ushered him into her office, sat down at her desk, and motioned him to a chair facing her. Then she folded her hands, schooled her expression to courteous attention and waited.

He hesitated. "Ms. Mulvaney, I'm not here to spoil anyone's plans." His words were deliberate, considered. "But I should tell you that there are some potential problems if you move into the Brock house."

"For whom, Mr. Scott? You or me?"

"For neither one of us, I hope. I came to tell you what I'm doing, find out what you want to do and see how we can work this out in everyone's best interest."

That would be a first. Her own experience had been that, no matter how reasonable they might sound, people were rarely interested in compromise. But he was being polite, even sounded sincere, so she might as well listen. "How do you propose to do that?" she asked coolly.

"I don't know." He grinned and shrugged, palms up. The gesture roughed up his sophisticated veneer, making him look boyish. In spite of herself, she felt the tug of attraction. "There has to be a way, if we both work at it." He spread his hands. They were big, tanned. Instantly, she remembered the strength in his handshake.

"Let me explain a little about my project," he went on, and Mickey's gaze flew back to his face. "A group of investors, myself included, are renovating some of the West Village houses along Shepherd Drive. Most of these houses are rental properties now, because the original residents moved out years ago to get away from the traffic. But plenty of the older families still live right off Shepherd, and they're interested in keeping West Village just as it is now. A safe, quiet place." He put an emphasis, subtle but unmistakable, on the words. "We're also trying to attract younger people to ensure the neighborhood's future. One of the things the residents are worried about is that deterioration will begin on Shepherd, then spread into the interior." The cool gray eyes bored into her.

She was careful to keep her expression blank. He sounded pleasant, reasonable. Plausible. But then, so did a lot of other people when they were trying to con someone. Like a whisper of cold air, a memory of her stepfather brushed her mind.

She forced her concentration back to what the man in front of her was saying. By deterioration, he meant places like Harbor House. He'd get to the bottom line in a minute. Then he'd make his demand. She already knew what it was going to be. *Stay out of West Village.* She waited.

"That's where our project, Village Walk, comes in," he was explaining. "We buy up the houses along Shepherd and renovate them. Then we lease them to merchants and craftsmen for art galleries, specialty shops, restaurants. It'll be like a shopping mall, but the stores will be in separate houses, old, attractive ones. Eventually we'll fill up four blocks in all, two on each side of the street."

"Four?" Mickey frowned, trying to remember. "I saw only two renovated blocks when I was there yesterday."

"That's Phase One." His voice took on a note of pride, and he straightened his tie. It was silk, a maroon-and-gray paisley. She was sure it had cost him plenty. Her eyes strayed just above the starched collar of his snowy shirt to the corded muscles in his neck. This man didn't spend all his time behind a desk. He was tough. Physically, professionally, every other way. Well, so was she.

"Phase Two will take in the two blocks across the street," he went on. "The Brock house—the one you're looking at— is the last house on the corner of the second block of Phase Two. My partnership wants to buy all these houses so they'll be maintained and managed together. That way, we'll preserve this part of the West Village neighborhood."

"And make money for yourselves, of course." She knew she probably sounded rude, but she'd heard enough. Some people genuinely feared what a halfway house would do to their neighborhood, but in his case, the bottom line was profit. It was business, no more, no less. Well, her business was to protect her girls, and there was nothing more important than that.

She saw the anger flash at the back of his eyes. Then, just as quickly, it was gone again. His response wasn't the least apologetic. "I make a living putting together development packages," he said reasonably, and grinned. "If I can't produce a profit, I'll be out of business." The grin was wide, engaging. Contagious.

Mickey didn't bite. She planted her hands on the desk, palms down. It was time to lay out all the cards. "I think I understand, Mr. Scott. What you're saying is that a halfway house has no place in your project. Am I right?''

This time the control didn't slip an inch. He leaned back, as though assessing her, and took off his glasses. The gray eyes collided with hers and she nearly jumped at the impact. *Face it,* she told herself. *This man is a hunk.* But she still didn't trust him, not as far as she could throw him. And he was a big man.

He didn't answer her directly. ''This entire section will be commercial, Ms. Mulvaney. I can't imagine that you'd want the Brock house. The—'' he hesitated, as if unsure of what to call them ''—residents of your halfway house wouldn't have the normal neighborhood environment I'm sure you try to give them. There are bound to be other homes around here that are suitable.''

''None with that kind of room,'' she shot back. ''Let me tell you what *I'm* doing, Mr. Scott. I run a halfway house for teenage girls who have, or used to have, substance-abuse problems. They come from juvenile homes, drug-treatment centers, families who have lost control, as referrals from psychologists—you name it.'' She ticked them off on her fingers. ''They all need help. We try hard to give it to them, and sometimes we're able to do some good. Harbor House is the only place in Houston filling this particular need, and this house—'' she waved a hand around her ''—only holds four girls. For every girl we take in, there are at least fifty more we turn away for lack of space.''

His eyes were still fixed on her, pulling at her, but she fought the distraction. ''The house on Shepherd was built for a very large family,'' she said. ''When we move there, I'll be able to take in twice as many girls right away, and by renovating the attic, I'll end up with room for at least twelve.''

Absently, he rubbed his hand along the line of his jaw. A strong jaw, she noted. A stubborn jaw. He didn't speak, only kept looking at her. Maybe he really was listening. "Shepherd Drive may not provide the quietest residential environment," she went on, "but the rest of West Village will, and there, at least, the girls won't be constantly exposed to the things we're trying to keep away from them."

"Ms. Mulvaney—" he began, but then the front door opened and closed again, interrupting what he had been about to say.

Must be M.C., Mickey thought, unaccountably relieved. Instead, Lisa Parigi, at thirteen the youngest resident of Harbor House, appeared in the doorway.

"Hi, Mickey. I'm home." She was a beautiful child, with huge dark eyes timid as a fawn's, flawless skin and hair of a rich dark brown, drawn back from her heart-shaped face into a single braid. She spotted Cameron Scott and pulled back. "Oh, sorry. Didn't know you had company."

"That's all right, Lisa." Mickey smiled at her. Not for worlds would she make Lisa think she was angry with her. The girl was so insecure that she sought approval under any circumstances. And with nobody at home to care for her, that craving for approval was one of the reasons she had succumbed to drugs in the first place. "Lisa, this is Cameron Scott. Mr. Scott, Lisa Parigi."

"Nice to meet you." Lisa's voice was breathy with shyness, but she met his eyes, even managed a tentative smile.

Good, Lisa, Mickey silently cheered. Then she looked back in time to see him return the smile and caught her breath. This was a real smile. The cleanly defined planes of his face had softened, and the gunmetal eyes had suddenly turned warm. She felt something inside her thaw in response.

"I'm glad to know you too, Lisa," he said gently. Even to Mickey, the warmth in his voice sounded genuine. Lisa responded like a flower unfolding to the sun, her smile widening and delicate color staining her cheeks. Then, as if catching herself, she lowered her long black lashes again, hiding her expressive dark eyes.

"How'd basketball tryouts go?" Mickey asked.

Lisa's face clouded. "Not so good. I didn't make it." Her face brightened. "Joni did."

"Good for Joni. And good for you for trying out."

"Thanks. I'll have supper ready in a little while."

"Okay, honey. I'm eating here tonight. I'll be there in a minute."

Lisa nodded, shifted the bag of groceries to her other arm and headed toward the kitchen, her dark braid swinging against the back of her neck.

"What are we having?" Mickey called after her. She prayed that whatever it was, it would be edible. Even if it wasn't, they'd have to eat it—and appear to enjoy it—to keep from hurting Lisa's feelings.

"My specialty. Lasagna." The voice came from the kitchen, but almost immediately Lisa reappeared in the doorway, a worried frown creasing her forehead. "Is that okay?"

"Sounds great," Mickey said.

Satisfied, Lisa nodded and disappeared again.

Mickey sat gazing at the empty doorway. Lisa had come a long way since she'd been here, but Mickey knew only too well how far she still had to go.

"How old is she?" Cameron Scott asked abruptly.

"Thirteen." Mickey felt her defenses go up again. Her girls were none of this man's business.

He grimaced, surprising her. Maybe he didn't intend to sit in judgment after all. "How long has she been here?"

"A month," she answered stiffly.

"How long will she stay?"

"Five more months, at least, maybe longer. Six months used to be the longest we could keep the girls, but the State Rehabilitation Commission recently allowed for longer stays when we think it's necessary."

"What'll happen to her then?"

Mickey's mouth twisted in frustration. It was a question she asked herself at least once a day. "In her case," she said reluctantly, "I really don't know. She has no parents, and she's been shuffled from one cousin's house to another for the past ten years. She's not a discipline problem. She only wants to please. If we've helped her enough, she may do fine. But without a stable home situation, it's anyone's guess."

She stopped, wondering why she'd told him so much. He just sat there, but his mouth had hardened, and she saw trouble in the clear eyes. She watched him in some consternation. He seemed genuinely concerned. And he was disarming all her defenses.

"Excuse me, Mr. Scott," she said. "You were about to say something."

He seemed to recall himself. "Only that I've taken up enough of your time." He put on his glasses again and stood. "Thanks very much for talking with me. I'll get back with you soon."

She stared at him. "But we haven't decided anything," she protested.

"No. But I didn't expect to do that the first time around." He smiled with an amusement she instinctively knew was genuine. She also knew he'd enjoyed throwing her a curve.

He picked up the attaché case. "As I said, we both know what we want. Now we'll just have to come up with a solution."

What did he mean, a solution? "I don't see how. We can't both have what we want." She heard the challenge in her voice, and a slow flush crept up her face. This time the rudeness hadn't been intentional.

He only raised a brow. "I wouldn't say that," he replied mildly. "There's nothing that can't be worked out. Eventually." To her horror, she felt her hostility draining away, realized that a small part of her wanted to believe him. Even to like him. Not knowing what else to do, she shook his outstretched hand.

As he turned to go, a sound like the opening of a rusty gate issued from the direction of the out box on Mickey's desk. A moment later a furry yellow head appeared, then Rooney climbed out and leisurely stretched his enormous frame. Padding to the edge of the desk on his thick paws, he leaned sociably in Cameron's direction.

"Hi, old fellow. Where'd you come from?" He reached to scratch behind Rooney's notched ear.

Emitting a creaky meow, Rooney leaned into Cameron's hand and began to purr.

Cameron stroked the length of his back. "You like that, don't you?" Another meow. The purring grew louder, and Rooney pivoted back and forth, rubbing his sides against the stacks of paper on the desk.

"He's quite a character. Have you had him long?" With one long finger, Cameron began scratching Rooney's back, just at the base of his tail. The tail began to lash.

Mickey, recognizing the signs, stared in fascinated horror. She knew she should warn the man; it was the decent thing to do. "Quite a while," she said. "Years."

"I used to have a cat," Cameron said. "An old tom. He looked mean, but he was really gentle." He began to stroke Rooney's back again. "Like this one."

Sure, Mickey thought. "His name's Rooney," she offered helpfully. At his questioning look, she smiled. "The name seemed to go so well with mine."

By this time Rooney was in ecstasy. His tail was whipping back and forth and he was purring like an antique diesel engine. In his delight he tilted his head skyward, exposing a full view of the gleaming front tooth.

Cameron scratched his back again. "Rooney, is it?" He smiled reminiscently. "Mine was named—I forget." His hand stopped for a second as he looked away, searching his memory.

It was going to happen. Mickey braced herself as Rooney turned his head and fixed Cameron with one-and-a-half baleful eyes.

"I remember now," Cameron said. "It was—"

Like a snake, Rooney struck, clamping his abundant set of sharp teeth onto one of the defenseless fingers dangling so near.

"Ouch!" Cameron jerked his hand away. He stared in outrage at Rooney, who wore a look of smug malice.

For one electric moment no one moved. Then Rooney sat down, extended a hind leg and calmly began to groom himself. It was too much. Before she could stop herself, Mickey dissolved into helpless laughter.

In the next moment, Cameron astonished her by joining in. His laughter was warm, rich. There was nothing forced about it. It rang with genuine, if rueful, amusement. Even in the midst of her own mirth, she felt another pull of unwanted attraction.

"I take it all back, Rooney." He set down the attaché case and examined his finger. "I'll never accuse you of being gentle again."

"I'm so sorry," Mickey hastened to say, horrified at herself and guiltily aware that she'd exceeded the boundaries of courtesy by a mile. "Let me see." She took his hand and examined his fingers. The skin wasn't broken. *How beautifully shaped the hand was*. Quickly, she let it go.

"It's perfectly okay." Still chuckling, he picked up his attaché case again.

She followed him to the front door, her face scarlet with embarrassment. "Rooney wasn't angry," she explained. "He just didn't want you to stop petting him. It was really an excess of affection, if that's any consolation."

"It is. I'll consider this a sort of initiation." His words were the only indication that he knew she could have warned him. She was relieved he didn't seem to hold it against her.

Halfway out, he turned to her. "I'll call you back to set up another meeting." The amusement still lurked in his eyes. "Without the cat."

"Of course," she mumbled.

"Goodbye, Ms. Mulvaney." His smile broadened. "I enjoyed meeting you...most of the time." Then he turned and walked rapidly down the cracked sidewalk to a bright red Mustang convertible, parked on the street in front of the house.

Mickey shut the door, leaned against it and tried to overcome her mortification. Good thing he hadn't let the incident faze him. In fact, nothing had fazed him. She thought about him and tried to assess him objectively.

She came to the obvious conclusion. Cameron Scott was a tough man. She had seen it in his eyes. But she could handle that and his temper, too. She was used to dealing with anger. His concern for Lisa was something else, though. It had been genuine. He couldn't have faked it, not like that. The problem was, she didn't know how to deal with caring, not when it came from the opposition. And his sense of humor had in some ways been the most disturbing thing of all. He was actually able to laugh at himself. She had the uncomfortable feeling that, Rooney notwithstanding, he'd won the first skirmish.

She took a deep breath. All this was irrelevant to the big picture. She'd known it would happen, of course. It was the NIMBy syndrome. *Not in my backyard.* It was always a factor. But the Brock house was perfect. Size, location, price. It had seemed that, for a change, destiny might actually be on her side. She'd even hoped that this time things might go smoothly, but they rarely did. Well, she'd overcome worse situations before. She'd work this one out somehow.

Straightening, she went to join Lisa in the kitchen.

CAMERON SCOTT SHUT the door of the Mustang and turned the key in the ignition. The finely tuned engine responded with a muffled roar. But instead of putting the car into gear he let it idle while he studied Harbor House. He frowned at the large, jagged cracks and the buckled sections in the concrete walk. The sidewalks were one of the first things he'd replaced in Village Walk. If Mr. Brock retained ownership of his house and leased it to Harbor House, they probably wouldn't have the funds to fix the walks.

On the other hand... He ran a practiced eye over the modest frame structure. It was freshly painted a sparkling white, and the dark-green shutters hung trim and square with the windows. The lawn had been recently cut—manicured, really—and beds of shrubs and bright flowers camouflaged the battered brick piers that supported the house. The interior had been neat, colorful, well-kept, even though it had obviously been decorated on a tight budget. Someone cared enough to make the place attractive and appealing, doing the best they could with limited funds. In spite of the crumpled sidewalk, the stained roof tiles and the ancient air-conditioning unit looming awkwardly from an upstairs window, he couldn't in all honesty say the place looked neglected. It looked like a real home.

It wasn't what he'd expected to find. Maybe it wasn't what he'd wanted to find. Nevertheless, it didn't change anything. If Harbor House moved into one of the buildings in Village Walk, it would still be operating on limited funds, outside his control. And if Village Walk was going to succeed, it needed uniform supervision and generous funding—the kind only a commercial venture could provide.

He eased the Mustang into first gear and put his foot on the gas. The car purred into life, responding instantly to his touch as he maneuvered it through the late-afternoon Houston traffic. For a wonder, the traffic hadn't yet begun to tie itself into its usual knots, but he knew he was bound to hit a snag before he got back to the office. Ordinarily he wouldn't even be driving this time of the afternoon. He usually worked until six-thirty or so, then headed home after the clogged thoroughfares had cleared a little. He consoled himself that at least he could use his driving time to think. In fact, right now he needed it. The Harbor House situation might be easy to analyze; Mickey Mulvaney was not. At least, not as far as he was concerned.

With a clarity that jolted him, her image sprang back into his mind. Although she was beautiful, the term didn't begin to describe her. Striking was a much better word, with her magnolia skin, Indian-high cheekbones and black blunt-cut hair that swung provocatively along the line of her jaw. Her eyes defied description. They were a clear, startling blue, unadulterated by even a trace of any other color. The overall effect was definitely one to ruffle a man's composure.

But he'd bet money she didn't think of herself as pretty. With all the other defenses she'd mounted against him, she hadn't used her looks at all. Throughout their interview her expression had remained wary, the fascinating eyes veiled by the black lashes, and she'd graced him only once with the slightest upcurve of those firmly compressed lips, until she'd slipped and laughed outright. Her voice was cool, surprisingly husky, but she spoke as if the words didn't come easily. Her rudeness had even managed to rile him, something that didn't usually happen, though he'd caught it so fast he hoped she hadn't noticed.

Everything about her radiated determination, strength, as though she'd had to fight for what she had accomplished. He couldn't help wondering what her story was.

He headed the Mustang onto the loop and swore at the bumper-to-bumper traffic that heralded the daily jam. Earlier in the day he could have been back at his office in a few minutes. Now he'd be held up for at least half an hour. It happened all the time in Houston. He squeezed into the right-hand lane between a black Ferrari and a battered green pickup and resigned himself to stop-and-go progress for the next five miles.

Almost immediately, he was thinking about Mickey Mulvaney again.

Of course, he couldn't judge her by the way she'd reacted to him. He'd expected her to be defensive when she found out why he was there. What he hadn't been prepared for, what had really thrown him, was the lightning change in her when the girl, Lisa, had come in. In an instant the hard-boiled front had fallen away like a discarded garment, and she'd all but physically enveloped Lisa in a warmth and protectiveness that was almost tangible. Her behavior went way beyond mere professional caretaking. It was obvious that she was personally committed to this girl's welfare.

What she'd also done, he admitted wryly to himself, was multiply her appeal by at least ten. When the cat bit him, he'd caught another glimpse of the woman behind the mask, with the same effect. The fact that she was probably unaware of her desirability did nothing to diminish it. Even now, remembering, he felt his body respond.

But for almost the entire interview she'd kept her defenses firmly in place. At some point in her life, Mickey Mulvaney had obviously had quite a struggle. With a curiosity that surprised him, he found himself wanting to know about it.

That brought him to her father, and what part he played in this confusing, unorthodox situation. Cameron definitely wanted M.C. Mulvaney in on the next meeting. Maybe he would be easier to deal with, and, after meeting him, Cameron might be better able to understand what made the man's daughter tick. Right now, besides his hunches, all he really knew about her was that she didn't back away from a fight. He'd confused her, he knew, by shutting off the discussion when he did. But after assessing the situation, he'd realized he needed time to lay his plans. He hadn't meant to make her think he was laughing at her, even though, as it turned out, it had served her right. Remembering her laughter, he decided it was almost worth having been bitten by the damned cat. When she laughed, she was beautiful. *And so damned desirable . . .*

He shook his head. Where had that come from?

He tried to back off and look at himself. He appreciated femininity, no question about it. He'd dated a lot of women since Cathy left—an entanglement or two, a few he'd really liked. But none quite right. After his marriage fell apart, he'd never looked very hard for another wife.

He still couldn't understand what had gone wrong. Two promising young people from two very respectable families who had even been friends. Cathy's parents had lived in West Village, and Cameron had grown up with her. At first everything had been fine. Then, a few years into the marriage, Cathy, always acquisitive, had grown restless and unhappy during the time Cameron had really had to struggle to make a living for them. He'd stuck it out, as he'd learned to do with everything, believing he could do something, one more thing, to salvage the situation. Until the day he'd found out she was having an affair with one of his business partners.

He had never quite figured out what happened. He'd stopped loving her long before the marriage ended. Maybe they'd been too young. Something he'd done, something he hadn't done... If a marriage as promising as theirs had failed, what chance had any marriage?

He braked as the taillights of the car in front of him flashed a warning, and forced his attention back to the problem at hand. He would try to do what he did best: work out something satisfactory for all parties involved. In this case, though, he wondered if he could. He hoped so. He didn't want to be the bad guy. Mickey Mulvaney was working hard for something important. She deserved to have a bigger place. And so did the girls, he thought, remembering Lisa. Yet if he succeeded in preventing Harbor House from moving into West Village, they just might have to remain in the smaller location. Surely there were other places in Houston that would be just as suitable as the Brock house. There had to be. Hell, if necessary, he'd find one himself. But the problem remained the same. For a lot of reasons, he had to try to keep Harbor House out of Village Walk.

Of course, Mickey Mulvaney would fight back. A vivid image of her, back to the wall, chin out in defiance and blue eyes ablaze, sprang into his mind. But he found himself not wanting to put her there.

Crazily enough, he wanted to make her laugh again.

"KEITH, I'M HOME." Penny Rhodes let herself in the back door of their spacious two-story brick house, newly painted an elegant taupe trimmed in white. She had seen his BMW in the garage.

"I'm upstairs," a masculine voice called. "I'll be down in a minute."

Penny set down her packages and surveyed the kitchen. Bleached hardwood floors, a wide butcher-block island with built-in grill, natural pine cabinets artfully finished to bring out the grain. As always, when she looked at the results of her imagination and handiwork, she felt a rush of pride. She glanced through the doorway into the interior of the house. Light, space, proportion...and the perfect blend of traditional and contemporary furnishings to bring out the best in the old structure. She'd inherited her mother's exquisite taste and her gift for putting it all together. To give credit where credit was due, Penny had had every advantage possible. Every material advantage.

The move to West Village had been a wise one, she thought for the hundredth time. It was a good place to start. As a fledgling interior designer, she had a reputation to build. So far, she was doing very well. Her clients included more and more of Houston's young professionals. Soon, if her life went according to plan, she'd be designing interiors in the palatial older homes on Memorial Drive or in River Oaks. But first, her own home had to reflect her taste and her ability. And she knew it did.

She heard footsteps overhead and moved into the entryway to meet Keith when he came down the stairs. She smoothed her skirt and patted her sun-glitzed hair, even though she knew the trendy, sideswept bob hadn't been disheveled by so much as a strand.

Keith stepped off the stairs, slight, dark, alive, a smile of greeting lighting his eyes. He radiated vitality from every cell. He had poured that vitality into his career, and it had landed him a job with one of the largest, most prestigious law firms in Houston. Now it was earning him a solid reputation as one of the city's most promising trial lawyers.

He took her in his arms and kissed her. "Hi, hon. How was your day?"

"Fine, darling." She reveled in his closeness. Even after five years of marriage, his touch still moved her. "We chose paper and paint color for the Elmores' dining room today, and I found a really nice walnut secretary for the Princes' living room. Donna seems pleased."

"I can't imagine why she wouldn't be." There was pride in his voice, and his hands lingered on her arms.

Flushing with pleasure, she caught his hand. "Keep me company while I fix dinner. I bought lobster and fresh asparagus."

"Sounds great." He followed her back into the kitchen.

She busied herself, preparing the asparagus for steaming, splitting and cubing the lobster tails, laying out ingredients for the herb sauce. "How did it go today?" She brought down a copper sauté pan from the overhead pot rack and set it on the range.

"We settled the McWherter case. It was iffy there for a while, but finally we settled for six hundred thousand. In my book, that's good news."

The McWherter case was Keith's first big solo assignment, and according to all reports, he had handled it well. She wasn't surprised. He was good, and she knew it. "That's wonderful, darling."

"It just worked out, that's all."

How like him to downplay his own achievements, she thought.

He opened the refrigerator and brought out a bottle of Chardonnay. "Want some?"

"Please." She threw a dollop of butter into the sauté pan and began to stir as it melted.

He half filled two wineglasses and handed her one.

She smiled. "To your settlement." She touched her glass to his. "I'm proud of you."

"Thanks, hon. By the way, I visited a minute with Tom today. He was working in his yard when I drove in."

"Oh? How is he?" Tom and Helen Mayes were the perfect neighbors—kind, congenial, helpful. They were much older than she and Keith, mid-sixties, maybe, and their two children were already married and gone. Which suited Penny just fine.

"He's okay. By the way, he told me a bit of news." Keith swirled the wine in his glass, seeming intent on watching it go around. "Do you know the Brock house?"

"The big one on the corner?"

"That's it. Brock had a big family, eight or ten kids, I think, but his wife's dead now, and all the kids are grown.

Anyway, Tom told me Brock's going to lease it to some halfway house."

Penny stopped stirring the butter and looked up. "Halfway house?"

Keith raised his eyes to hers. "You know. One of those places that serve as a midpoint between institutions and the real world. Some are for substance abusers, some for the mentally retarded—"

"I know what they are." She put down her wooden spoon, splattering the spotless range top with butter. "I can't believe it. That house is supposed to be part of the Village Walk project."

"Tom seemed pretty sure of his facts." Keith was still watching her. "After all, Cameron's group doesn't own the house yet. It still belongs to Brock. They've been trying to talk him into selling, but apparently he's decided against it."

"Who's going to live there?"

"Teenage girls."

She froze. "Teenage girls?"

"Yes. Alcohol and drug-abuse problems, Tom said."

"Do you mean to tell me there's going to be a whole houseful of disturbed teenage girls a block and a half from here?"

"Looks like it."

"Keith, we can't let it happen." Her stomach knotted. *Teenage girls*. A whole flock of unwelcome memories stirred in the back of her mind. "The neighborhood will go to pot," she added lamely.

He grinned. "Is that a bad pun?"

She made a quick, impatient movement. "It's not a joking matter, Keith. You know how I feel."

"Yeah." The tiniest edge of regret was in his voice, but she ignored it.

"We have to stop it, that's all," she said flatly.

To still her nervous movements, he caught her hand in his. "I don't know that we can do anything about it. Legally, a halfway house can go in just about anywhere it wants to."

"We have to try. Call Cameron. He has to do something about this." She could hear her voice climbing. "He promised us—"

"Hold it, Penny." Keith tightened his fingers on hers. "He didn't promise us anything. He has no control over this. He can't force Brock to sell to him, you know. But if it'll make you feel any better, I'll call Cameron tonight and discuss it with him. After all, maybe it won't be so bad."

"No, Keith." She gripped his hand. "Think. You know how hard I've worked on this house." She gestured around her. "It's got to look good, my career depends on it. We've sunk a lot of money into it. If the halfway house devalues the neighborhood, we'll lose our investment. We'll have to sell our house for nothing, if we can sell it at all. Besides, you know Cameron wants to keep the neighborhood attractive enough that more young people will move in."

He shrugged. "But I'm not so sure it'll hurt the neighborhood. After all, it's just a bunch of teenage girls—"

"Teenage punks, you mean," she interrupted, deliberately fanning her own anger. "Alcoholics, dopeheads. Some of them have probably been prostitutes, or still are." The smell of scorching butter rose from the pan. Hastily, she turned off the burner.

"Penny." His voice hardened. "Halfway houses do a lot of good. People get the kind of care in them they wouldn't get anywhere else."

"I know," she said helplessly. Poor kids. Of course they had to be cared for. Didn't she know it? But not in this neighborhood. Not now. Not when things were going so well for her and Keith. Not when she'd have to see them, know how miserable they were. Wonder where they had come from . . .

"Take it easy, honey." Keith's voice gentled again. "I'll call Cameron in a little while, see what I can do."

Her anxiety ebbed. Keith would work it out. He always did.

He took her in his arms, his dark eyes shining with his love for her. And she loved him. God, how she loved him. They made the perfect couple, the perfect team. They were complete with each other—without children. She'd long ago resigned herself to being unable to have them, and he'd loved her enough to marry her anyway. He'd mentioned adoption at first, but she couldn't bear the thought.

She thought of the miserable girls in the halfway house. She thought of her own adolescence, fought the sharp stab of pain. In spite of everything, she'd managed to put the pieces of her life back together. Now everything was going according to plan. She was all Keith needed, all he would ever need. She would make sure of it.

She lifted her face for his kiss.

BRANDY WILLIFORD DAWDLED, savoring her last cigarette. When the manager of Baker's Ice Cream Parlor had said she didn't need to come in this evening, she'd been glad at first. Then she'd remembered that when she got to Harbor House, she'd still have all her chores to do. And those didn't pay.

She walked slower and slower, even considered hiding out somewhere until the time she normally got off work. Considered, then thought better of it, because she was uncomfortably sure she would get caught. Mickey didn't miss much, and what she did, M.C. spotted. Anyway, she didn't want to get in trouble right now. She planned to stay right here, at Harbor House, doing what they told her, making them think she was going along with it all, until her time was up. Then she'd be gone so fast they wouldn't even have time to blink, and she could do what she wanted. She'd learned how to move out of these places.

She made a face. Boy, had she been stupid. When she first went to the drug-rehab center, she'd fought everyone and everything like crazy. Then she'd finally caught on. If she kept on fighting, she'd never get out. So she'd learned to play the game. Oh, yes, she'd learned to play it, giving them the answers they wanted to hear, doing just enough of what they wanted to make them let her out. She'd learned manipulating people wasn't hard at all.

Now, though, she wondered just how completely she was fooling the people at Harbor House—Mickey, M.C. and especially that psychologist. She sat there and listened and didn't say much, but sometimes Brandy had the feeling she knew exactly what she was thinking and just didn't choose to call her on it. Brandy couldn't imagine why not. Everybody else always had.

The late October sun slanted through the trees and the tiny breeze made a kaleidoscope of changing patterns in the leaves. Most were still green, she noted, but some were beginning to show the bright reds, oranges and yellows of autumn. They'd make a good collage, or maybe even a fabric design. She'd used the same colors in her last art project, a watercolor. Her teacher, Miss Foy, had liked it, and now she wanted Brandy to enter some sort of art contest. To represent the school in the regional competition, she'd said. For some reason Miss Foy thought she was good. Brandy hadn't really said yes or no, but she thought she might do something just to keep her off her back. Or then again, she might not. Just because she'd decided to play the game didn't mean she had to get carried away with it. If she didn't want to, nobody could make her.

In fact, she reflected, taking a deep drag and blowing the smoke into the hazy October air, nobody could make her do anything. She knew that now. Just that day the campus drug connection had offered her some dope. She'd told her no, along with some pretty specific instructions as to what she could do with her stuff. If the girl tried it again, there'd be some trouble. Nobody was going to lay that junk on her again, at least not until she decided it was time. She wanted to stay clean for a while.

The cigarette had burned down nearly to the filter. Too bad. She didn't get paid until tomorrow. She hoped she could bum some from Leslie, who always had a few stashed away. She flipped the filter into the street, smoothed the denim miniskirt she'd bought with her last paycheck over her curved hips and slowly, deliberately turned the last corner toward Harbor House.

CHAPTER THREE

"WHAT'S THE MATTER with you, girl?" M.C. Mulvaney demanded. "You've been up and down three times in the past five minutes. Sit still, will you?"

"Sorry." Mickey walked back from the living room window and plopped into the nearest chair, but she couldn't keep from glancing at her watch. One fifty-five. Cameron Scott was coming at two o'clock—he'd talked to M.C. this morning.

"Relax," M.C. said. "He's not due for another few minutes yet." He eyed her shrewdly. "Come on. What's bugging you about this guy?"

"I don't like him." But that wasn't entirely true. She felt her cheeks grow red and hoped M.C. wasn't reading her mind as easily as he usually did. She'd found herself *wanting* to like Cameron Scott. In fact, she'd had to keep reminding herself he was in the enemy camp.

"Why not?" M.C. persisted. "Rooney liked him, didn't he? After all, he bit him." M.C. grinned, coaxing a reluctant answering smile from Mickey. "Anyway," he went on, "you only talked to him for twenty minutes. He sounded reasonable over the phone."

"He did to me, too." With a quick gesture, she tucked the heavy mass of black hair behind one ear. "But I don't think he understands, or cares, what we're trying to do. He lives in a different world."

"Didn't he tell you he wanted to find a solution that would be okay for everybody?"

"Sure. That's part of his job. But his first concern is to make a profit. He's a businessman, after all." She knew it had to be true, although one corner of her mind didn't want to believe her own words.

"That he is, but I think we ought to give him the benefit of the doubt. After all, he's willing to talk to us. That's more than a lot of people would do. Come on, honey." M.C.'s voice held a tincture of sadness. "You can't go through life being suspicious of everyone."

Mickey only nodded, a little abashed. He was right, of course, but sometimes it was difficult for her to remember.

When the knock sounded she jumped to her feet, but it was M.C. who moved to answer the door. She heard Cameron Scott's deep-timbred voice. Then he was in the room, seeming to fill it, making M.C. look even smaller and wirier than he was.

She'd thought she'd steeled herself against the physical impact of the man, but she'd been wrong. This time the suit was black with the tiniest of charcoal pinstripes, the tie a rich red with discreet gray florets. But once again the expensive outfit failed to camouflage the set of his broad shoulders, his muscular body. Just as the smooth exterior failed to hide the rough strength she knew was there.

"Ms. Mulvaney, how are you?" He extended his hand. She took it, hoping he didn't notice that her palm was damp.

"Mr. Scott." She released his hand as quickly as courtesy allowed.

"Have a seat, Cameron." M.C. indicated the sofa, and Mickey noted without surprise the ease with which her father used his first name.

"Thanks." He sat down, completely relaxed, and looked around. "Where's your man-eating cat?"

Mickey's lips twitched in spite of herself. "You're safe. He's asleep in my office, in the out box."

"Smart cat," Cameron said. "He could give lessons to a lot of executives I know. How's Lisa?" he asked abruptly, catching her off guard.

Her gaze flew to his. There it was again. Concern that she could swear was genuine. She hadn't imagined it the other day. "She's fine."

"Tell her I said hello." He gave her a quick, quizzical smile, and the warmth in it beckoned to her.

"I will," she said, touched in spite of herself. "Thanks for asking."

"Now, Cameron," M.C. said briskly, "let's put this thing on the table and talk about it." He grinned like the Cheshire cat. In spite of her nerves, Mickey had to smile.

Cameron matched M.C.'s grin. "That's what I came for, Mr. Mulvaney."

He gestured expansively. "Call me M.C."

"M.C., then. Thanks." Cameron began his pitch.

Mickey sat quietly, listening, sensing real rapport between the two men. She wondered if M.C. was being fooled. In their brief adult acquaintance, she'd never known him to be taken in, but Cameron Scott was a persuasive man. She found herself watching Cameron's hands. Large as they were, they were surprisingly mobile, emphasizing his words, drawing pictures in the air to illustrate a point.

"I've looked at the whole picture, and I just don't feel that it would be in anyone's best interests for you to locate in Village Walk," he finished.

"As I told you before, Mr. Scott, I don't believe that's true," Mickey cut in before she could stop herself.

He swung his gaze toward her, and she felt the air charge between them. This man had steel in him, she reminded herself, and a temper. She watched as he brought it under control.

He sighed. "In spite of what you believe, Ms. Mulvaney, I'm sympathetic to your work, and I was very impressed by what I saw here the other day. But I've got to be frank about the reality of the situation."

"I understand that. I'm just not sure your idea of reality and ours are the same." What was there about him that brought out all her defenses? She didn't look at M.C., not wanting to see the chagrin on his face as all his painstaking PR work flew out the window, but she had to be as honest about the situation as she could. "I'll be frank, too. There are no zoning laws that would prevent our coming in. If Mr. Brock wants to lease to us, you can't legally keep us out."

"That's true," he said reasonably. "But I can hardly believe you'd put Harbor House where it wouldn't be welcome."

Her laugh was short, humorless. "Mr. Scott, can you tell me any place in Houston where we *would* be welcome?"

M.C. intervened. "You're both right. But if we could work things out between us, it would save us all a lot of grief in the long run."

M.C. the diplomat, Mickey thought, *trying to regain the ground I just lost for him.*

Cameron nodded. "That's why I'm here," he said simply. "I have to protect my own interests, but I also do a lot of arbitration. Over the years I've worked out some tough situations. You can check me out on that."

"I already have," M.C. said.

Cameron grinned. "Somehow I figured you would."

"Cameron," M.C. said seriously, "I can almost promise you there won't be a problem with Harbor House in the neighborhood. Mickey runs a tight ship." His pride shone in his eyes. "We do good things here."

Mickey flushed with mingled pleasure and embarrassment. In spite of her cherished independence, she still needed M.C.'s approval the way a growing thing needed the rain. But Cameron Scott's eyes were on her again, probing her secrets.

"What about it, Ms. Mulvaney?" he asked.

"M.C.'s right," she admitted. She disliked boasting, but facts were facts. "We've done very well with our girls in the two years we've operated Harbor House. While they're with us, they don't often get into much trouble. Of course, there's no guarantee there'll be a happy ending. There's a better chance of that when there's some sort of a home situation for them to go back to," she added, "and many of them just don't have it."

"Like Lisa," he said quietly.

"Yes. We're the bridge back to reality," she explained, warming to her subject. "The girls are already on the mend when we get them, but we try to better equip them to deal with the world outside. I think the most important thing we offer is care. We try to let them know that, for a little while at least, somebody cares about where they are, what they're doing, what happens to them. And it works." As always, when she talked of her work, she forgot everything else. She was barely aware that Cameron was listening intently, his gaze fixed on her face.

"You obviously feel strongly about what you do," he said thoughtfully, his eyes lingering on her.

"Halfway houses can save children, Mr. Scott." By now, Mickey was atop her favorite soapbox and had completely forgotten the original discussion. "When I was growing up—"

Catching herself, she bit off the words and darted a guilty glance at M.C.

"Never mind, sweetheart." The words were gentle, but she could see the pain in his eyes. She never meant to hurt him, but it seemed that sometimes she couldn't help it. Cameron Scott's see-too-much eyes were looking from one to the other of them, obviously speculating. Well, it was none of his concern.

"We rarely have severe discipline problems," she went on. "In a way, we're just like any other family in any other neighborhood. There's never a *guarantee* there won't be a problem. But you take that chance with any neighbor, not just with halfway houses."

"I don't doubt it," Cameron said. "But whether there's a problem or not, the neighborhood is going to think there is. West Village is at a crossroads right now. It's either going to deteriorate or it's going to get a new lease on life. I'm here to see that it survives."

"How can you speak for the West Village residents?"

"I *am* a West Village resident," he said.

She stared. "You live there?"

"Yes. I was brought up in the Village. My parents still live in the family home about three blocks off Shepherd, and a couple of years ago I bought a house near them and remodeled it."

"I see." This changed the whole picture. "So that gives you two reasons to keep us out, Mr. Scott." She kept her tone casual, but shot him a challenging look. "One financial and the other personal."

"Mickey," M.C. interjected. She ignored him.

Cameron didn't answer right away. For the life of her, she could see nothing hidden in his eyes. She could even see the tiny spark of anger she knew she'd kindled.

"That's true, Ms. Mulvaney," he finally said. "I owe it to both my investors and my neighbors to represent their interests the best I can. But I also love West Village because I grew up there. To tell you the truth, I won't make the money on the Village Walk project that I will on some of my other deals, but as long as it preserves the Village, I don't care." He folded his arms across his chest. "It'll be worth it to me."

"I hope so," Mickey said grimly, trying with only limited success to nurse her distrust. *Damn the man*. She kept trying to peg him, but he just wouldn't stay in the slot.

"Enough oratory." The disarming smile again. "As I've said, I'm not trying to sabotage your operation. In fact, I'll help you all I can. I'll even help you find another place."

Mickey felt a sharp flare of anger, but she fought it down. As M.C. had often told her, it would get her nowhere. "That's very nice of you, Mr. Scott," she said, trying to keep her annoyance out of her voice, "but M.C.'s already looked, and the Brock house is the only one he's found that will really suit our needs."

"Tell you what." M.C. sat forward, steepling his fingers together. "We'll make a deal with you, Cameron. We'll stay open to other possibilities if you'll do something for us."

Mickey's mouth fell open, but the look her father gave her was guileless. At the edge of her vision, behind Cameron's back, she saw a large yellow shape come sailing through the doorway at about knee level, then stroll leisurely into the room. One corner of her mind registered it, but she was too distracted to pay much attention.

"What's the deal?" Cameron asked.

"I want you to come around as often as you can in the next two weeks, to see how we operate," M.C. went on. "No strings attached. Then you can make a first-hand report to your investors and your neighborhood homeowners' association, or whatever you have over there. I think you'll be pleasantly surprised."

Cameron was silent a moment. "I'd like that," he said finally. "I don't know much about what you do here, but I want to learn." He threw a glance in Mickey's direction. "In fact, I think I'm going to enjoy it."

M.C. flashed his piratical grin. "Done, then. We'll table the discussion for two weeks and hope to see you soon. As a visitor."

Mickey listened helplessly. This time M.C. had really lost his mind. They needed to act fast, to go ahead and sign the lease, to move in and just take the heat. They'd done it before. Why waste time playing games?

Cameron Scott hoisted his powerful frame from the sofa. She rose, and he took her hand. She lifted her gaze to his and saw interest there. *In her, as a woman.* Something closed up inside her. He'd just have to look elsewhere. She wasn't interested, especially not in someone she might soon be fighting tooth and nail. But now he smiled at her, a real smile this time, and in his eyes were things she could only sense. Steadiness, durability. Substance... She was suddenly conscious of an odd hunger inside.

"Since I'm going to be around a lot," he said, "do you think we could make it Cameron and Mickey?"

"Of course," she stammered, caught off guard again.

He nodded. "Goodbye, then." His eyes lingered on her. "I'll look forward to—" Suddenly he broke off and looked down, then sidestepped with the speed and grace of an Olympic skater.

Mickey looked in time to see Rooney's jaws snap like bear traps on empty air.

"Not today, buddy," Cameron said mildly.

Ears flattened, Rooney howled his disappointment. Mickey felt the laughter bubbling up inside her.

M.C. was grinning. "Nice move, Cameron," he said admiringly.

Chuckling, Cameron relented and bent down to scratch Rooney's head. The old cat closed his eyes so tightly even the slits were almost invisible and dissolved into one continuous clanking purr. "I'm not about to let him connect again," Cameron said. "He's got way too many teeth."

"The trick is to keep your eye on him," Mickey warned, sternly suppressing her laughter.

Deftly, he removed his hand. Rooney looked as if he might go into attack mode again, then, apparently realizing he'd milked the situation for all it was worth, sauntered off, tail in the air.

"See you later, old man," Cameron called after him. "As I was saying, Mickey, I'll be looking forward to seeing you soon." The laughter was still in his eyes, and she knew it was mirrored in hers.

Her own amusement faded as she she watched M.C. usher him toward the door. Her mind screamed "Watch out," but her feelings whispered something else.

She turned abruptly and walked back to her office.

"WHATCHA DOING, M.C.?" Joni Jefferson's voice came from behind him.

"Hi, Joni." Without looking around, he spoke from the innards of the 1978 Chevrolet that served as his and Mickey's extra car. "Just trying to keep this thing going another year." It wouldn't last forever, he knew, but it would have to do until they could afford another one.

"Let me see." Joni stuck her head under the hood.

"All right, Miss Curiosity. Do you see that thing right there? It's a carburetor. I'm trying to fix it."

Joni looked, then rapidly lost interest. "M.C.?"

"What, sweetheart?"

"Will you take us to get some ice cream later?" She slanted her black velvet eyes at him. "Please? If you do, I'll pull weeds in the front flower bed tomorrow."

M.C. chuckled. Joni was a natural con artist. She had learned it from the same teachers, and in the same place, he had—the streets. Yesterday it had been pot, today it was ice cream. That was the thing you had to remember about these kids—they were like normal teenagers, except that, at heartbreakingly young ages, they had learned more about the rough side of life than most normal adults ever glimpsed. "Don't try to con a con man, Joni," he said. "We'll see. First I've got some stops to make."

"Can I go with you?"

"Nope. Not this time." M.C. pulled a bandanna out of his pocket and wiped his hands. "Joni?"

"Sir?"

"Did you do your homework?"

"Yes, sir."

"All right, then. Go check in with Mickey. I think she's got something she needs you to do."

Reluctantly, Joni went. M.C. went into the house, washed up and slipped on a fresh shirt from the extras he always kept there. He wanted to look halfway presentable, at least.

He got into the car and started the engine. It coughed a couple of times before it caught. He listened a moment, then, with a grunt of satisfaction, put the car in gear. The first thing he was going to do was to take another look at the Brock house. And if Brock was in, he was going to talk to him.

A potential powder keg, he mused. Bad business. They'd run into it before, in other neighborhoods. And Mickey was a fighter, there was no doubt about it. Sometimes he deplored that quality in her. It wasn't his way. He'd learned very early that you could work around a problem without fighting. *Any* problem. Lay a little groundwork, keep at it, and you got along fine. If he could only teach that to Mickey. If he could only have those lost years... He shut out the thought. He'd learned long ago that "what ifs" did no good. But he'd vowed to make it up to her, and he'd die trying.

Of course, the real sparks were flying between her and Cameron Scott. Mickey didn't like him, M.C. reflected between exasperation and amusement, not one little bit. Granted she wasn't good at camouflaging her feelings, but he'd rarely seen her take such an instant dislike to anyone. Ironically, from what he'd seen of Cameron Scott so far, he seemed to be a reasonable man, with a reasonably long fuse. M.C. liked him, and his instincts about people were practically infallible. They'd had to be. Otherwise he wouldn't have survived his childhood. Good thing he hadn't turned to a life of crime. He spared himself a moment of quiet pride. What a criminal he'd have made.

He turned the last corner onto Shepherd Drive. Of course, some of Mickey's reaction to young Scott might be because he was a good-looking man. Mickey generally tended to keep men at a distance. M.C.'s fists clenched around the steering wheel. Then, deliberately, he made them relax. He repeated the motto he'd learned to live by: What's done is done. Don't look back. Fix the future. *Fix it.*

He pulled up to the curb in front of the Brock house. Probably 1930s vintage, he gauged, a two-story dark red brick. Big. Run-down in spots, but nothing he couldn't repair. A spacious yard with huge oaks and shady, private corners. The whole place had a solid look to it, a comfortable look. According to his sources, the Brocks had raised a family of ten in this house. This was it, he thought. Perfect for Mickey. And right now, her happiness was the most important thing in the world to him.

He looked down the long driveway. No cars there; Brock obviously wasn't home. He'd intended to touch base with him, to tell him how much they wanted the house, to assure him personally that it would be well taken care of. M.C. believed in touching bases.

In fact—he swung the car in an illegal U-turn and headed down a side street—just for grins, he was going to touch another base. It couldn't hurt, and might even do some good. He was great with the ladies.

Five minutes later, he was there. Before he touched the doorbell of the trim beige frame house, he took a quick, assessing look around him. Everything about it and the surrounding yard was perfectly in place. Not the tiniest chip of paint was peeling from the exterior of the house. No speck of dirt smudged it anywhere. In spite of the late October nip in the air, the impatiens in the front beds were blooming in regimented splendor. No blade of grass poked its head above its freshly edged fellows. It probably wouldn't dare, M.C. thought.

As usual, he'd done his homework. He knew all about Jessamine Cunningham. She was an old-maid schoolteacher with a lot of inherited money, and she ran the neighborhood. A tough nut to crack. But if he could somehow win her over, they would have hurdled one of the biggest obstacles they faced. And he had supreme confidence in his own abilities. He pushed the doorbell.

The lady who answered the door looked about as he'd figured she would. Tall, thin, with a very erect back. Graying hair pulled back into a no-nonsense bun. Faded green eyes that could slice a diamond in half. M.C. knew the type. She probably still took grown men by the ear occasionally, just for practice.

In spite of himself, he felt a twinge of nerves. The last time he'd felt like this was when he'd stood before his adult daughter and asked to be taken back into her life. This was going to be almost as great a challenge. But, he reminded himself, he loved a challenge.

He cleared his throat. "Miss Cunningham?"

"Yes?" Her tone was not exactly frosty, but close. The green eyes strafed him from head to toe. He couldn't remember ever having been given so thorough a once-over, not even in his misspent younger days.

He shifted uncomfortably, then caught himself. He squared his shoulders and mustered all his Irish charm, knowing he was going to need every ounce of it. This one would never stoop to anything so vulgar as being impolite, but she'd never give an inch to anyone unless she chose. And that was where he came in.

"Miss Cunningham, my name is M.C. Mulvaney," he said smoothly. "I understand you're the president of the West Village Homeowners' Association."

"That's correct." Her tone didn't soften, and she didn't offer her hand. If anything, her back grew straighter.

"I'd like to talk to you, if I may. I'm from Harbor House."

"Oh, yes. I've heard of it." The cool voice suddenly turned to ice. *Here we go,* M.C. thought.

"Miss Cunningham," he said, "I understand there is some neighborhood opposition to Harbor House's moving into West Village." He was careful to keep his grammar correct—he'd managed to soak up the basics, along with a lot of other things, in his various forays in and out of school. At times it served him well. "It's natural for people to feel that way," he went on. "Most do, until they find out more about us. I'd like to explain what we do and answer any questions you might have."

Pointedly, she looked down at her watch. "I'm sorry, young man, but I'm afraid I don't have the time to talk with you right now. Perhaps another day."

In a gesture his daughter would have recognized instantly, M.C. put his hand over his heart. "Thank you, ma'am," he said, his tone a model of gentle sincerity.

Miss Cunningham looked a little startled. "I beg your pardon?"

"It's been a long time since anyone called me a young man," he said, his hand still over his heart. He gave her his most winning smile.

He was rewarded by the briefest flash of humor in the flinty eyes, a little quirk at the corner of the prim mouth. The first crack in the armor. It was a tiny one, but that was all he'd ever needed. He congratulated himself.

"Young man," Miss Cunningham repeated with emphasis, "when you're my age, everyone else *is* young." Again that slight unbending, the hint of a smile.

"By the way," M.C. said, widening the crack just a little, "your impatiens are beautiful. How do you grow them so evenly? Mine always get a little spindly." *Probably threatens to pinch them if they don't behave,* he thought.

"Thank you." Miss Cunningham's expression thawed a bit more. "I feed them regularly with plant food. And if they become unruly, I simply pinch them back. You must try it," she added kindly.

There was a moment of total silence. If he laughed, it would ruin all his careful groundwork. He mustered every ounce of control he possessed. It was close, but it worked. "Thank you, ma'am," he said when he could trust himself to speak. "I'll be sure to. I realize you don't have time to visit with me now, but would you be able to spare me a few moments sometime soon? We've learned from experience that the sooner we sit down and talk about this, the better off we'll all be."

"Very well, Mr....Mulvaney, is it?" Again Miss Cunningham was the quintessential schoolteacher.

"Yes, ma'am."

"I feel it only fair to warn you that I'm unalterably opposed to having a halfway house in this community. However—" she impaled him with her gaze. "I'll never let it be said that I was unwilling to listen to another person's viewpoint."

"No, ma'am."

"Be at my house tomorrow afternoon at three o'clock. We'll discuss this matter for thirty minutes, no more. I've another meeting at four-thirty, and I must have an hour to get ready. Don't be late."

"No, ma'am," M.C. said humbly. "Thank you, ma'am." He wasn't lying. He truly was grateful.

She'd given him all the opening he was going to need.

STRAINS FROM "The Brady Bunch" theme seeped through the solid shiplap walls that separated Harbor House's living area from Mickey's office. Leslie was watching reruns and had the volume turned up much too loud, but Mickey hadn't asked her to turn it down. She was in the midst of her weekly meeting with Connie Allen, the consulting psychologist, and the noise would effectively muffle their confidential conversation.

"You don't need to whisper," she told Connie. "In fact, you can scream if you want to." In the two years they had worked together, Connie had become a good-friend.

Connie's generous mouth stretched into a wide grin. "I'd like to, but I'm supposed to be the one in control, remember?" She opened a battered notebook crammed with loose papers and spread it across her lap. "So Leslie got to watch TV today? She must be doing better."

Mickey nodded. "Thank heaven for small favors." Several weeks ago Leslie had fallen in love, to the complete detriment of her normal good behavior. She had neglected her duties, forgotten her homework, even broken curfew, with the result that she had spent a lot of time on restriction... and away from the object of her affections. It was only in the past week or so that she'd seemed to realize what she was missing, and why, and had begun to straighten out her behavior.

"Love can be a wonderful thing sometimes," Connie commented. "In this case it's dangerous. Leslie's a motherly, caring little soul. She wants a home and family of her own so badly she can taste it, and that's what scares me."

Mickey grimaced. "Something else to worry about. Teen pregnancy."

Connie shot her a look. "Don't even say it."

"I take it all back." Mickey found one of the few clear spaces on the desk and knocked wood. "What about Brandy? Has she started talking to you yet?"

"She's giving me what she thinks I want to hear." Connie adjusted the frames of her oversize glasses. "She doesn't mean a word of it, but she's gotten pretty good at faking."

Mickey sighed. "I guess that's progress. At least she's not being disruptive."

"Now we only have to worry about what she's thinking." Connie smiled grimly. "Or plotting." She turned over a few pages in the notebook and began making notes.

If anyone could reach Brandy, Mickey thought, Connie could. During counseling sessions, Connie listened, responded when appropriate, guided wisely and missed nothing. The short blond hair, the big, seemingly guileless blue eyes behind the large-framed glasses, the freckles, the youthful face all made Connie seem as young as the girls she worked with, and they tended to trust and confide in her as though she were one of them. The big problem was that Brandy didn't trust anyone, especially not anyone in a position of authority. In the few short months they would have her, Connie would have a difficult time penetrating Brandy's defenses.

So much to do with Brandy, so little time. And what about all the ones Harbor House couldn't hold? The ones Mickey couldn't even try to help? She had to do something. She *would* do something. "We've got to have more room," she blurted out, smacking her open palm on the desk. The impact was a little harder than she'd intended. It overturned her pencil cup, and before she could catch it, the contents clattered loudly across the desktop and onto the floor. Feeling foolish, she watched them fall.

Connie looked up. "So I see," she said in a brisk, professional voice. "Would you like to talk about it?"

Mickey grinned. "Don't try your psychological tricks on me. There really isn't anything to talk about right now. The executive board's meeting tomorrow to approve the proposal for the Brock house, and M.C.'s been working out the details. But we still have one small obstacle—the united citizens of West Village." She leaned over and began retrieving pens and pencils.

"What else is new?" Mickey heard the acid in Connie's voice even as she ducked under the desk after a yellow highlighter. Though Connie tried not to show it, she got every bit as frustrated as Mickey at the stumbling blocks that forever seemed to slow their progress. "Who's the one most opposed to it? Or should I say, who does M.C. have to win over?"

Mickey sat up before she answered. "A developer, a man who lives in West Village." Thinking of Cameron, she could feel the hard-to-identify emotions she'd felt before, and hoped she sounded noncommittal. Connie was much too good at picking up on things people didn't say. "His name is Cameron Scott. He's their unofficial spokesman. He also wants to buy the Brock house himself, to use in a project of his own."

"So? M.C. can talk to him."

"Unfortunately, M.C. seems to like him. So does Rooney. He bit him."

"No kidding?"

"Yep. You know Rooney only bites the ones he loves. You should have seen the guy's face." Remembering, Mickey dissolved into laughter again.

"How did he take it?" Connie asked.

"Very well, actually," Mickey said, wiping her eyes. "Considering he probably wanted to strangle Rooney. The next time he dodged him pretty fast."

A low tap, barely audible above the blare of the TV, sounded on the office door. Connie looked a question at Mickey, who shrugged and closed her notebook. The girls at Harbor House knew they weren't to interrupt a meeting between Mickey and Connie. "Come in," Mickey finally said.

The door opened tentatively, and Leslie poked in her head. "Someone to see you, Mickey. His name's Cameron Scott."

CHAPTER FOUR

MICKEY'S FIRST REACTION was dismay. Her second was annoyance at M.C. It had been his bright idea to invite the man over. The least he could do was be here to entertain him. She knew she was being irrational, but at this point she didn't care.

Avoiding Connie's too-perceptive eyes, she looked up to answer Leslie. Then she caught the expression on the girl's face and felt a sinking in the pit of her stomach. Being in love herself, Leslie was seeing romance everywhere—in this case between Mickey and Cameron. "He's a real hunk, Mickey," Leslie said in a stage whisper. "Where'd you find him?"

Mickey started to correct her, then realized the futility of even trying. She let out an explosive breath and shot her what she hoped was a quelling look. "Just show him in, please."

Leslie disappeared, and Mickey finally dared to glance at Connie, who was watching her with a thoughtful expression. For the first time, she wished her friend wasn't quite so good at her job.

She stood. Normally her height, or lack of it, didn't bother her. Now, for some reason, she felt determined to give herself every possible advantage. As Cameron Scott came into the room, she was glad she'd risen.

Today he wasn't wearing one of the expensive, perfectly tailored ensembles that enabled her to dismiss him as just another wealthy businessman. He wore casual slacks and a short-sleeved plaid sport shirt. Once out of those elegant suits, he looked like a linebacker. Seeing his bare arms and muscular shoulders, she knew her speculation about his powerful physique had been right on the money. A vivid image of him, tousled, perspiring, grinning, galloping across the turf for a backyard touchdown teased her mind.

"Hello, Mickey," he said easily, as though they'd been on a first-name basis for years.

Mickey shook the extended hand. "Hello, Cameron." She forced herself to use his first name. "This is Connie Allen, our consulting psychologist. Connie, Cameron Scott."

They shook hands. "Are you part of Harbor House, too?" he asked.

"More or less," Connie answered. "I work here part-time as a counselor. I'm under contract to Harbor House and several other facilities in town."

"I see." He straightened his glasses, and Mickey found her own gaze tracing the smooth, firm line of his jaw, the cleanly defined profile. "I'm here to learn about halfway houses," he confessed frankly. "Right now I don't know much, but I have a feeling that Mickey and M.C. will remedy that."

Connie laughed. "You'll learn more than you ever wanted to know."

"I hope so," he said, and Mickey found herself believing him. Today the steel that usually lay just beneath his courteous exterior seemed to be less in evidence, as though he were deliberately putting himself in the role of observer. Still, he radiated a quiet strength that was as unmistakable as it was evident.

He glanced at Connie's notebook and at the papers spread across Mickey's desk. "I've interrupted you," he said. "Finish what you were doing. I'll wait outside."

Mickey was about to seize the opening to forestall him, even for a few minutes, but Connie blithely betrayed her. "We were through, just visiting." She shot an amused glance at Mickey. "I have to be at Social Services in half an hour." She stood and reached for her purse. "I enjoyed meeting you, Mr. Scott."

"My pleasure," Cameron said cordially.

Mickey mumbled a goodbye, swearing an oath to inflict a slow death on Connie the next time she saw her.

Connie smiled sweetly. "Bye, Mickey." Then she was gone, leaving Mickey alone in the office with Cameron Scott. The silence stretched until she thought she would scream. He didn't offer to break it, just kept looking at her with a knowing half smile on his face.

Finally, because she couldn't think of anything else, she blurted out what was foremost in her mind. "I didn't really think you'd come." Then she cursed herself for how it sounded.

"I said I would, remember?" He sounded a little surprised.

"Of course," she said hastily. Apparently, as far as he was concerned, his word settled the matter. "Everything's pretty routine," she told him. "You'll probably think you're wasting your time." She kept her eyes glued to the plaid of his shirt. It was a pretty pattern, really, mostly reds and greens, with a thread of bright yellow running through it.

"Not at all," he said. "I'm sure routine is what you hope to maintain. By the way," he added as if in passing, "I know what you're doing, and it won't do you any good. I don't discourage easily."

Her gaze flew to his face. There was mischief there. Pure, little-boy mischief. She could only stare foolishly at him.

The mischief melted into that lurking amusement that played such havoc with her senses. "Look," he said, "you might not believe it, but I really do want to learn about Harbor House. Why don't you start by explaining the basic operation to me, then show me around, if that won't interrupt things too much?"

Twenty minutes later Mickey felt as though she'd never talked so long, so nonstop, in her life. She'd taken him upstairs, downstairs, even around the yard, all the time trying to tell him how Harbor House worked. And every minute, she was acutely conscious of him behind her, beside her.

She knew she was talking too much, because her mouth was dry. But he didn't seem bored. He listened and from time to time asked questions, intelligent, perceptive ones that made her stop and think about her answers. Damn him anyway. As they came back into the living room and she walked with him to the front door, she felt strung out and exhausted.

"I think I've covered just about everything," she said. "I'm sure you'll have more questions when you see us on a routine basis." Somehow, the idea didn't seem to disturb her the way it once had.

"I intend to do that." Something in his voice made her look up at him, and she saw an odd expression on his face. "You know, you're really to be commended," he said.

"I beg your pardon?" She couldn't quite believe her ears.

"This place is so—so needed," he added lamely.

Before she could stop herself, Mickey laughed aloud. "Yes, we think so, too."

Suddenly he was laughing too. "Sorry. That was a pretty silly thing to say. I suppose it just really dawned on me." His gaze lingered. "And by the way," he said, still in that matter-of-fact voice, "I love the way you laugh."

For a moment she couldn't say anything at all. "I—"

"I know what you're thinking," he interrupted before she could say anything else. "But at this point, if I criticized Harbor House, I'd be lying."

There he went again. If ever a man seemed to operate with candor and honesty, it was this one. "Thank you," she murmured.

"You're welcome." His smile told her he knew he was confusing her. "When does the night manager come in?"

Mickey looked at her watch. "Any minute. Why?"

He was looking at her keenly. "I'm taking a chance on undoing any goodwill I may have earned today, but I have an idea. Let me take you to see a house I think might be suited for your operation."

Involuntarily, she stiffened.

He saw it and put out a restraining hand. "Please," he said. "All I want you to do is look. What can that hurt?" It was a simple request, made eloquent by the expression in his eyes.

Mickey wanted to refuse him, to tell him he was wasting his time, but there was no way she could say it without sounding unpardonably rude. "All right," she finally agreed, knowing beforehand it was a mistake. "I'll go with you. To look," she added with emphasis.

The qualification didn't bother him in the least. "Great." Grinning broadly, he caught her arms and squeezed them.

His hands were warm, incredibly strong. Deep inside her, an alarm went off. Without thinking, she pulled away and stepped back, putting space between them. When she realized what she'd done, she went hot with embarrassment.

He stood there watching her, puzzlement plain on his face. He said nothing, nor did he make any move to touch her again.

Mickey turned her head away. "I—I thought I heard the night manager coming in the back." Without looking at him again, she walked quickly toward the kitchen.

Ten minutes later, seated uneasily in the soft bucket seat of his Mustang, listening to the muted roar of the big engine, she wondered what on earth had possessed her. She'd worked through all the old problems so many years ago. Yet this man, who against all reason invited her trust, had frightened her with his touch, had brought back all the old knee-jerk defenses.

And she knew that the main reason he'd frightened her was that she'd wanted him to touch her.

EXCEPT FOR the most desultory of small talk, they drove in silence. A faint aroma of new leather still clung to the Mustang's dove-gray interior, and computer numbers winked at Mickey from the instrument panel. From the look of it, the car could practically cook and serve breakfast. But she was unable to appreciate its fine points or relax against the deeply padded upholstery. The console that separated her from Cameron Scott wasn't enough. He was too big. He seemed to fill the entire car. She hugged her door, hoping her uneasiness wasn't too obvious, and kept her gaze focused on the passing scenery.

They were entering a neighborhood a mile or so from West Village. In fact, it was much like the Village; the wood-frame and dark-brick houses were the same vintage, built mostly in the twenties or thirties, adaptations of Federal, Colonial or Tudor architecture, with an occasional bungalow sandwiched in between. Like the Village, it had been a respectable, even substantial neighborhood. But now there were differences.

On some houses the paint was faded, beginning to peel. On others the grass grew tall against the buildings and around the trees, as though someone occasionally mowed but didn't bother to edge. Abandoned children's toys, their once-bright colors faded, lay scattered here and there in the yards among other debris. Some of the houses displayed Apartment for Rent signs on the front doors. The community atmosphere, the well-cared-for aura that pervaded all of West Village, was absent. Mickey knew this neighborhood well. She had come here not more than a year ago in search of one of her errant Harbor House charges. She wondered if Cameron was aware of the differences.

She glanced at him. Obviously not. He was draped over the wheel, studying the street signs, gray eyes intent behind the steel-rimmed glasses.

More than halfway through an intersection he hit the brake, then hung a sharp right. With no more than the barest squeal of tires, the car made a right-angle turn that lacked only a few degrees of being perfect. Before Mickey could retrieve her stomach from where it had landed somewhere in the back seat, he had pulled over in front of a house and cut the engine.

He turned to speak and, seeing her expression, grinned. Gone was every trace of the businessman. There was no hint of apology. Instead, he looked unconscionably pleased with himself, like a small boy who had just landed his model airplane without demolishing it. This was a side of Cameron Scott that she'd only glimpsed, and the effect was irresistible. Without thinking, she smiled back, right into his eyes.

For a second neither spoke. The gray eyes fixed on her were laced with humor and lurking warmth. She felt as though he were inviting her to come along and have fun with him. She was tempted. Oh, she was tempted. She didn't know how to respond, but her body knew. She felt a current of desire ripple through her body like a breeze over a still pond.

A long second passed before he finally broke the silence, his voice a little husky. "Sorry. I almost missed my turn." He patted the dash and looked around the interior of the car with obvious affection. "Doesn't she handle great?"

The moment was gone. "Just great," Mickey said, feeling relieved and a little bereft at the same time. "Do you drive like this with all your clients?"

The grin broadened. "Sure. People tell me my professional image calls for a more sedate car, but I'd wanted a Mustang convertible since I was in high school. As soon as I could afford it, I gave it to myself as a reward."

She should have condemned his priorities, particularly since the price of this car would pay for clothes, tuition, electric bills, you name it, for Harbor House for no telling how long. But somehow she couldn't. He seemed to enjoy himself so much.

She looked at the house. It was a large two-story structure, painted white but beginning to flake in spots. It sat squarely in the middle of the block, flanked by smaller but relatively well-kept homes. A large realtor's sign was posted in the front yard. Across the street, on the corner, stood a convenience store. As they watched, two boys came out, shouting and laughing, and gave an exuberant high-five to a young man standing near the bus stop.

Cameron opened his door and unfolded his long length from the driver's seat. By the time Mickey found the belt release, he had opened her door and was waiting. When she got out of the car she nearly bumped into him and had to force herself not to back away. There was just too much of him.

Cameron unlocked the front door and led the way into the large living room. "The owner's willing to sell or lease," he said. "He just wants the property to produce some sort of income."

"How much is he asking?"

He named the monthly payment. "One-year lease minimum, but I think he'll take any reasonable offer."

He stood aside to let her precede him. They went all over the house, downstairs and upstairs, not missing a room, even a closet. He kept up a running commentary, occasionally referring to a multiple listing sheet he carried in his hand.

She noticed that he lacked the typical salesman's hype. He spoke as though he was giving serious thought to what he was saying. Once or twice she even caught him pointing out the house's disadvantages. Almost, she thought, as if he were really trying to find them a place as satisfactory as Brock's house, not just something, *anything,* to get them out of West Village. Maybe he'd really meant what he'd said about solutions being his specialty. In fact, he only mentioned the Brock house once, to tell her it was located on a smaller lot. The remark was accompanied by a sidelong glance and a grin that verged on being sheepish. She caught herself watching his mobile, well-formed mouth as he talked, and had to remind herself to remain objective about him.

The end of the tour brought them back to the empty living room. He said nothing, but she knew he was waiting. She took a deep breath and walked over to the window.

"It's a good house," she said without preamble. "If it were located anywhere else, I'd seriously consider it."

"What's wrong with the location?" Apparently he hadn't expected her objections to come from that direction. "It's a lot like West Village."

"Look over there." She pointed through the window toward the store. "Do you see that?"

He stood behind her and followed the direction of her finger. He was very close to her, but for some reason, his nearness didn't seem to disturb her so much.

"Sure." He frowned. "I saw it when we came in. Maybe the convenience store's not so good, but it's also right next to a bus stop. Anyway, in Village Walk you'd have—"

"Not the store. See the guy standing near the bus stop?"

"Yeah?"

"He was in the same spot when we came up."

"The bus is late." He looked at her as if to say, so what?

She shook her head. "That's not it. A dozen buses could come by and he wouldn't leave. He's not interested in catching a bus." She shoved down the anger, the frustration, and made her voice level. "He's a pusher."

Total silence. When she looked at Cameron, he was staring at her as if he'd been poleaxed. "You've got to be kidding."

"I wish I were."

"You don't know it for a fact." His voice was peremptory, almost angry. But she could see in his eyes that he knew it was true.

"Trust me."

He said nothing, just looked at the youth across the street, then at her, then back across the street.

"He's lining up future customers. He starts by making friends with them, then moves up to free drug samples."

"I see." Cameron was still staring at the young man across the street. He leaned one hand against the wall, as if for support, and watched without speaking. Three children, two boys and a girl not more than ten or eleven, came down the sidewalk. They passed the youth, and he smiled and said something to them. Two walked by without stopping, but one of the boys hesitated, apparently listening, before hurrying to catch the others.

"See?" Mickey didn't even try to keep the bitterness from her voice. "They've been warned, of course, and they're cautious, but even so, he's making progress with one of them."

Before Cameron could answer, a flashy, late-model car pulled up to the curb. The young man sauntered over to it and leaned down to talk through the window. After a few moments he got in, and the car drove away.

Cameron straightened, ran a hand through his hair. "I'll be damned." He couldn't seem to say anything else. He looked around the cavernous, dusty living room, then back out at the street. Lightly, he struck his fist on the window-sill. "I feel really... stupid," he finished.

"Don't." Mickey's anger was draining away. Strangely, she wanted to comfort him. It occurred to her that one of the things she found most appealing about this man was his readiness to accept blame, to admit fault or ignorance. In her experience, not many men were like that. "That's one reason drug education programs are so important. For everyone," she finished gently.

"You've obviously dealt with this quite a lot...." Underneath his tone she could still hear his anger.

"Yes." She met his eyes. "I have." His look sharpened, so she looked away before he read too much. "It doesn't get any easier," she said. "There aren't any rules. You just learn to handle it any way you can. In some cases you can help. Even if you help only one kid, it's worth it. Believe me."

He looked back at the street as if he were still doubting what he'd seen. "Point made," he said. "I'll keep trying to find another house, but I'll reserve judgment until you've seen it. In fact," he added grimly, "in future I'll reserve judgment about a lot of things."

The ride back to Harbor House was for the most part made in silence.

M.C. WAS RIGHT ON TIME. He knew better than to show up one minute late. Or one minute early, for that matter. He glanced accusingly at the impatiens, no doubt the last of the season, blooming in multicolored order in the impossibly tidy beds, and straightened his tie. For this meeting he had donned a suit, something he rarely did for anyone. This time he was going to need all the ammunition he could get.

He tracked the second hand of his watch. When it hit number twelve, he rang the doorbell. He almost jumped at the promptness with which it was answered.

"Mr. Mulvaney." Jessamine Cunningham was immaculate in a navy dress with a white collar, fastened with a gold bar pin. "Please come in." Her eyes flicked over him, taking due note of the suit, he was sure. Although her voice was as well modulated as ever, her tone was strictly business. There was no trace of yesterday's fleeting humor. As he followed her inside, M.C. shrugged inwardly. He was a patient man. Doors that had been opened once could always be opened again.

Miss Cunningham stood by to allow him to enter her parlor—there was no other word for it. It certainly wasn't a living room in the true sense of the word; obviously no everyday living went on here. He stole a glance around. Antiques. He was no expert, but he suspected these were good ones. Accessories, in perfect taste. Paintings and prints everywhere. Art books on the tea table. M.C. filed away the information. One never knew when the most irrelevant scraps of knowledge might come in handy.

"Please sit down, Mr. Mulvaney." Her gesture was straight from a European court.

He took a Queen Anne wing chair and sat down. Carefully.

Miss Cunningham took a seat opposite him. Her back, he noted, did not touch the chair. "As I told you yesterday, Mr. Mulvaney, you have thirty minutes," she said. "I'm willing to listen to you for that long. But I must warn you that it's most unlikely I'll change my mind."

"I appreciate it, ma'am," he said seriously. "Let me tell you a little about what we do, and then you can ask me any questions you like...."

Twenty-five minutes later, he was beginning to wonder if at last he'd met his match. Miss Cunningham hadn't budged an inch. Oh, she'd been polite enough, but she'd fired a barrage of the most penetrating questions he'd ever had to answer, and even his most persuasive arguments hadn't seemed to faze her.

He knew his time was running out. He had one shot left, and, being M.C. Mulvaney, he was going to take it.

"I understand you've taught school," he said.

She inclined her head. "That's correct."

"Tell me, have you ever taken a child everyone else had given up on and changed the direction of his life?"

He was rewarded by seeing the faintest gleam appear in the green eyes. "Certainly," she said. "Many times. It's part of a teacher's duty." The gleam grew stronger. Pride. "I've discovered potential in students when no one else knew it was there, including themselves," she said. "Of course," she added, "they had to be taught discipline."

"Of course," M.C. agreed. *Like the impatiens,* he thought. He leaned forward in his chair. "We're doing the same thing at Harbor House, Miss Cunningham," he said. "The only difference is that, with many of these kids, there are no loving families or—" he paused meaningfully "—one-in-a-million teachers to help them."

He thought he caught an arrested expression in her eyes, and the thin skin across her angular cheekbones washed with the palest color.

"We feel the same commitment to our girls that you felt toward your students," he went on, "to give them the best chance possible. West Village . . . your neighborhood," he said with subtle emphasis, "is the kind of place that can help us give them that advantage. I won't lie to you, Miss Cunningham. Sometimes our girls do get into trouble. But there's a risk of that with any normal family unit. It's a chance every parent takes by having children in the first place."

She looked at him thoughtfully. "I see your point, Mr. Mulvaney," she finally said, "and I'm sympathetic to what you and your daughter are trying to do. You're to be commended."

"Thank you, ma'am." M.C. felt as though he should stand up and salute. But he knew what was coming next.

"However, I am still unable to change my position," Miss Cunningham went on. "Having a houseful of troubled teenagers in West Village is simply not in the best interests of the neighborhood. My neighbors look to me to guide them in these matters, and I must not betray their trust." Was it his imagination, or did her voice sound a little less firm? He couldn't tell. "You must try to understand," she said. She glanced at her watch. "And now, if you'll excuse me. . . ."

M.C. rose. Like any good general, he knew when to retreat. "I do understand, Miss Cunningham," he assured her with all the sincerity at his command. "And I appreciate your candor. I'll be going now. Thank you very much for your time." He inclined his head in the courtliest of little bows.

She nodded graciously in return, then moved to show him to the door.

"By the way," he said as if in passing, "I couldn't help noticing your art. You have quite a collection." He turned to watch her face.

"Thank you." Sure enough, the gleam of pride reappeared in her eyes. "I inherited some pieces from my family, but some I've purchased for myself over the years."

He decided to explore this particular road a little further. He could fake an interest in art—in anything, if he had to.

"This piece, now." He pointed to a landscape hanging just inside the parlor doorway. He didn't have the foggiest notion as to the identity of the painter, or even the time period. He tried to look knowledgeable, hoping she would give him a clue.

She came through like a champ. "A Ruisdael," she said. "Seventeenth century. A reproduction, of course, but a good one. It was one of my father's favorites."

"It's beautiful," M.C. said truthfully. He scoured his brain and fished up a name. "I've always admired Van Gogh."

Miss Cunningham sniffed. "An untidy painter. And, I might add, an untidy man."

Oops, M.C. thought. *Can't win 'em all.*

"Seurat, now..." Miss Cunningham moved to another reproduction on the adjoining wall. "So tidy, such a beautiful effect. His technique, you know."

"Technique?" M.C. decided to probe further. Besides, by now, he was thoroughly enjoying himself.

"Yes. His pointillism, of course. He originated the method," she supplied helpfully. She indicated the myriad microscopic dots of bright color that brought the painting to life.

"Of course." M.C. spotted a pen-and-ink drawing resting on an easel on a nearby desk. It was a small work, a woodland scene showing a stag at bay, muscles knotted along his powerful frame, antler-crowned head raised in challenge. It was a simple drawing, but every line radiated energy and power. And it was composed of innumerable tiny dots of ink. No color, but... M.C. decided to act on the intuition he was famous for. "Pointillism?"

Miss Cunningham actually smiled. "Young man, you have a good eye."

"Thank you, ma'am," he said modestly. "Whose work?"

Her smile faded, and she hesitated a moment before she answered. "My niece's, actually. She did this when she was only sixteen years old."

"Amazing." M.C. was genuinely impressed. The drawing was powerful. "Has she pursued her art?"

"No. She's not with us anymore." Miss Cunningham's voice held traces of an old sadness. "She died not long after she did this piece."

"I'm sorry," M.C. said simply. And he was. For Miss Cunningham's grief, and for the young life that had been ended so prematurely. She had been just about Brandy Williford's age....

Suddenly, M.C. had one of his periodic strokes of genius. "One of our residents is an artist, ma'am," he said quickly. "I've not seen any of her work, but her teachers tell us she has real talent."

"Oh? How old is she?" The question might have been polite conversation, but M.C. didn't miss the tiny note of interest in Miss Cunningham's voice.

"I believe she just turned sixteen."

"I see." There was a small silence, during which M.C. congratulated himself. He even amazed himself sometimes.

Miss Cunningham glanced down at her watch. "Mr. Mulvaney," she said in faint surprise, "you'll have to excuse me. I'm going to be late."

"My fault, ma'am," M.C. was quick to say. "I was so interested in our discussion that I forgot the time."

"That's quite all right," Miss Cunningham returned graciously. "I should have been watching it more closely." She seemed to recall herself. "By the way, I trust I've made myself quite clear regarding my position on the halfway house?"

"Perfectly, ma'am."

"Good. However—" the look she gave M.C. would have been coquettish coming from anyone else "—if you would care to come back another time to discuss art? Perhaps for tea..."

Bingo. "I'd be delighted," he said, giving her another little bow. In all his patchwork of experiences he couldn't ever remember taking tea with an elderly maiden lady, but there was a first time for everything. "I'll call before coming to make sure it's convenient."

"And someday you may bring the girl, too. She might enjoy seeing the paintings and drawings. Now, good afternoon." She dismissed him with a nod that was positively regal.

As M.C. headed back down the walk to his car, he was hard put not to skip in triumph. She had actually let him stay a full fifteen minutes past the allotted time. And had invited him to come back, to bring Brandy.

Miss Cunningham might not know it yet, but he wasn't through, not by a long shot.

CHAPTER FIVE

"HI, CAMERON. C'mon in."

"Thanks, Joni." Cameron stepped inside. At first Mickey had made the girls call him Mr. Scott, but he'd insisted they use his given name, especially now that they were growing used to him. They ought to be, he reflected. He'd been around often enough in the past couple of weeks. His mouth twisted into a wry smile. He'd learned more than he'd ever dreamed possible. And he'd failed to find another satisfactory place for Harbor House. He dreaded what he was going to have to tell Mickey today.

"How's school?" he asked Joni.

She shrugged, but didn't answer. Her normally cheery expression was closed, mulish.

"What's the matter?"

"Somebody called me a—" She paused. "Never mind."

"You can tell me," Cameron said gently. "I think I've heard it all by now."

She told him. The term was short, obscene, and had to do with Joni's race, among other things. The ugly words fell from her lips as casually as if she were giving him the time of day.

With difficulty, Cameron suppressed his shock. Oh, he'd heard the expression before, plenty of times. But not from the mouth of a pretty fifteen-year-old, especially one at whom it had just been aimed.

Here it was again, that other world. The one Mickey had shown him two weeks ago, where the friendly young man at the bus stop had turned out to be the neighborhood drug pusher. He'd known that world existed but always before had managed to keep it at a safe distance. Lately, he was being forced to face it. Not in New York, not in L.A., not in the news, nor even in the parts of Houston where he'd known it was there, but right under his very nose. Suddenly he felt light-years more naive than the youngest of these kids.

He looked at Joni. Anger burned in her eyes, but beneath it he could see the hurt. No child—and for all her street smarts Joni was still a child—should be on the receiving end of such filth. "Who called you that, Joni?" he asked tightly.

"One of the white girls at school."

"What did you do?"

Joni studied her feet. "I slapped her."

Good for you. He caught the words just before they left his mouth. "Then what happened?" he asked instead.

The mulish look faded into one of pure misery. "Now I'm in trouble. Mickey's on the phone with the principal."

Feeling horribly out of his depth, Cameron searched his mind for the right thing to say. "I'll tell you something, Joni," he said finally. "I used to fight a lot."

"You did?" Diverted, she looked up at him.

"Yeah. I had a reputation for being the kid with the quickest temper in the school. All someone had to do to pick a fight with me was look at me wrong."

"Wow." Joni's eyes grew round. "I thought you went to a rich kids' school."

Cameron winced. Was that how they saw him? "I don't know that you'd exactly call it a rich kids' school, Joni, but it really doesn't matter. Kids fight in any school." *But I never had that kind of provocation,* he reminded himself. *If I had, I'd have probably killed somebody.*

"Anyway, I learned that there are better ways to solve problems," he said aloud. "It's not easy, but if you had just kept your cool, the other girl would be the one in trouble right now."

"Yeah, I know." Joni shrugged, and though the defiance was still there, it seemed to have faded a little. "It just happened before I could stop myself."

"Well, maybe it won't go too badly for you." He touched her shoulder. "Just keep working on your temper. You'll be better off in the long run." Even to himself, he sounded shallow, sanctimonious. Who was he to give such assurances? His childhood experiences had been normal kid stuff, give or take a few incidents. Hers must have been hell.

"C'mon, Cameron," Joni said. "Mickey's in her office."

He followed her through the house. In the living room Lisa sat curled up in an overstuffed chair, watching TV. Leslie called a greeting from the dining room, where she was working on a science project. A basket of tennis rackets stood in a corner, a soccer ball resting beside it. The kids here seemed so normal, so wholesome that it was hard for Cameron to believe they'd ever been in trouble for anything more than being late to class. But today, with Joni, was just one more reminder of how ignorant he was of the whole situation.

The door to Mickey's office was closed, but he could hear her voice. She was presumably talking on the phone to the principal. Joni walked right up and knocked, but Cameron stayed back, telling himself not to eavesdrop. He couldn't hear her words, anyway, just the husky, clipped cadence of her speech.

In a minute or so, he heard her hang up the phone. "Come in," she called. Joni went in but didn't bother to close the door behind her.

Cameron knew Mickey couldn't see him, and he knew this was none of his business. He told himself that he ought to let her know he was here, at least. But he didn't move.

"Joni." Mickey's voice was level. "I talked to Mr. Griffin."

"What'd Old Lizard Face have to say?" The bravado in Joni's voice didn't quite mask the unease.

"He's giving you five days of detention. If it happens again, you'll be suspended."

Joni's response was descriptive, explicit.

Cameron grimaced. He'd heard that one, too.

Apparently Mickey was more accustomed to such language from children than he was. "Language like that will just earn you more demerits, Joni," she said evenly.

"But, Mickey," Joni protested, "Cindy called me a—"

"I know what she called you. The principal will deal with her. But it doesn't change the fact that you hit her. Now you have to accept the consequences."

"She deserved it," Joni said sullenly.

"Maybe so. But you shouldn't make judgments about what other people deserve, and you can't go around dishing it out to them. All you can do is be responsible for yourself. Now, listen to me a minute...."

Leaning against the wall, arms folded, Cameron listened, too, while Mickey talked. Sensibly, reasonably, as if to a peer instead of a child. The heart-stopping warmth he always saw in her dealings with Lisa was just underneath her tone, but less in evidence.

After Mickey finished, she allowed Joni to vent her spleen without interruption. At the end of the tirade, she responded with positive comments, meant to reinforce and bolster confidence, not to confine or destroy. Implicit in every word she said was that she, and Harbor House, were there to help, but in the long run, Joni's life was Joni's responsibility.

Cameron listened in awed humility. Mickey had just laid out a formula for life that anyone could take a lesson from. The sheer strength of the woman staggered him. Compelled by the desire to see her, he inched up just enough to look through the half-open door. Focused as she was on Joni, Mickey still didn't see him. He found his gaze playing over the beautifully shaped planes of her face, the sweep of her black lashes against her porcelain skin, the almost painful intensity in her eyes. She gave all of herself to her work, and more. Irrationally, he found himself a little jealous. If he could evoke that kind of response from her, even once....

"Just think before you react," she reminded Joni. "Use common sense. If you hadn't hit Cindy, she would have been punished instead of you, and you wouldn't be in trouble now."

"That's what Cameron said," Joni mumbled.

"Cameron?" Mickey looked up quickly. He moved into full view, and the flash of pure blue as her eyes met his hit him like a body blow. Just before her guard came up, he saw one millisecond of startled welcome. He felt ridiculously pleased.

"He came to see you," Joni explained.

"I'm sorry," he put in, stepping forward. "I didn't mean to intrude. I followed Joni back, and—"

"It's all right," Mickey said. "Come in. Go ahead with your chores, Joni. I'll be with you in a minute."

Obediently, Joni disappeared. Mickey indicated a chair and he took it, directing a malevolent look at Rooney, ensconced in his usual spot in the out box. Following recommended procedure, he scratched the prescribed area on his head. "Hello, Rooney, you old—"

"Ah, ah," Mickey interrupted. "Remember the children."

"The children, my eye. They know more swear words than I do."

She laughed, and the clear, musical sound was everything he remembered. "That's probably true, but we have to remember to set an example."

"I'll try to keep that in mind, especially with him." He nodded toward the sleeping cat. "Joni told me what happened." He smiled. "At least I seem to have told her the right thing."

"It's nice to hear what I say reinforced," she said, "even if you did say it first. Maybe we should hire you as an assistant counselor."

He looked away from her mouth and, with an effort, concentrated on what she was saying. "I wouldn't know where to begin." He spread his hands. "I'm beginning to think I don't know anything at all."

She sobered, and it occurred to him that her face would be fascinating no matter what her mood. "These kids relate to their peers, their parents, their teachers, the whole world differently from the way others do," she explained. "They operate from a different frame of reference. That's the thing you have to remember."

"I suppose so." He shook his head. "Like Joni," he mused. "She's cute and likable. And just now, without turning a hair, she used language that would make a Green Beret turn pink."

"But that's all she's known," Mickey pointed out. "Have you ever noticed the little scar along her jaw?"

"No, not really."

"It's from a knife fight. By the age of twelve, she'd already been in several of them. That's about the time she got into drugs. It's an old story. She never had a father she knew, and her mother was a heroin addict. She had to support them both by stealing, or whatever she could find to do." In her habitual gesture, Mickey tucked her hair behind one ear. "The fact that she only slapped the girl today means we've made a great deal of progress. Two years ago she'd have gone after her with a knife."

He was shocked into silence. Watching Mickey's face, he realized that she spoke of these horrors as if they were the norm. Maybe they were, as far as she saw it. Speaking of different frames of reference, what was hers? What lay under that tough, matter-of-fact facade? When he'd touched her the other day, she'd jerked away from him as if he was an ax murderer. He was certainly no authority, but he'd be willing to bet next year's profit that, at some point in her life, she'd been abused. An ex-boyfriend, maybe. He was stunned at the surge of protective anger that flooded him. One way or another, he intended to find out the particulars. If she ever spoke to him after today...

"If these kids are so tough," he said, only half-joking, "why don't they just take a knife to you?"

"Every once in a while, one of them does." Her half laugh didn't do much to soften the stark statement. "By the time we get them, most of them behave themselves," she hastened to add, seeing his face. "They may commit minor infractions, like Joni did today, but basically they want to stay here. And if they come to us from the streets..." She took a deep breath. "They don't usually want to go back.

The problem is finding a way to teach them that life doesn't have to be an endless round of knife fights, sex for hire, guns and drugs, that it's possible for them to build new lives for themselves. And they *can* do it, if they work at it." Her face glowed with absolute conviction.

Did you do it, Mickey? he wanted to ask. *Did you have to build a new life for yourself?* He decided to risk it. "How did you get into this kind of work?" he asked casually, hoping to catch her off guard. Immediately the wariness was there again, just behind her eyes. Was it only because she saw him as a threat to what she was trying to do? Or was it because he was a man? He'd have to be more careful next time he touched her.

Next time. With a small shock he realized that he hoped there would be a next time. He could feel the desire, an irresistible undercurrent pulling at him beneath all their careful, civilized words.

"I...it interested me." She clipped off the words, and he saw the defenses click back into place.

"And M.C.," he said, still keeping his tone casual. "How'd he get involved?" He might be pushing his luck, but he was determined to get a lead on what made her tick. M.C. was her father. It occurred to him that M.C. could probably provide him with some answers.

"M.C. got interested after I was already into it." Her words were delivered in the same even tone, giving nothing away.

So that was a touchy point, too. A remembered fragment of conversation tugged at a corner of his mind, something between her and M.C. about her growing up.... Could M.C. have been part of the problem? Impossible. He dismissed the thought the instant it entered his mind. If that had been the case, they wouldn't be working so comfortably together now. He knew by instinct, if nothing else, that it wasn't true. Of course, M.C. actually worked *for* her, which in itself was a little strange. She seemed very fond of him, but she didn't treat him like a father. More like a friend.

A mystery here. He decided to let it go...for the moment. "It seems to have worked out well for both of you," he said conversationally. "However it happened, you're both very good at what you do."

"Thank you." Her tone changed, lightened.

He glanced at his watch and rose as if he'd suddenly remembered something. "I've got to be going now," he said. "It's later than I thought. I need to go back by the office."

Her relief was so obvious he almost laughed. A little hurriedly, she led the way back through the house into the living room. Now it was Brandy Williford who was draped over the old overstuffed chair, watching TV, one foot swinging idly back and forth. A sketchbook lay on the floor in front of her. He saw with amusement that, when she spotted him, she straightened. Lately she'd been doing her best to flirt with him.

He smiled at her. "Hello, Brandy."

"Hi, Cameron." Brandy rose from the chair, her natural grace almost making up for the too-short skirt and the sleazy rayon tank top. She smoothed the skirt, hands lingering over her hips, and thrust out her chest. "How're you doin'?" Her full mouth pursed into an adolescent approximation of a sultry pout. *Must have been watching Madonna videos,* he thought, his amusement growing.

"I'm fine, Brandy," he answered cordially. "How are you?"

"Just fine." She looked up at him through lashes heavy with too much mascara. "I haven't seen you lately. Why don't you come around more often?"

Cameron suppressed a smile and tried to keep his tone noncommittal. "I've been around. I guess you just weren't here." He glanced down at the sketch pad. "Are you drawing something?"

"It's nothin'." Her clumsy flirtation deflected, Brandy became a sullen child again.

"May I see it?" Cameron held out his hand.

Lifting one shoulder in a shrug, she handed him the pad.

The sketch was simple, perfunctory. But he easily recognized the figure of Leslie, bent over her work on the dining room table. Form, line, composition—there was real talent here. "It's good, Brandy."

"Thanks." The girl's face showed momentary pleasure. "I gotta go now," she mumbled, grabbing the pad and heading for the stairs.

"I told you we should make you an assistant counselor," Mickey said from behind him, her voice warm with approval.

He swung around in surprise. "How's that?"

"You handled that just right. Deflected her flirting without hurting her, then praised her for the one thing I hope is going to be her salvation."

"I was serious. She's talented."

"Yes, she is. Everyone who's ever seen her work says the same thing. But the problem is convincing her."

"What's to convince? Can't she see how good she is?"

Mickey hesitated. "Unfortunately, it's not that simple. It's all in self-perception. Brandy has practically no self-esteem at all. And if she doesn't believe in herself, nothing anyone else can say is going to convince her she's any good."

"I see." Add another bit to his newly acquired store of knowledge. In the past few weeks, he reflected ruefully, the term *live and learn* had taken on an entirely new meaning.

Mickey walked with him to the front door, and they stepped onto the porch. It was almost evening, and the November air was chill. She tilted back her head, closed her eyes and inhaled deeply. "Someone's burning leaves somewhere."

"Yes. I love the smell." He watched light and shadow play over her face. Desire, sharp and bittersweet, moved inside him.

"So do I," she said.

In silence, they stood for a moment on the porch, savoring the aroma.

Their gazes caught, held. Was it his imagination, or were Mickey's defenses down just a little? He found himself hating what he had to say, irrationally wanting to protect her. From what? The world? Or, more accurately, *her* world? How laughable. She was far better able to take care of herself within its boundaries than he could ever be. Even so, he wanted to take her in his arms, to soothe away the resistance, the barriers. He wanted to show her a different world, a world of laughter, love, joy. But he knew she wouldn't let him. Not yet. Maybe not ever, once he'd told her what he had to tell her. The truth. He'd built his whole way of life on it.

But he couldn't quite bring himself to break the peaceful silence of the moment.

"It's been more than two weeks," she said, breaking it for him. "You've seen how we operate. What are you going to do?"

Leave it to her, he thought ruefully, to be so blunt. He had to clear his throat to speak. "Mickey, I'm going to be perfectly honest with you. I'm going to tell my people the whole story. The good things and the disadvantages, every one of them. I'm going to tell them that I've come to have the highest respect for you, and admiration for what you do."

She said nothing, just waited, but he sensed her stiffen. He could barely muster the courage to say the next words. "But I also have to tell them I'm still not convinced it's best for anyone concerned if Harbor House moves in. I can't tell them one thing and believe another."

"Then I'll be honest with you." She met his gaze squarely, and he could see that as far as she was concerned, the lines of battle had been drawn. "I'm going to do what I have to do, regardless of what you, or anyone, thinks or does. My responsibility is to my girls. You can't keep us out, and there's nowhere else for us to go. We'll sign the lease next week, then we'll move in as soon as we can."

"That's your decision, and I can't blame you for it." He chose his words with care. "But if you do move in, you've got to remember that you've virtually assured us that there'll be no problem. I consider West Village, and Village Walk, to be my responsibility. As long as you're good neighbors, fine. If not, I'll do what I have to do." He paused. "I'll try to be fair to everyone concerned. That's all I can promise."

The light of war dimmed in her eyes, leaving an expression he couldn't quite read. "I suppose I'll have to live with that." Suddenly she looked exhausted. Vulnerable.

And he was doing it to her. It saddened him beyond words. Then, from nowhere, the need hit him again. To touch her...

Remembering the other time, he took it slowly. Holding her eyes with his own, he reached up and grazed her cheek with his finger. Her skin was softer than he'd imagined. He inhaled sharply. Her fragrance—light, fresh-scrubbed— teased his nostrils. She said nothing, didn't even flinch, just stood there, her eyes still unreadable.

For a long moment after his hand had dropped, he remained, looking at her. Then he turned and headed back down the sidewalk toward his car.

He'd lost the first round, he thought as he slammed the door. Somehow he'd known he would. Nothing short of handcuffs would keep Mickey Mulvaney from doing what she thought she had to do. It seemed that she'd had to fight for everything she'd ever had. If he could only... But he couldn't. His responsibility lay in other directions. *For now*.

He hadn't quite explored all the possibilities. There might be a chance that Village Walk's deed restrictions would prevent the move, but it was a long shot. He'd have to check them again, call his lawyer to make sure. And if he couldn't stop Harbor House from moving in, he could at least keep working with both sides, try to arbitrate, mitigate, find solutions acceptable to everyone.

He'd always prided himself on his ability to solve dilemmas, but he was beginning to have his doubts about this one.

And then there was Mickey.

He turned the key to start the Mustang. Either way he looked at it, this dilemma was his own.

"SO THERE'S NOTHING we can do?" Mechanically, his hand moved from stack to orderly stack of papers on his mahogany desktop, straightening edges that were already exactly aligned.

"All right, Mike," he said. "Thanks for checking." He hung up the phone. Mike Sabatelli was a good lawyer. If he said they had no recourse, they didn't. Besides, the man had only confirmed what Cameron already knew.

The real problem was that Houston had no zoning laws, and everything was up for grabs. A whorehouse could go in next to a Presbyterian church. The only check to the city's sprawling, unruly growth lay in the individual deed restrictions that most residential areas possessed. West Village had them, all right. Cameron had studied them, when he'd undertaken the Village Walk project. The trouble was that they had been drawn up when most halfway houses were still a half century into the future. They simply didn't cover this situation. Now the same lack of zoning restrictions that had allowed him to put in Village Walk would allow Harbor House to come in.

He cursed his own arrogance. He'd thought he could control Village Walk without having to worry about the out-of-date deed restrictions, had thought he could get the entire project in place without opposition.

He wadded up the piece of paper he'd been doodling on and threw it at the wastebasket. It fell short by two inches, bouncing feebly on the thick beige carpet. So much for arrogance.

He took off his glasses and pinched the bridge of his nose, not wanting to think about having to break the news to his investors and neighbors. Particularly his neighbors. He thought of Miss Cunningham, then decided he'd wait on that one awhile. Resolving instead to call his biggest investor, then work from there, he picked up the phone again and made himself dial the number.

"Mort Jacobs, please." The developer's booming voice came over the wires. "Mort? Cameron Scott. Listen, something's happened with the Village Walk project. I don't know that it'll affect us in the long run, but I thought you should know...."

Ten minutes later, he hung up the phone, wincing. Mort Jacobs, who enjoyed a reputation as one of Houston's shrewdest, most successful businessmen, had not been pleased. He'd agreed with Cameron that it wasn't an unmitigated disaster, but he'd made it quite clear that he considered the problem—and the responsibility for finding a solution—to be Cameron's.

Deciding he'd still rather face a whole battalion of Houston businessmen than Miss Cunningham, Cameron decided to call his other investors next.

He was looking up the first number when the intercom buzzer sounded. "Line one, Cameron," Vicky said. "Miss Cunningham."

Wondering what he'd done lately to enrage the Fates, he picked up the phone. Was this just one of her periodic check-in calls, or had she actually heard the news already? Perversely, he hoped she'd already heard. He'd rather field her anger than have to break the news to her himself.

"Cameron, I talked with Mr. Mulvaney a few days ago." She sounded pleased with herself.

"Yes, ma'am?" Oh, boy. She didn't know. He was going to have to tell her.

"A most charming gentleman," she added, the tiniest of lilts in her voice.

"Yes, ma'am." *No kidding,* Cameron thought grimly. The only surprise was that M.C. had managed to charm Miss Cunningham so completely. He must be even better at it than he'd thought.

"We had quite a nice discussion, actually," Miss Cunningham said. "We share an interest in art."

"That's…great, Miss Cunningham." *Art?* He rolled his eyes heavenward. No question about it, he'd underestimated M.C. Mulvaney by at least half.

"I want you to know, however, that I told him in no uncertain terms that I was unalterably opposed to having a halfway house in West Village." Her tone indicated she believed she'd settled the entire matter.

"Uh...actually, Miss Cunningham, there's been...ah...a new development." Why was it that he could talk on equal terms with any professional man in town, but Miss Cunningham could make him stammer like a schoolboy? "They're moving in anyway."

Dead silence on the other end of the line. "That's impossible," she said finally, in stunned accents. "I told him exactly how I felt about it."

With grim amusement, Cameron reflected that it was probably the first time in her life she'd ever been disobeyed. "I'm afraid it's going to happen," he said. "Did Mulvaney actually promise you they wouldn't move in?"

Silence again. "Now that I think about it," she said slowly, "he only thanked me for my time. Then we began discussing art. I don't suppose he actually lied to me...."

"No, I'm sure he didn't. Both he and his daughter have dealt squarely with us from the beginning." He realized it was a relief to be able to defend Mickey and M.C. "I was impressed with the whole operation after I learned more about it, but I also told them I didn't think it would be in anyone's best interests, theirs included, for them to move into West Village. Ms. Mulvaney told me they were going to make the move anyway."

"We must have some legal recourse," Miss Cunningham protested. "The deed restrictions—"

"Are outdated. They don't cover halfway houses because there were no such things when the subdivision was built."

"You can't mean it!" Incredulity and horror mingled in Miss Cunningham's voice.

"I wish I didn't." But he wasn't so sure. "I just finished talking with my lawyer. He says we have no legal recourse at all. We can sue, of course, but it might take years. In the meantime, West Village and the Walk project would get a lot of unfavorable publicity, which we don't want. It may not be all bad," he added. "Harbor House may turn out to be a good neighbor." *Which was what he was hoping . . . .*

"According to your attorney, we have no choice." She still sounded stunned.

"You're right," he said heavily. "We have no choice at all."

There was a small, pregnant silence. Cameron held his breath.

"Well, I've never cried over spilled milk," she said finally. As she spoke, he could hear the habitual no-nonsense, authoritative tone creeping back into her voice. "We'll just have to make the best of it."

"Yes, ma'am."

Another little silence ensued, this one ominous. "But I'm going to have a thing or two to say to Mr. Mulvaney," she added. Each word dropped like a perfectly formed little stone.

Cameron said his goodbyes and hung up the phone. In spite of his doubts about M.C. Mulvaney, he pitied him. He wondered if the man had any idea of what he was facing.

He sat back against the soft leather of his desk chair and stared at the giant wall map with its bright pink and yellow demarcations. He'd felt morally obligated to try every way he knew to keep Harbor House out of West Village, and he'd failed. Now, not entirely to his surprise, he realized that one corner of him was glad. Harbor House—and Mickey—deserved a chance.

Mickey. She probably hated him. He had a vacation coming up, would be gone a few weeks. It probably wouldn't hurt if he were out of her hair for a while. Then, when he came back . . . Who knew? He certainly didn't.

Rousing himself, he flipped through his Rolodex for the name of the next investor on his list.

M.C. MULVANEY RANG the doorbell of Jessamine Cunningham's house for the third time in as many weeks and braced himself. He had a major fence to mend with her over the decision to move Harbor House, and he knew he was in for it.

It was a real shame, because up to then he'd been well on his way to winning her over. It couldn't be helped, he supposed. After all, it had been Mickey's decision to make. He was sure he could heal the breach, but with Miss Cunningham, he knew it was going to require major surgery. He also knew that he was going to have to take his lumps.

Well, that was all right, too. He straightened. Never let it be said that Melchior Caedmon Mulvaney couldn't handle anything for the sake of a higher goal, even a tongue-lashing from the most intimidating woman he'd ever run into.

Hearing her clipped, staccato footsteps approaching the door, he took a firmer grip on the portfolio he held in his hand and swallowed. Loudly.

She opened the door. He'd thought he was prepared, but when the faded eyes speared him like laser beams, he quailed where he stood.

"Mr. Mulvaney." Never in his life had he heard his name pronounced quite like that. She made no move to step aside, nor did she ask him in.

M.C. pulled his courage around him and scraped together every last bit of wit, charm, persuasiveness he possessed. Even though they were moving in under protest, it was still vital to Harbor House's welfare, and therefore to

Mickey's, that the neighborhood accept them eventually. And, he reminded himself, that was where he came in.

He coughed politely. "Miss Cunningham, I have some news for you."

"You needn't have bothered, Mr. Mulvaney. I've already heard it." The green eyes never wavered. "But I would like to take this opportunity to tell you that I take it amiss, *greatly* amiss, that you disregarded my express wishes on the matter." She folded her arms. "Particularly when I felt we understood each other so well."

"I realize that, Miss Cunningham, and I'm more sorry than I can say." He spread his hands in a gesture of apology. "As far as I'm concerned, we did have a good understanding, and I'd like to think we still do."

"I'm sorry, I'm afraid that's impossible, given the circumstances." She made as if to close the door.

"Miss Cunningham?"

She stopped the door a little too quickly, as if she hadn't really wanted to close it. He took due note.

"I'd like you to know that we explored every other option open to us before we made this decision," he said. "I told you once before that we're totally committed to providing our girls with the best opportunities possible, no matter what it takes. There was no other place for us to go. We had to move into the Brock house, for the sake of the girls."

He was watching her closely, but as yet could detect no softening in the implacable eyes. "Now we have to fulfill an obligation to you to be the best possible neighbors. We run a—" he groped for the word that would carry the most weight with her "—disciplined organization. Ask Cameron

Scott. He's visited us several times, and he liked what he saw."

"I believe he mentioned something to that effect," she unbent enough to say.

Good, M.C. thought. *Cameron's been putting in a word for us, even if he did try to scotch the project.* "I'd like you to visit, too, to see how we operate and what we do for our girls."

"I'm not sure about that." The expression was still unyielding, the posture poker-straight. But the blue-veined hand relaxed on the door, allowing it to swing open the tiniest bit.

"Miss Cunningham," he said, trying to pour all his accumulated years of persuasive skills into this one moment, "you told me once that you were always willing to listen to another viewpoint. I know it was a shock for you to hear that we'd gone ahead with our plans without your consent, but I'm asking you now to forgive us because of our own needs, and to give us a fair chance." He raised his hand to his heart. "I think I know you well enough to be sure that you'll do that."

Now, at last, he saw the change, the microscopic softening in the expression. "I'll consider it," she said.

He breathed an inward sigh of relief. He'd rounded the top of the mountain. From now on the going might still be rocky, but at least it would be downhill. *God, I'm good,* he thought modestly.

"When we're finished, I'll personally escort you on a tour of the house." His hand lingered over his heart. "And I brought something to show you." He indicated the portfolio. "Do you remember the young lady I told you about, one of our residents, who is artistically inclined? Let me show

you her work. Her teachers think she's very talented, but of
course you would know better than they...."

PENNY RHODES PLUMPED UP the pillows on one of the living room sofas. It was covered in an English floral chintz she
was particularly proud of.

"All right, Cameron," she heard Keith say from the
phone in the study. "Thanks for calling."

It was late for a call, almost nine-thirty, and something in
her husband's voice set off a faint warning in the back of her
mind. "What did Cameron say?"

Keith turned, and the look on his face made the warning
sound louder. "He says he couldn't talk the halfway house
people into relocating anywhere else," he said flatly, his eyes
on her.

She said nothing, just stood there holding the cushion,
staring at him.

"They signed the lease this week and will be moving in as
soon as they can fix up the house. Penny?"

"I heard you." Mechanically, she replaced the pillow on
the couch, setting it at just the right angle. "Cameron wasn't
supposed to let this happen."

Keith shrugged. "He couldn't do anything about it. The
deed restrictions in West Village are out-of-date, and the law
says they can move in anywhere they want."

"What are we going to do?" The panic rose inside her,
sending her voice higher, threatening to choke her.

"We can't do anything." The patience in Keith's voice
was barely controlled. "We'll just have to make the best of
it. After all, it's not the end of the world." He moved toward the door and picked up his briefcase. "Look, I've got

to go back to the office to pick up some files I need for to-night. Back in a little while, okay?''

''Of course.'' Automatically, Penny presented her cheek for his kiss.

After he'd gone, she stood for a long time, staring out into the darkness.

But she didn't see anything at all.

CHAPTER SIX

"PUT THEM IN MY OFFICE, please, Leslie," Mickey directed.

"Okay, Mickey." Her arms full of files, Leslie headed toward the back room in the Brock house that would now serve as Mickey's office.

Finding a stray stepladder, Mickey set down the armload of files she was carrying and stopped for a breather. Moving day was always chaos. The movers had come this morning, bringing over all the heavy furniture. Tonight, after six weeks of M.C.'s concentrated engineering, six weeks of hard labor, six exhausting, hectic weeks of moving everything from toasters to couch cushions piecemeal and trying to operate from two locations at once, her girls would sleep under a new roof. Now, ten days before Christmas, Harbor House would begin its official life on Shepherd Drive.

She wiped the perspiration from her forehead, pushed her hair back and looked down at herself. She didn't know which was grubbier, the faded, torn jeans she wore or the holey T-shirt, and she knew she had dirt on her face.

But she didn't care. God, she didn't care. She sent up a silent prayer of thanks for this spacious, welcoming house that radiated the benign spirits of the huge, happy family who had lived here, this house that was perfect for her and her girls. For the first time she could remember, she felt within sight of her dream.

She inhaled the smell of fresh paint that permeated every corner of the house. Better than perfume. They hadn't changed the structure or the floor plan; the maintenance agreement with Brock prohibited it, and they couldn't afford it anyway. Besides, they hadn't needed to. It was exactly right as it was.

But there had been shoring up, repairing, refurbishing, painting and papering tasks aplenty, and for the past six weeks, M.C. had been working his own particular brand of magic on the house. Assisted by Mickey, the girls, the regular staff and the assorted helpers he somehow always managed to pick up, either for token wages or for free, he had transformed an outdated, decaying hulk of a house into something miraculous. Now the walls sparkled with fresh color, the newly refinished floors shone, and the spacious, high-ceilinged rooms fairly beckoned them to make it a home again. It was theirs now, hers and her girls'.

She stood just inside the front door and surveyed her domain. Space, and plenty of it. Now they could accommodate eight girls. Twice as many as the old location had held. She couldn't take in the whole world, but now, at least, fewer of the turndowns would haunt her dreams. And when M.C. finished the attic, she could accommodate four more.

They weren't finished, of course. For that matter, they probably never would be. She could hear pounding coming from the second floor, where M.C.'s crew was still working on odds and ends. But at least they'd been able to move in. They were home. Edward Brock had come by yesterday to see for himself what they'd done with his house. With the suspicion of moisture shining in his eyes, he'd pronounced himself pleased. For Mickey, it was as good as a blessing. She only hoped—prayed—that the rest of the neighborhood would come to feel the same way.

Her gaze traced the graceful curves of the staircase in the entrance hall. It appealed to some small romantic corner of her soul that she hadn't even known existed. She visualized the Christmas tree that would stand beside it. They would have to hurry with the tree, she reminded herself. She would buy one this week and hope they could locate the box of ornaments in time. A Christmas tree was a must at Harbor House. Sometimes it was the only bright spot in existences normally defined in shades of black and gray.

M.C. walked past her, heading for the stairway with a long one-by-six over his shoulder. Joni shadowed his heels, with Lisa close behind her. At the foot of the stairs he set down the board, pulled out his bandanna and wiped his face. "Just baseboards and molding, then Leslie and Brandy's room will be ready to paint," he said. "Probably tomorrow. They'll have to camp out with Joni and Lisa tonight, though."

"No problem. They've got their bedding, and the mattresses are already upstairs. Since tomorrow's Saturday, we should be able to start painting early. I've already picked up the paint." Mickey reflected that it was good for the girls to help. It gave them a sense of accomplishment and made them feel the house was theirs, too. Besides, she and M.C. needed all the help they could get.

"Did you get the blue for our room?" Joni piped up.

"The very one," Mickey said. "The one you and Lisa picked out." She exchanged an amused glance with M.C. That particular shade of cornflower blue had been Joni's choice. Lisa had wanted yellow at first, but Joni had managed to con her into going along with the blue. Mickey had salved her own conscience by allowing Lisa to choose curtains and spreads of a bright yellow, blue and green plaid.

M.C. snapped his fingers. "I forgot something. Joni, make yourself useful." He grinned at her. "Go get the box of nails from the front seat of the car, please."

"Yes, sir." Joni, ready to do anything for her idol, turned and sprinted down the hallway.

"Happy to be here, honey?" Mickey laid a gentle hand on Lisa's hair.

"Yes, ma'am." The sweetness of Lisa's smile could pierce the coldest of hearts. Joni would always land on her feet. It was kids like Lisa the world could gobble up. If only someone would love Lisa the way she needed to be loved....

"Do you like the curtains and spread?" she asked aloud.

"I think they're beautiful," Lisa said softly.

"Good. Do me a favor, will you, please? Start unpacking the boxes of kitchen stuff." Mickey gave her a last pat. "Sooner or later, we're going to have to start cooking again."

As Lisa disappeared into the kitchen, Brandy walked past, head down as usual.

"Brandy." The girl was still Mickey's greatest worry. She was showing improvement in manners, dress and general behavior, but both Mickey and Connie Allen knew there was still a wall around her, impenetrable as glass. Sometimes it almost seemed to Mickey that it was a mirror, and she was seeing herself as she'd been at Brandy's age. They had to break through it. They simply had to.

"Ma'am?" Brandy raised her head, but didn't quite look Mickey in the eye.

"I really love the colors you've chosen for your room." Brandy, with her eye for color, had picked a subtle, luminous shade somewhere between apricot and terra cotta, then had managed to find curtains and a spread in a complementing Southwestern motif from the local bargain store.

Leslie, occupied with the intricacies of being in love, had been only too happy for Brandy to take care of it.

"Thanks." Brandy ducked her head again and walked on, but Mickey thought she heard a note of gratification in her voice. Actually, Mickey realized with a small shock, she really did look different. Her makeup was less garish, more becoming to her coloring, allowing her natural beauty to show through. Her T-shirt was a soft green that accentuated her hazel eyes. Though it might have been an accident, her jeans were definitely not as tight as the ones she'd worn when she first came to Harbor House. And she'd told M.C. just the other day that she'd decided to enter the art contest. Maybe she really was changing.

M.C. looked at Mickey with his knowing eyes. "Regrets?"

"No." She'd never meant anything more in her life. "None at all."

"Good." He nodded as if satisfied.

"What about the neighbors? Have you met any of them yet?"

"Yep. I've met the people directly in back of us, and the families next to them. They were a little hostile at first, but I think they're settling down now. I'm even hoping Miss Cunningham will come around. She liked Brandy's pictures."

"That's a good sign."

"I'm going to take Brandy to see her."

Thank you, Lord, for M.C., she whispered to herself. It occurred to her, not for the first time, that in addition to the Lord, she ought to thank M.C. himself. Her thoughts skittered away. She would someday.

M.C. stuffed his handkerchief into the back pocket of his khakis. "As soon as we come to a stopping point on the construction, I'll make a few more visits. If I can get to know just a few families, maybe one at a time..." He winked at her. "Divide and conquer, as somebody said." He looked pleased with himself.

"We'll plan the open house for February," she said. "Maybe by then they'll have found out we're not poison. Some of the West Village people probably know our advisory board members. That should help, too."

"Not to worry, sweetheart." M.C. picked up the board and hefted it to his shoulder. The strength in his small, wiry frame never ceased to amaze her. "I'll have them dropping by for breakfast before it's over." He headed toward the stairs, whistling.

Mickey had no doubt he would. She felt good, right about the move, but it would be a real bonus if the neighbors could accept them.

Which brought her to one neighbor in particular.

She gathered up several almost-empty paint cans blocking the front door and set them against the wall a little harder than necessary. Since she'd told Cameron Scott they were moving in over his objections, she hadn't seen or heard from him, not once in six weeks. She'd wanted to hate him.

On the other hand...there was no reason for him to maintain contact, not really. He hadn't lied to her, not that she'd known. He'd been forthright about his doubts from the beginning, then had expressed his opposition honestly. After all, by moving in, she'd gone directly against his clearly stated wishes. In the end, she hadn't even been able to dislike him. And inside, she knew that one of the problems had been her own; she'd been on the verge of letting down her guard. When he'd touched her like that, he'd made her feel as though she were losing all her hard-won control....

The girls still asked about him. That hurt, too. If there was anything her girls needed, it was permanence in their lives, a sense of continuity, a knowledge that someone who offered them kindness and affection one minute would still be around the next.

So much for Cameron Scott, she'd told herself, mentally washing her hands of him. She'd tried to dismiss the lurking hope that he would come back around anyway. When he hadn't, she'd tried to stop thinking about him at all. And had succeeded, except at odd moments. Like now.

To distract herself, she allowed her gaze to play over the elegant lines of the staircase. She enjoyed it more every time she looked at it.

"How's it going?" The voice, cheerful, casual, spoke from just behind her.

Mickey jumped. She couldn't help it. Even before she turned, she knew whose voice it was.

She tried to still her pounding heart, compose her features, but she couldn't stop the rush of gladness that flooded her. *Where have you been?* she almost said, then realized in the nick of time how ridiculous it would sound. Cameron Scott owed her nothing, least of all an explanation.

She swung around, hoping nothing showed in her face. "Hello." She tried to make her voice sound as if he'd been by yesterday. Which was just as well, because when she met his eyes she could do nothing, nothing at all, just stand there, stupidly frozen, staring back at him.

"I've been out of town," he said. "I just thought I'd drop by to see how the move was going."

With a great effort she pulled herself together. "Fine," she said. "Come in." He looked fit. Relaxed. Maybe he really had been gone.

Stop it, she told herself. She didn't have to make excuses for him. It shouldn't really matter to her one way or the other.

He stepped inside, looking around as if he were really interested. She stole a glance at him. He was wearing Levi's that sheathed his long, muscular legs like a second skin and a faded denim jacket that picked up the bluish gray of his eyes behind the steel-rimmed glasses. She grew acutely conscious of her own grubby state.

He put his hands in his pockets, leaned back and rubbernecked like a tourist. "You've really worked miracles here." She could hear surprise in his voice.

It must have been his tone. Suddenly she was angry. What was he doing here? For six weeks he hadn't shown his face. Then he walked in as though he'd never been gone and casually threw out a compliment. "No miracles," she said shortly. "Just a lot of hard work."

He shot a quick glance at her. She flushed.

"I'm sure it was," he said. "But what in the world did I say to make you angry?"

"Nothing," she mumbled like a disgruntled teenager, feeling the red stain her cheeks.

"Not true." He didn't raise his voice, but she heard the change in it. For some reason it made her want to shiver, but the feeling wasn't unpleasant. "Tell me, and I'll be glad to apologize." He paused for a half count, as if considering, then a quick grin transformed his face. "Unless, of course, I don't think I owe you one."

His words coaxed a reluctant smile from her. "You don't owe me anything. I assumed you'd lost interest in the project," she went on lamely. "The girls missed you...." She stumbled to a halt, wanting to scream with frustration. Now she was whining.

"I missed them, too. And why did you think I'd lost interest?" He seemed honestly surprised.

"What was I supposed to think? The last time I saw you, you told me you couldn't approve the move to West Village. I moved us in anyway. Then we didn't see you for six weeks."

"I told you. I was out of town. And now that we're neighbors, I'll be more interested than ever." Amusement was still tugging at the corners of his mouth. "Come on, let's start over." He held out his hand. "Good day, Ms. Mulvaney," he said with exaggerated formality. "How have you been these past six weeks?"

She knew a fleeting surge of the old annoyance that she could never stay angry at him, but it died immediately. She couldn't help it. She laughed.

His hand was still extended toward her, and she couldn't resist putting her own into it. He held it, the contagious laughter still in his eyes. She remembered the last time. His touch had made her forget to pull away, had haunted her dreams for a long time afterward. In her memory, a man had never touched her like that before.

Looking at him now as they laughed together, she could see the desire for her in his eyes. "How about a tour of the house?" she asked quickly, taking her hand from his.

"Sure. That's what I came for."

Is that really what you came for, Cameron Scott? "Come on, then," she said. "I'll give you the deluxe version."

"Cameron!" Joni's exuberant shout echoed down the hall. "You're back! Where were you?" She came bounding up, a happy grin on her face.

"I've been out of town." He grabbed Joni's shoulders and shook her playfully. He was sticking to his story, at least. "How've you been?" he asked.

"Fine. We moved without you." Joni's tone was faintly accusatory.

"I know." He grinned. "Moving's a lot of work. Why do you think I left? Do you think I'm dumb or something? Hi, Lisa."

"Hi, Cameron." She didn't jump up and down like Joni, but Mickey could tell from her smile that she was pleased to see him, too. Mickey didn't know whether to be glad for the girls' sakes that he'd come back or resent him for dabbling in their lives so casually, raising false hopes in everyone. *What hopes?* She reminded herself that she had none, false or otherwise.

This tour was a little different from the one she'd given him before at the other house. This time it was as if she were showing him her own house. He didn't say much besides asking an occasional question, but his questions were always incisive, to the point. She could feel his gaze on her and could tell he was listening closely to every word she said.

When they'd finished downstairs they climbed the wide, sweeping staircase, Mickey in the lead. Without thinking, she trailed her hand over the rail, enjoying the sweep of its fluid lines.

"It is beautiful, isn't it?" he said. She turned to find him watching her.

"Yes, it is." Self-consciously, she let her hand drop.

They followed the sound of hammering down the upstairs hall to the room Leslie and Brandy would share, where M.C. and his crew were replacing the last of the baseboards.

M.C. rose from where he was nailing quarter-round molding to the bottom of the baseboard. "Hello, Cameron," he said cordially. "It's been awhile. Enjoy your trip?"

Mickey shot Cameron a startled look. So he really *had* taken a trip. Trust M.C. to know.

"As a matter of fact, I did." Cameron shook hands. "How'd you know?"

"I called your office last week to invite you to come by and see the progress we're making," M.C. explained, "and your secretary said you'd gone on vacation."

Mickey turned scarlet to the roots of her hair as Cameron threw her an amused I-told-you-so look.

"I met friends in Dallas," he said. "Then we flew out to San Francisco. I hadn't seen them in a while. It was a good trip."

Was one of them a woman? What did she care? It was none of her business anyway. "I'm glad to hear it." She forced her tone to be gracious.

"By the way, Mickey," M.C. interjected, "today's already the sixteenth. There's a tree lot a couple of blocks over. I'll pick one up tomorrow."

"I'll buy it," she said. "I've always liked to choose my own."

"I guess you had to do it often enough." There was pain, sudden and raw, in M.C.'s voice. He laid his hand on her shoulder.

She managed to keep herself from flinching, but stiffened in spite of her best effort. Quickly, M.C. took his hand away. "Sure you don't want company?"

"No, you have enough to do, and I really enjoy picking them out." She wanted to kick herself. "Thanks anyway," she said, desperate to banish the hurt from his eyes. "By the way, do you know where the box of ornaments landed?"

"No telling. But I'll look." As always, he was putting the incident behind him, but she could see the effort it cost him.

And she knew that Cameron Scott had picked up on the exchange—on all of it.

With a sense of *déjà vu,* she walked out onto the porch with him to say good-night. Except that this was a different house, the porch was twice as big and a lot of water had gone under the bridge. And Cameron himself? He was still an enigma to her. Reason told her his interest had to be strictly professional. Instinct told her it was personal. She knew he wanted her; she could see it in his eyes. Well, a lot of men had wanted her. And there lay a dead-end street. She'd found that out a long time ago.

The December night was clear and cool but not biting. Nat "King" Cole's voice, muffled but unmistakable, drifted from an upstairs window. "...From now on, our troubles will be out of sight...." On a night like this, with the new house nearly ready, with this man standing beside her, Mickey could almost believe it.

"Will you stay here tonight?" Cameron asked.

"Yes. M.C. will be finished with the room tonight, and all of us are going to start painting early in the morning."

"Your new residents. When will they come in?"

"M.C. says he'll be finished with the second-floor bedrooms by mid-January. Then we'll take in four more girls. The attic will take another six months or so, since he has to work on it in his spare time."

"He's a lot of help to you, isn't he?"

"I don't know what I'd do without him," she said simply.

"You two seem to be close. Why do you call him M.C.?" The question was sudden, direct.

She glanced at him sharply. "I—it just happened that way." She bit off the words. She wasn't about to discuss M.C. with anyone. She never had, not even with M.C.

himself, and she wasn't about to start now. Especially with Cameron Scott. "Now, if you'll excuse me, I'd better say good-night. They'll need me to tell them where to put everything in the kitchen—"

"Whoa." He held up a hand. "They can spare you for another few minutes. It's really nice out here." His voice beckoned irresistibly. "Come here and look at all the stars."

She hesitated, tried to make herself walk back into the house. But she waited just one second too long. Giving in, she walked with him to the edge of the porch and looked up.

The stars were a million tiny jewels strewn by a celestial hand across the sable sky. "You can't often see them this clearly in town," he said. "This looks like the night sky on the beaches in summer."

He was leaning against the porch column, watching the sky. Faintly, she could see his profile against the darker shadows beyond him. Firm jawline, solid chin, strong straight nose, except for the small irregularity where she suspected it had been broken. Not a perfect profile, she conceded, but it spoke of strength, character. Tenacity.

"We went to Galveston sometimes, when I was small," she said. "I remember the stars." She looked up at the sky. Those trips were some of the few happy childhood memories she possessed, and she hoarded them inside herself like a small cache of diamonds. For a moment she forgot he was there and allowed the remembered images to immerse her. Sunlight, heat, sand, water—the salty, cleansing water that washed away the guilt, the hurt, the anger, leaving only a happy, carefree little girl.

"My folks have a house on Bolivar Peninsula, right across the ship channel from Galveston Island," he said. "I'll take you there sometime. Just for the day," he added quickly, seeing her expression. "We'll go to Galveston first, shop the

Strand, then go over to the Peninsula where it's quiet. There aren't many people on the beaches in the off-season, and you can find a lot of shells. How's that sound?''

"It...sounds like fun.'' She wanted to go. How she wanted to go with him.

"Good,'' he said, as if it were settled. "We'll plan it sometime after Christmas. Until then, how about dinner some night next week?''

"I—'' He'd caught her off guard again. "I don't think so. As you can see, I'm pretty snowed under.''

"Come on,'' he coaxed. "I know a little place not too far from here that serves the best hamburgers in town. I won't say a thing about Harbor House or the Village Walk project.''

Damn him for being so appealing. "We'll see.''

"I'll take that as a definite maybe.'' He moved a step nearer.

Mickey couldn't move. She felt detached from her normal self, lost in a world where everyday rules didn't apply. A little as she used to feel at the beach . . .

"You've got dirt on your face.'' Cameron's voice had blurred, gone out of focus. In a gesture so casual, so natural that it didn't even occur to her to jerk away, he reached up and scrubbed the smudge from her cheek. His thumb was warm, rough against her skin.

Then, just as casually, just as naturally, he slipped his hand under her chin, lifted her face and kissed her, his lips light on hers for so brief a moment that she half thought she'd imagined it.

She felt the need, hot and sweet, rise inside her and flood her veins. The sheer urgency of it staggered her. And on its heels, the guilt. *C'mon, honey.* The voice arose from the murky memories of her childhood. *Got a kiss for dear old Dad?*

When she reacted, it was with the only defense she knew—emotion. "I'm not interested, Cameron," she icily.

Even in the dim light on the porch, she saw the anger flash like ignited gunpowder at the back of his eyes. It was gone just as quickly, but it left them stern, austere.

"Aren't you presuming something?" he asked, a bite to his tone. "A kiss doesn't mean a marriage proposal or even a proposition. The last time I checked, it meant an affectionate exchange between two people who like each other. I'm sorry you took it for anything else."

She came to herself in a rush. "I—I beg your pardon," she stammered. How could she explain what she didn't understand herself? He frightened her. No, she corrected herself, what he made her feel frightened her.

He drew a long, slow breath. "Mickey." He reached down and in a simple, open gesture took both her hands in his. "I don't know what's bugging you, but you have no reason to be afraid of me. I know we've had our professional differences, but I enjoy your company, and I think, in spite of yourself, there are times you enjoy mine. Right?"

Mickey was miserably silent. She couldn't say no, because what he'd said was true. But she couldn't make her lips form the words to admit it. She finally nodded, a single small motion.

He brought her hands up, interlacing their fingers. "Look," he said. "No strings, no promises. Just let yourself enjoy something for a change. I'll call you next week."

Before she could refuse, he was gone. All she could see was a shadowy form moving away from her, down the sidewalk toward his car.

She didn't go in right away. She felt exposed, vulnerable. She needed time to corral her scattered emotions.

She didn't know what to do about Cameron Scott. She'd thought the problem had resolved itself when she'd moved Harbor House into West Village against his wishes. Now he was back, with the promise of more to come.

She was almost tempted to do as he asked—for once in her life let matters take care of themselves, with no strings of guilt, fear, responsibility attached. But she couldn't. She knew how destructive dead-end relationships could be.

And she also believed, as strongly as she'd ever believed anything, that Cameron Scott couldn't possibly be interested in any other kind of a relationship with her.

CHAPTER SEVEN

ON THE SATURDAY AFTERNOON before Christmas, Penny Rhodes was working.

She picked up a stem of silk iris from the table beside her, snipped an inch from the bottom and inserted it into the arrangement she was designing. She fluffed a leaf or two, stood back and critically inspected her work. Perfect. Mrs. Lynch would love it.

Creating custom artificial flower arrangements was just one of several personal extras Penny provided her clients. It was good business practice. But it was also pure pleasure for her and the best therapy she knew. Even after the worst day imaginable she could sit down to work with flowers, and the knots of frustration inside her would gradually unravel and the threads of her life would resume their usual orderly pattern. It was doubly gratifying to see the arrangement in place, the perfect finishing touch to a room she had planned to the last square inch.

She stepped back a few feet and gave the colorful mix a last once-over. Satisfied, she replaced the leftover blooms and greenery in labeled sacks and carried them toward her workroom, actually the third bedroom of the house. The second bedroom served as a guest room, intended for visits by both sets of parents, but so far only Keith's parents had used it. She'd come to realize that it was unlikely hers ever would.

As she passed the living room, she glanced at the Christmas tree. Every color-coordinated ornament hung in its appointed spot on the perfectly symmetrical artificial branches. The open house, held two nights ago, had gone well this year; it should generate business. Only a few more days, she thought with relief, and the whole Christmas hassle would be over.

She went back into the kitchen and picked up the shears to put them away. With her hand halfway to the drawer, she stopped as a sudden yen struck her to arrange fresh, growing things, this time for herself. While most of the flowers in the yard had succumbed to the first cold snap, there should still be enough blooms in the greenhouse to make a stunning arrangement for the Satsuma bowl on the dining room table.

She walked through the den and down into the glassed-in room that she and Keith had added when they'd remodeled. He loved gardening as much as she, and they both spent time here after work or on weekends, clipping, watering and fertilizing the plants or just simply enjoying the wealth of greenery.

The morning had been cool, but now bright December sunshine poured through the glass, making the room almost too warm. Penny walked to the outside door and opened it, letting the fresh air circulate among the plants. Stepping out onto the redwood deck, she took a deep, appreciative breath of the crisp air and ran a diagnostic eye over the backyard—the neatly pruned shrubs along the borders, the manicured patch of grass in the center, the small fountain bubbling in one corner.

Even to her critical eye, it was perfect. Leaving the door open, she went back inside the greenhouse to look for flowers to cut.

She had gathered three sprays of oncidium orchids when she heard a tiny squeak. She looked up, but saw nothing. She decided she'd imagined it.

Just as she was snipping a piece of maidenhair fern, she heard it again, just outside the greenhouse door. A second later a minute ball of black-and-white fur slipped around the doorjamb into the room and stopped a few feet away, regarding her with eyes that were perfect circles of blue. A scrap of a kitten, barely old enough to leave its mother.

Penny wasn't all that fond of cats, or any other animals, for that matter. She started to shoo it away.

But then she made the mistake of looking at it more closely. Its fur was soft and silky; its feet, four tiny white stockings; and its velvety nose sported one black dot on the very tip. In spite of herself, Penny extended a hand. The kitten began purring loudly.

"Go home," she finally said halfheartedly. The kitten's purring escalated several decibels. She waved her hand in a shooing motion, but the cat stayed put, its perfectly round blue eyes darting back and forth in perfect time with her movements.

As soon as she stopped, it came nearer.

"All right," Penny told it as she stood. "You win. Stay if you want to, but I'm going inside."

The kitten followed her.

"You can't come in," she said sternly. "That's all there is to it. Now, go away."

The cat sat in the doorway and looked up expectantly.

She was pondering her next move when the patio door slid open and Keith stepped out.

"Who are you talking to?" He looked down and saw the kitten. "Well, hello there." His mouth widened in a grin. A fatuous grin, Penny thought irritably. Bending, he stroked one finger along the kitten's nose and across the top of its head. It arched its back, purring like a microscopic motorboat.

"Don't encourage it, Keith, or it'll never go away." But she leaned down to watch it.

Before he could answer, a noise on the driveway made them both look up. A girl dressed in jeans and a T-shirt, her dark hair caught back in a long ponytail, was walking toward them. She carried herself with the leggy awkwardness of dawning adolescence, but Penny could see that she was beautiful.

As she drew nearer, Penny studied her. Classic bone structure, skin so fair it was almost transparent. But what transfixed her were the girl's eyes. Except for their deep brown color, they were like the kitten's. Wide open. Wary. Vulnerable. A familiar expression. One that struck an unpleasant chord in the innermost corner of Penny's being. *Was she . . . ?* It was the old question she always asked herself. Of course not. No chance. But Penny recognized the look in this girl's eyes. She'd been hurt, expected to be hurt again. Penny knew. She'd been there herself.

No one needed to tell her. This girl was from the halfway house.

Penny felt her insides twist painfully. She glanced at Keith, but his eyes were on the girl.

"There you are." She pointed at the kitten, who was weaving in and out of Keith's legs. "I'm sorry." Her voice was soft, tentative. "I thought she was too small to go so far. Was she bothering you?"

Penny stood frozen, speechless.

"No, she's fine," Keith said. He looked curiously at the girl, who had knelt and was reaching for the kitten. It batted at her hand with a tiny paw, missed and fell over onto its back, exposing a tightly rounded little stomach. The girl laughed softly, and Keith smiled at her.

"I'm glad nothing happened to her," she said. "It took me a long time to earn the right to keep her. I sure wouldn't want to ruin things now." She picked up the kitten and held it to her face, gently rubbing her cheek against its soft fur. It curled into her cupped hands. Penny watched, unable to help herself.

Suddenly the girl's brown eyes widened, and color washed across the delicate skin of her cheekbones. "I'm sorry," she said again. "I didn't mean to be rude. I'm Lisa Parigi. I just moved into the big house on the next street over."

"We know." Penny had found her voice, but it sounded small and cold. Keith shot a glance at her.

"You mean—" He was obviously unsure of how to say it.

"Harbor House," Lisa supplied. "We've just been here a week. The new house is great. We've got so much more room than we had before." Her voice was still muted, and she spoke in short bursts, as if she were nervous.

Certainly, she was making Penny very nervous. She wished the girl would leave.

Lisa looked beyond her to the deck, the orderly design of the yard. "Gee, it's pretty here," she said. "You must have to work hard to keep it up. M.C. should see it—he'd love it."

"Who's M.C.?" Keith asked.

"He's a counselor. Well, he's also kind of a general repairman. Actually, he's Mickey's father." Her brow wrinkled. "But that doesn't help, because you don't know who Mickey is."

Keith chuckled. "No, but I'll bet you'll tell us," he said. Penny looked sideways at him. *Don't encourage her, or she'll never go away,* she wanted to tell him. But this time she couldn't say the words aloud.

"Mickey's the director," Lisa said. "She said I could have Half-pint if Rooney liked her, but I'd have to take care of her. I don't mind," she added. "It's not like work or anything."

"Hold on," Keith said, laughing. "One thing at a time. Half-pint?"

Lisa smiled down at the tiny animal, which had fallen asleep against her chest. "That's her name. It's what Pa called Laura on 'Little House'." There was a terrible wistfulness about Lisa's smile. It tore at Penny's insides.

"Now," Keith said, "Who's Rooney?"

"Rooney's Mickey's cat," she explained. "She brings him to work sometimes. He's old and cranky, and sometimes he bites people. But he loves Half-pint."

"Do you . . . like Harbor House, Lisa?" Keith asked.

Like it? Penny thought. *What a stupid question. How could anyone like being in a halfway house?*

"Sure," Lisa said without hesitation. "It's home to me. I don't know where I'd be if I weren't there." She glanced at a cheap plastic watch on her wrist. "Uh-oh. I need to get back. It's my day to clean the living room, and everything is still a mess from the move. Thanks for being so nice about Half-pint."

"You're welcome, Lisa," Keith said. "Glad you found her."

"This is a nice neighborhood," she said. "We're trying to be on our best behavior, since we weren't really invited." Her eyes widened again, as if she realized she might have said too much. "I have to go. Glad to meet you," she added hurriedly, then turned and headed down the driveway, the kitten still clutched protectively to her chest.

Just as she got to the street, she turned. "Could I come back sometime, just to look at your yard?" she called.

Penny took a breath to answer—

Keith beat her to it. "I think that would be all right, Lisa."

"Thanks," Lisa called back.

When she was halfway down the block, Penny shook her head. "I knew it."

Keith was looking after Lisa. He turned to Penny, a thoughtful look on his face. "Knew what?" he asked.

"They'll be over here all the time."

"Maybe," he said absently. "Really, she seemed very nice. Just like any other kid."

"But she's not any other kid. She's from the halfway house."

Keith looked at her sharply. "That's no reason to condemn her out of hand," he said, as sternly as he had ever spoken to her. Her heart sank. The girl—the halfway house—they were already causing problems between her and Keith.

He studied her. "What is it, Penny?"

She looked away. "Those children—I—nothing."

"You act as though they're . . . I don't know. Evil or something." His bewilderment showed on his face. "It's ridiculous. No matter how much trouble they've had, they can't hurt you."

You're right about part of it, Keith, she thought. A bitter sadness welled up inside her. *Of course they aren't evil. They're poor unfortunate victims of adults' unthinking acts. But you're wrong about the other part. They can hurt you. Oh, yes, they can hurt you.* "Of course they can't," she said dully.

"I can't bring myself to shut this girl out, and I can't believe you can either. Penny. . ." He put his arm around her. "What are you afraid of?"

I'm afraid you wouldn't love me if you knew the truth. She leaned against him and shook her head. "Nothing," she said, wishing with all her heart that she could tell him.

"HARBOR HOUSE." Mickey said brightly, clamping the telephone receiver between her shoulder and her chin while she made the last note on a case report.

"Mickey?" The smooth baritone made her pen stop in mid-scribble. "Cameron Scott."

"Hello, Cameron." She felt her pulse jump, then cursed herself. Why did she let him affect her this way?

"Did I interrupt you?"

"I'm just finishing a report." She fought the urge to tell him she had to go. That kiss, that one simple kiss, had haunted her dreams for many nights.

"Why are you working so late the week before Christmas?"

"Why shouldn't I? The work's got to be done, whether it's Christmas or not."

"Do you ever give yourself any time off?"

"Certainly."

"When?"

She thought, but honestly couldn't remember. Maybe there hadn't been a last time. Time off was a luxury she'd been promising herself for years; it just hadn't happened yet. Vaguely, she wondered what she would do with it if she had it.

"I can't remember, but it's not important," she said, deciding to rise above the whole issue. "What's important is that the work gets done."

"I see." The amusement in his voice told her he knew he'd won. "I promised you a hamburger with no shoptalk. Remember?"

"Yes." She'd been afraid he'd call, had hoped he wouldn't. It would've been so much simpler if he'd stayed away. She'd finally managed to stop thinking about him, but when he'd reappeared at Harbor House, he'd thrown her emotions into turmoil all over again. And the kiss had frightened her. "Look, Cameron, I—"

"No excuses. Do you have other plans tonight or don't you?"

It would have been so easy to lie. "No," she said before she could stop herself. "No plans."

"Good." His satisfaction came clearly over the wires. "I'll pick you up around seven. Will you be there at the house?"

"Yes. I do have work to do, in spite of what some people think." His soft, infectious chuckle made her realize she'd deliberately provoked his laughter, just to hear it. "I'll be here until then," she went on. "M.C. brought us both to work this morning, so I don't have my car. You can just drop me home afterward."

"By the way, where is home?"

She told him where her apartment was located.

"Does M.C. live with you?"

"No. He has his own place in the same complex."

"Do you carpool with him?"

"That's right. He takes one week, I take the next. It saves gas."

"Makes sense to me. I'll see you in a couple of hours."

Mickey hung up the phone, telling herself she was an even bigger fool than she'd thought.

JUST AS Mickey had imagined it, the tree stood framed by the curve of the stairway, a perfect little fir whose branches twinkled with tiny white lights and held a most eclectic assortment of ornaments. Presents had already begun to appear under its lower boughs. Its spicy fragrance cleansed and sharpened the air. "Silent night"... The strains of the ancient carol drifted faintly from a radio playing somewhere in the back of the house.

"It's beautiful," Cameron told her.

"Thanks." She was inordinately pleased that he liked the tree. "I put the lights on and the girls did the rest." She always chose the tree and allowed no one but herself to put on the lights. It was her bit of self-indulgence.

"Where did you get the angel?"

"Brandy made her." She touched the Renaissance-style angel gracing the top of the tree. It was made of papier-mâché, but Brandy had wrought miracles with the humble stuff. She had brought the angel to life, given movement to the voluminous folds of her gown and the sweep of her wings, imbued the delicate face with an other-world serenity.

"She's a work of art."

"Yes, isn't she?" Mickey sent up a silent prayer that this gift of Brandy's could somehow point the way to reaching her.

"This one?" Cameron touched an exuberant clown ornament, painted in bright, primary colors, hanging near the top of the tree.

Mickey smiled. "Joni's. She just finished it this afternoon."

Cameron chuckled. "I should have guessed."

She pointed to an old-fashioned glass Santa Claus, made in the European style. "This is Lisa's," she said. "It belonged to her grandmother. Probably the only thing she has from her family.''

"And this one?'' His finger traced a wooden carousel horse.

Mickey felt the familiar sadness. Time helped, but it never seemed to erase it entirely. She hesitated before she answered. "A girl who came to us the year I opened Harbor House. Her name was Melissa. She stayed three months, then ran away. She died a year later in a Dallas hospital from a drug overdose.'' She touched the ornament. "We couldn't help her.''

"I'm sorry.'' The sympathy in his voice reached inside her, pulled at her control. She didn't want it.

"It's part of my job,'' she said. "I learned my lesson with Melissa, promised myself I'd never get that involved with a child's problems again. But sometimes you can't help it, I suppose. With Brandy...'' To her horror, she felt tears, as unwelcome as they were unexpected, prick the backs of her eyelids. She never cried. She had found out when she was a tiny child that it didn't do any good. Quickly, she blinked them away, but not before he'd seen them. What had gotten into her?

"The girls always leave, whether we've helped them or not,'' she said, deliberately making her tone light. "They can't stay here forever.''

"But every year, when you put up the tree, you remember them.'' He spoke very softly.

"Yes.'' In silence, they looked at the tree. At the other ornaments, each from a girl who had lived at Harbor House, wherever it had been at the time. Reminders, some bright, some bittersweet, of the ones who had stayed their time, then moved on, for good or ill.

"Do you ever hear from them?''

"Sometimes." She half smiled. "Some keep in regular touch. A few never look back. For them, the time here is an unpleasant memory. Some we hear about later—second-, thirdhand." Briefly, the shadow touched her face again. "As I've said, the news isn't always good."

"I can imagine." There was infinite compassion in his voice.

"Sometimes it is," she hastened to add, her face clearing. "We even have a few who are making important careers for themselves. That's when we know we're doing good things."

As she spoke, he watched her. In the diffused light from the tree, her face held a quiet pride. "Every time I come here, I realize all over again how much good you do," he said softly. *But at what cost to herself?* he wondered. *Part of my job,* she'd said. He'd seen the agony on her face when she talked about the girl they had lost. And when she'd mentioned Brandy, she had blinked back tears. Was it because she'd once been in the same boat? Was she trying to save the world by sacrificing herself? He was beginning to wonder.

Unable to help himself, he touched her shoulder. She didn't stiffen, and he was glad she apparently accepted the touch for what he'd meant it to be—a simple gesture from a friend.

For a moment, she didn't speak. "I've learned to be grateful," she said finally. "Every single child we've been able to help is a gift."

He couldn't take his eyes from her face. He'd always thought her stunning, but now he saw another dimension, an added inner beauty, that stole his breath away. Felt, too, a strange envy of anyone who could know with certainty the good they had done. It moved him unbearably.

After the briefest of intervals, he dropped his hand. If he'd touched her any longer, he would have taken her into his arms. "Come on," he said. "Let's go for the hamburger. Better grab a jacket, it's cold outside. By the way—" he nodded toward the tailored navy slacks and Christmas-red sweater she wore "—I like the outfit. Red looks good on you." His eyes, lingering on her, said more than his words.

"Thanks." She'd never known how to respond to compliments, but she was glad she'd worn the sweater. When she'd freshened up a few minutes ago, she'd taken extra care with her hair and the makeup she kept here for emergency use. Ridiculously pleased, she went for her jacket.

The place Cameron had chosen was cozy, informal, crowded without being noisy. They headed for a booth toward the back of the restaurant, then ordered hamburgers and beer.

"You were right," Mickey said after the first bite. "This really is the best hamburger I've ever tasted."

"I told you. What will you do for Christmas?" He took a large bite of his burger.

"We'll have it at the house with the girls," Mickey said, surprised at the question. "Josie—she's the cook—is going to make most of the dinner this week and freeze it. We'll open gifts Christmas morning. Then M.C., the girls and I will put the rest of the meal together." She paused before taking another bite of hamburger. "The old table's too small for the room, but at least we're in the house."

"Harbor House is your whole life, isn't it?" he asked.

"I suppose so. Why shouldn't it be?"

"Call me silly, but other people have families, hobbies, other interests."

"I keep thinking that someday I'll have the time." She couldn't keep the wistfulness from her voice. "Until now, there just hasn't been any. First school, then graduate school. Since then, I've been trying to make Harbor House go. I do like to read...."

"And walk on the beach," he finished for her, smiling. "Family?"

"M.C.'s all I've got." She searched her mind for something to change the subject. She'd have to be careful. This man caught her with her guard down entirely too often. Or was it that he made her unwary enough to lower it?

"Your mother?"

"She died five years ago, just after I finished graduate school. She'd been sick a long time. I was glad she lived to see me get my degree. It meant a lot to her, and to me."

"Where did you grow up?"

"I was born here in Houston," she said. "Then—" She interrupted herself just in time and started again. "Then we lived all over."

"You said M.C.'s interest in your line of work was more recent than yours," he said. "What did he do before?"

"When I was a baby, he was a seaman. After that, I don't know," she said unwarily, then caught herself. "A little of everything, I think," she added hastily. "You know M.C. He can do anything."

"So it seems." His words were offhand, but he was watching her closely. Probing. Why on earth did he care?

"You seem to have grown up very self-sufficient," he remarked.

"I had to."

"I thought you had M.C."

"He was ... away a lot."

"He came home sometimes, didn't he?" His voice had sharpened.

"Yes," she said, forgiving herself the lie. He was asking too many personal questions. Unconsciously, she lifted a hand to bite her nails, then realized in time to drop it. "Have you lived in Houston all your life?" she asked deliberately. Knowing amusement filled his eyes. She wished he wasn't so damned attractive....

"In other words," he said gently, "it's time I minded my own business. Okay. The answer is yes. I grew up and went to school right here in West Village, actually. Happy childhood." He chuckled. "Undistinguished academic career. Hottest temper in school. Fortunately, understanding parents. That about sums up my young life."

"You had a hot temper?"

Her surprise made him smile. "Yeah. Trouble was, I was small for my age."

She thought of his well-muscled height. "You must have made up for it later."

"I did. But meanwhile, there were plenty of times my mouth got me in trouble, and someone, usually one of my bigger buddies, would have to bail me out."

She laughed with him, enjoying the sound of their united laughter.

"I learned the hard way to control my temper," he went on, "but it still crops up every now and then."

She remembered the fleeting glimpses she'd had of it since she'd known him and decided she didn't want to encounter the real thing. "You should tell that to Joni."

"I did," he said promptly. "The other day."

"See?" She smiled. "I told you we should hire you as an assistant counselor."

"Missed my calling. Anyway, I finished high school here, then went on to college. I was no scholar, but I finally learned that if I just kept plugging away, I'd make it. Plugging away is what I've done ever since."

He was deliberately minimizing his accomplishments, Mickey realized. She liked him for it. "Where will you spend Christmas?"

"With my mother and father. In the house where I grew up. It's only two blocks from where I live now."

"Just the three of you?" She ignored the sharp stab of envy.

"No. My sister, her husband and their three kids will be over, too."

The envy grew. "Boys or girls?"

"Two boys and a girl."

"Do you see them often?"

His face lit with pleasure. "As often as I can. I don't have any of my own, so I really enjoy them." At her look, he burst out laughing. "I was married and divorced several years ago," he explained, still chuckling. "No children."

"I'm sorry." She didn't know what else to say.

"Don't be. I wasn't scarred for life. It's worked out for the best." He waved a casual hand. "Anyway, the boys are old enough to humor me by throwing a baseball with me, and my niece already has her Uncle Cam's number."

"Uncle Cam?" Mickey lifted a brow.

"Well, yes." He looked a little sheepish. "She's only three, and Cameron's a little long for a youngster to start off with."

"I see." *What a father this man would make.* The thought came out of nowhere, startling her. "Were you a baseball player?" she asked hastily.

"All-state shortstop through high school," he admitted. "I went to the university on scholarship, but my eyesight wasn't good enough for the pros." His hand touched the glasses in his pocket.

"Do you wear those all the time?"

"No—"

"Just when I want to see." Laughing, they finished the corny line together.

"I don't need them all the time," he added, "only for close work or if my eyes are tired. But I don't need them for golf, and I can still play a mean game of sandlot baseball."

"Joni and Leslie are both very athletic," she said. "Leslie plays basketball and softball too."

"When the weather gets warm, I'll come over and we'll get up a game in the backyard," he said. "You've got plenty of room to lay out a small diamond back there...."

They finished the meal in comfortable camaraderie, all touchy topics successfully avoided. When they left the restaurant, she gave him directions to her small one-bedroom apartment.

When he insisted on walking her to the door, Mickey's nerves began to tighten. Since she rarely dated, she hardly ever had the problem of whether to ask a male friend inside.

She needn't have worried about what to say. He simply followed her in, too fast for her to thank him politely and close the door. "Just to make sure no serial killers are around," he said by way of explanation. "Or maybe I should worry more about your cat."

She laughed. "Rooney's probably retired for the night. He's a cranky old man and needs his sleep. Anyway, I'm perfectly all right. After all, I do this every night. Sometimes it's even later than it is now."

"Then this is one night I don't have to worry about you."

"Worry about me?" She faced him head-on. "Nobody has to worry about me. I've been taking care of myself for a long time."

"Too long, Mickey?" he asked gently. He caught her hand and drew her toward him.

She tried to make herself pull away but couldn't. She tried to resist the gentle pressure of his fingers on hers, but they were warm, strong. His gaze dropped to her mouth. Her breath slipped out of her lungs, and that crazy, out-of-control feeling started seeping through her veins again, frightening but impossibly sweet. She tried to fight it, to regain control, but couldn't. A small voice inside her reminded her that she'd known this would happen.

"No." She meant to say the word firmly, but it came out as a whisper. Then his lips came down on hers, and any lingering resolve evaporated into a flood of unwelcome desire. And underneath it, a vast, nameless hunger welled up from within her innermost self.

This time his mouth lingered, moved gently on hers. Need bloomed inside her, blotting out resistance, thought.

With an inarticulate sound, he angled the kiss deeper. As his mouth took hers, the blood began to pound in her ears. She felt her own lips soften, open. His arms went around her and pulled her close, and she felt the leashed strength in him. Fright and guilt pushed at her consciousness, but she was scarcely aware of them. She was lost in a world of sensation so new to her that she'd never even dreamed of its existence. Her hands came up between them to shove him away, but instead her fingers spread involuntarily across his broad chest. His hands began to stroke her back, and he pressed her against the length of his body. She heard a small, involuntary sound, then realized she had made it.

It startled her back into reality.

"No." This time the word came out with an edge of panic. The fear infused her arms with strength, and the guilt made her push him away.

He said nothing, didn't move. She stared up at the lean planes of his face, into his gray eyes. For the first time since she'd known him, their clarity was clouded. By desire. For a second he looked as though he was having trouble focusing them on her face. He reached for her. "Mickey?"

"No." She took a step backward. The panic pushed her voice higher. "I can't."

"Why? There's no one else, is there?"

"Of course not." She fought for balance.

"Then tell me." He spread his hands in bewilderment.

She took her gaze from his. "I don't . . . want it."

"That's not true," he said gently. "And if you're honest with yourself, you'll admit it."

For one long moment he stood there, silent, but she couldn't meet his eyes. "Merry Christmas, Mickey," he whispered finally. She sensed rather than saw him turn and leave. He closed the door quietly behind him.

The relief she felt was almost as keen as the regret.

As CAMERON DROVE AWAY from the apartment complex, he tried to quiet the clamor of his still-aching body. He'd had his share of women, but he couldn't ever remember wanting any woman as he wanted Mickey Mulvaney.

When she'd pulled away from him, he'd heard the panic in her voice, seen it in her eyes. He remembered that first time, when she'd jerked away from his touch. He might be a stranger to her world, but he wasn't the village idiot. Someone had abused her. He'd long ago become convinced that it hadn't been M.C., simply because she was obviously too fond of him, too at ease with him. But someone had. Who? And where had M.C. been?

Steering his way through the well-lighted streets of West Village, Cameron tried to fit the pieces together—the oblique references, the fact that Mickey called her father by his first name. *I guess you had to do it often enough,* M.C. had said when Mickey had insisted on choosing the Christmas tree herself. In spite of Mickey's evasions, it was obvious M.C. hadn't been around when she was growing up.

Cameron turned into his driveway and fought an unexpected wave of pure rage. From the indications, M.C. had deserted her. He got out of the car and slammed the door behind him with all the force he could muster.

He leaned against the door, counted to ten, took a deep breath. It wasn't his business. None of this was his business. Yet he was attacking the whole mystery with a compulsion that he couldn't understand.

It only occurred to him after he'd been staring sleeplessly at the ceiling of his bedroom for a good two hours that he was far too concerned about Mickey Mulvaney and her problems. Without realizing it had been happening, he had come to like her far too much. He was already in over his head.

Oh, great. He had to laugh at himself. Here he was, falling for a prickly, independent woman with an unknown past, a hundred hang-ups and a profession she was married to. A woman who obviously wanted no part of him.

No, he corrected himself, that wasn't entirely true. When he'd kissed her tonight, she'd most definitely kissed him back. Surprise number two: Mickey Mulvaney was a complete novice at lovemaking. At kissing, anyway. There had been no expertise there, only pure emotion. But there had certainly been that. At the memory, his body tightened again.

She was so strong, he thought. A survivor. More than that, a winner. She met life head-on and turned the bad into good for all the world to see. But she had love in her and a rare sweetness. There was also a huge vulnerability there, which she hid very effectively. He'd only glimpsed it from time to time—like tonight. He lay back, remembering her face as she'd lingered over each Christmas ornament. As she'd spoken of Brandy... She was hurting herself too much, and he found himself wanting to protect her.

He felt another stab of the blind, murderous rage at whoever had hurt her. And at M.C., for having allowed it to happen.

Life had been so simple before he met Mickey Mulvaney.

Cursing himself for a fool, he punched his pillow savagely and turned over to try to salvage what was left of the night.

CHAPTER EIGHT

HUNDREDS OF LOCKERS banged shut, cracking like so many rifle shots over the roar of nearly three thousand students changing classes. The noise level had escalated all through the day, so that now, between sixth and seventh periods, it was nearly unendurable.

Brandy stopped at her locker just long enough to retrieve her jacket and slam the door shut, adding to the general din. She already had all the books she needed to take home that night, so when the final bell rang, she wouldn't have to come back to her locker. That way she could avoid running into Kelly Sandifer again.

She clutched her armload of books a little closer to her chest. Tucked into a manila folder between her history and English books was the sketch she had done of Leslie.

It was already near the end of January, and the deadline for the art contest was coming up fast. She'd finally agreed to enter. Why, she wasn't exactly sure.

Miss Foy had asked to see some of her work to help her decide what to enter in the contest and, remembering that Cameron Scott had liked her sketch of Leslie, Brandy had brought it along. Actually, she still felt a little funny about the whole thing; she had never voluntarily cooperated with a teacher in her life.

She stood at her locker and scanned the crowd, then gradually eased into the slow-moving, chattering mass of students that flowed through the wide halls of the school. There was no hurry; class was just around the corner.

But Kelly Sandifer always stood at that particular corner.

The first time she'd approached Brandy with a joint, figuring her for a pushover who would be easy to pull back into the drug scene, Brandy had told her to get lost in the plainest language she knew. Which was plenty plain. Since then, Kelly had had it in for her. Every time she passed, Kelly taunted her with insults and thinly veiled threats. Though Brandy either ignored her or gave as good as she got, she had the uneasy feeling that somewhere down the line Kelly was going to try to get her, and get her good.

Not that Brandy didn't know how to take care of herself. The trouble was, none of the grown-ups knew what Kelly was up to. She had pushed drugs for a good while now without getting caught because she was smart enough to stay clean. She kept up her grades, had a real talent for buttering up teachers. Besides, her father was a lawyer and her mother stayed home and drove a fancy car, the same kind that Kelly drove. They acted like the all-American family or something. Kelly looked clean-cut, even dressed preppy. Not the way the grown-ups thought a drug dealer dressed.

A hell of a lot they knew, Brandy thought bitterly. Kelly was as bad as any street dealer she'd ever known. The kick was that she didn't need the money. She did it for fun. That made her a real lowlife in Brandy's book. But dangerous, because Kelly didn't have anything to lose. She probably figured her old man could buy her out if she ever got caught.

Brandy rounded the corner. Sure enough, Kelly was there, leaning against the wall with several of her sidekicks around her. With her frosted blond hair, stylish clothes and skin that

stayed tan even in the wintertime, she looked like some sort
of cheerleader.

And she was watching Brandy with a little smile on her
face and pure malice in her eyes.

Brandy kept walking, but every muscle in her body
tensed. The hall was crowded, so she couldn't move to the
other side without appearing obvious. Still, as Brandy got
closer, Kelly made no move, and for one split second of
wishful thinking Brandy wondered if Kelly was going to let
her off today with the silent treatment.

No such luck. Just as she was almost past, Kelly stretched
out a leg, stuck her foot between Brandy's ankles and, with
a motion that was finished almost before it started, sent her
tumbling headlong to the floor.

Books, folder, jacket went in all directions. For a minute
Brandy lay stunned, only vaguely conscious of the students
scrambling to avoid falling over her. Then, as awareness
began to return, she felt the hot bubble of anger welling up
inside her. She clenched her fists, forced it back. *Chill out*,
she told herself desperately. *She's not worth it.*

To her own surprise, it worked. She felt her temper begin
to cool, enough for her to hang on to it again.

She climbed painfully to her feet and, still dodging other
students, began to retrieve her scattered books. She saw the
English book first. It was right in front of her, along with a
couple of her notebooks. The history book lay a few feet
down the hall, almost in front of the art room door.

The manila folder. Where was it? Frantically, Brandy
looked around her, finally spotted it across the hall. Open.
The sketch was lying next to it—crumpled and torn from the
many feet that had trampled it.

She whirled to face Kelly, who was still leaning against the
wall, laughing with her cronies. *At her*. Inside, the rage

boiled up again, burst through the hard-held barriers and flooded her like hot lava.

Without saying a word, she knotted her fists and lunged.

"Ms. MULVANEY?" The precise voice coming over the phone heralded trouble. "This is Elaine Lawrence, the assistant principal at Sam Houston High School. I'm afraid there's a problem...."

Five minutes later, Mickey and Connie Allen, who had happened to be at Harbor House writing evaluations, were in Mickey's small, scuffed Chevy sedan, fighting the first wave of rush-hour traffic that clogged the streets between Harbor House and Brandy's school.

"What exactly did she tell you?" Connie asked.

"Only that there was a fight, and the other girl—Kelly, I think she said her name was—accused Brandy of starting it. Actually Brandy got in the only blow, but it must have been a dilly." Amazingly, a clear spot opened in front of them all the way to the intersection. Mickey, seizing her opportunity, barely glanced to either side before sailing through a light that turned red just as they passed under it.

Connie's only reaction was to put a hand against the dashboard to brace herself. "What did Brandy say?"

"Apparently she hasn't said much of anything." But that didn't mean she was to blame. Guilty or innocent, Brandy wouldn't bother to defend herself because she'd automatically assume no one would believe her.

By the time they drove in some fifteen minutes later, the school parking lot was almost empty, so Mickey parked in one of the faculty spaces near the front. She and Connie got out of the car and hurried up the broad walkway to the main entrance.

As they passed into the shadow of the massive brick building, Mickey shivered. She pulled her corduroy jacket tighter around her and looked up at the long rows of blank windows, unpleasant memories nagging at her. She'd known it was coming. It happened every time she walked into a school, which in her line of work was frequent. Sometimes it still caught her off guard. Maybe this time because of Brandy... Pressing her lips tightly together, she pulled open the heavy front door.

After the chill of the outdoors, the hall seemed overwarm, stifling. Only a few students still lingered at their lockers, retrieving or putting away books and gear, but the sights, smells, sounds were all too familiar. They came straight out of the bad old days, as Mickey had come to think of them. Her steps slowed involuntarily in the flood of unwelcome sensations that assaulted her.

During her school career she'd walked through corridors like this one, lived through scenes like this one, hating every moment of every single day. She'd had poor grades and no activities or friends to cushion the sharp, painful edges of her existence. She could still remember the feelings of worthlessness, of isolation, the belief that in all the world there was no one to take her side, to really care for her. Full of anger, devoid of self-esteem, she'd sought relief in trouble. A lot of it. If someone hadn't cared enough to make her want to turn her life around, there was no telling where she'd have ended.

But, luckily for her, someone *had* cared. Had shown her that there was another way to live. Slowly, very slowly, she'd begun to take control of her own life. It had taken years of effort, frustration and pain, but she'd finally learned that failure didn't have to be a way of life, that she could steer herself in whatever direction she chose. Not always easily or quickly, but eventually. And that was all that counted. In the end, her course had come straight, and she had come to know that life could hold its own rewards. It was just that being in a place like this brought back the bad times, if only for a few seconds.

Out of the corner of her eye she saw Connie watching her. Sometimes Connie's powers of observation were eerie. Mickey gave her what she hoped was a reassuring, take-charge smile and led the way across the tiled foyer to a door marked Office. A secretary ushered them through yet another door with the assistant principal's name on it.

When they entered, the silence that greeted them was complete, but a quick glance around told Mickey volumes. Mrs. Lawrence, graying and heavyset, gold-rimmed glasses settled firmly on her formidable nose, sat at her desk, writing. In a chair to one side, a girl about Brandy's age sat quietly, hands folded in her lap. She was dressed stylishly, her ash-blond hair caught back in a long clip. Her whole appearance was fresh, clean-cut, in spite of a puffy bruise on one cheek and a tear in her oxford-cloth shirt.

On the opposite side of the office, shrunk far back into the corner, dressed in magenta sweater and black stretch pants, Brandy sat, or rather slumped, radiating sullen defiance.

Mrs. Lawrence looked up and laid down her pen. "Ms. Mulvaney? I'm Elaine Lawrence." She stood and shook hands, giving Mickey a wintry smile. Mrs. Lawrence had a reputation for being tough but fair, but she was overworked. All the staff at Sam Houston were overworked; it was a huge school. Sometimes students simply slipped through the cracks. Especially students like Brandy, who came from places like Harbor House....

Mickey braced herself, introduced Connie, then got right down to business. "Thank you for calling me, Mrs. Lawrence. Now, could we start from the beginning?"

Five minutes later, the tale had been told—at least, Mrs. Lawrence had repeated Kelly's version, with a few contributions from Kelly herself. According to her, she'd been standing in the hall minding her own business when Brandy had passed her, tripped and decided Kelly had done it. "When she got up, she just jumped on me and hit me." The girl spoke in a soft, convincing voice, looking her elders full in the eye.

Brandy didn't say a word. Hadn't even moved, so far as Mickey could tell. She sat, arms folded, staring at the floor.

"Brandy, is there anything you want to tell us?" Mrs. Lawrence asked.

"She tripped me," Brandy mumbled without raising her head.

Mrs. Lawrence looked at her sternly. "The only witnesses have corroborated Kelly's story, and you hit her first." She turned to Mickey. "I'm sure you know how strict our rules are against fighting."

"Yes." Mickey's mind raced. She turned to Mrs. Lawrence. "Could the girls wait outside for a minute, please?"

The older woman nodded. Kelly rose at once. As she walked past, Brandy stood up, too, and Mickey saw the look that passed between them. Brandy's was full of a cold, dull hatred; Kelly's, pure triumph.

The exchange told Mickey plainer than words. Kelly had started the fight, apparently to get Brandy into trouble. The same thing had happened to Mickey herself once. The circumstances had been different, but the result had been the same: Mickey hadn't had a chance. Well, it wouldn't happen to Brandy, not if she could help it.

"Mrs. Lawrence," she asked when the girls were out of the room, "as the situation stands right now, what will you do?"

"I'll have to suspend Brandy." There was regret in the woman's eyes. "From the only evidence we have, she started it."

"And these witnesses, were they Kelly's friends?" Mickey would have bet her diploma on it.

Mrs. Lawrence shrugged, a little impatiently. "Who knows? Ms. Mulvaney, in a school this size, I can't begin to know everyone's name, let alone their relationships with other students. I can only go on what evidence I'm presented."

"Mrs. Lawrence, has either one of the girls been in trouble before?"

The older woman shook her head. "No. I've already checked." She indicated the two open folders on her desk.

"Brandy's a relatively new student here. What about Kelly?"

"Let's see . . ." Mrs. Lawrence consulted the files. "She's fairly new, too. But she comes from a respectable family, and she's a very good student." The implication was, of course, that, being from Harbor House, Brandy fit neither category.

Mickey bit back the angry retort that came so readily to her lips. It would only have made things worse. *Help, M.C.* But he wasn't here to show her the most diplomatic, persuasive way to handle the situation. She would have to deal with it the best way she could. Brandy needed her.

"Mrs. Lawrence," she began, "I know Brandy's past record, before she came here, is nothing to be proud of. Neither is her attitude, certainly compared to Kelly's. But you have to look at other factors, such as how far she's come. You can see the progress she's made, especially in her grades. And believe me, we've seen a tremendous improvement since she's been at Harbor House.'' Mickey leaned forward, fought the urgency in her own voice, made herself keep it level. "Mrs. Lawrence, you just said this is her first time in your office. You know, it's possible she's telling the truth.''

"Look at it from Brandy's point of view.'' Connie spoke up, the very voice of reason, and it comforted Mickey to remember that she wasn't in this alone. "She sees everything stacked against her,'' Connie went on. "She feels that it won't do her any good to defend herself. She's already pegged herself as a loser. That's the pattern we've got to break.''

They had Mrs. Lawrence's attention now, at least. Her stern features had grown thoughtful. If they could just make her see, Mickey thought. It was true that she didn't have time for an in-depth analysis of each case. But if she could just see....

"Brandy is doing well right now, even better than she was before she...had her problems.'' Mickey spoke with controlled emphasis, desperate to make the woman understand. "She's developed a real interest in her art courses, and that may be her salvation. But we're just now getting it through to her that she can have some control over her own life, that she can change it for the better. If that's destroyed, I'm afraid we'll lose her for good.''

"You're assuming Brandy is innocent,'' Mrs. Lawrence said.

"I'm utterly convinced Kelly tripped her.'' Mickey tried to put all the conviction she felt into her voice.

Mrs. Lawrence lifted a skeptical brow. "But whether Brandy started the quarrel or not, she's the one who turned it into a fight. She can't go unpunished."

"No, and she shouldn't. She'll be punished at Harbor House, too. But at least treat the girls equally. Assume they were both at fault, and punish them both." ·

"I don't know." Mrs. Lawrence frowned. "Brandy acts as though she doesn't even care."

"I know better." All too vividly, Mickey remembered how it had been with her. "Please believe me, Mrs. Lawrence. She doesn't even know it herself yet, but she cares a great deal."

The assistant principal looked intently at Mickey. She glanced at Connie, then down at her papers. The silence held, stretched taut.

"Very well," she said finally. "I'm willing to compromise. This time. I won't suspend anyone, but both girls will report to detention, Kelly for one week, Brandy for two. I'm sorry, Ms. Mulvaney." She held up a hand. "Remember, I have no evidence that Kelly tripped Brandy. And Brandy was the one who actually started the fight. I'll notify Kelly's parents." She copied a number from one of the folders, then closed both of them, stacking them neatly on the desktop.

It could have been worse, Mickey thought, giddy with relief. So much worse.

As they stood to go, Mrs. Lawrence took off her glasses and leaned back in her chair. "Ms. Mulvaney."

"Yes?"

She eyed Mickey levelly. "I trust you'll speak to Brandy about this incident. I don't want to see her in my office again."

"I understand," Mickey said. "Thank you, Mrs. Lawrence. You may have just saved a child."

AN HOUR LATER Mickey stood in the driveway, talking with Connie through the open window of Connie's car. Brandy had already gone up to her room, where she would spend all her time for the next week. During the talk they'd just had with her, the whole story—the sketch, the incident in the hall, her prior run-ins with Kelly—had come out, bit by painful bit. Although Brandy hadn't accused Kelly outright of pushing dope, she'd said enough that Mickey knew it as well as if she'd been told. She was conscious of a deep thankfulness. Not only had Brandy refused to be drawn back into the drug scene, she had trusted her and Connie enough to tell them what had happened.

"So that's why she was so upset," Mickey mused. "When Kelly tripped her, it ruined the picture she was taking to art class."

Connie rested her forearms on the steering wheel. "You believed her, then, when she said Kelly started it."

"There's not a doubt in my mind."

"Mine, either. I saw Kelly's face, too." Connie grinned. "I also saw it when she found out she was being punished along with Brandy. And Brandy's, when she realized she wasn't going to suffer alone. I realize it's most unprofessional of me, but I'll have to say it did my heart good."

Mickey chuckled. "Mine, too." She sobered quickly. "Kelly's really going to be after her now."

"True. Anything you can do about it?"

"Not really. There's no proof of any of this, just what Brandy told us, or hinted at, and my own strong hunch. But I intend to have another little chat with Mrs. Lawrence sometime in the next few days. Then, if something else happens, we'll at least have laid a little groundwork, as M.C. says. By the way, thanks for backing me up. Without M.C., I was afraid I'd blow my cool."

"You didn't need me, or M.C. You did fine on your own." Connie aimed a glance at Mickey. "You were much more protective with Brandy than you were with Joni when she got into trouble," she remarked.

"I know," Mickey admitted. "But Joni wasn't faced with suspension. And she . . ."

"She wasn't about to fall back into the Black Hole," Connie finished.

"Right." Mickey tried to smile, but it came out a grimace.

"I saw your face when you walked into the school. Was it that bad for you?"

Mickey gave a short laugh. Counselors were supposed to be diplomatic, but sometimes Connie didn't mince words. "Pretty bad." *The understatement of the year.*

"What turned you around?"

"Not what. Who." Mickey buttoned her coat to keep out the raw night air. "A school counselor. She kept believing in me until she finally forced me to believe in myself. I had a lot farther to go than Brandy, but I finally made it."

"I've never seen you get so involved with one of your girls. Is Brandy so different from any of the others?"

"No. Yes. I don't know, really." Mickey shrugged impatiently. "I just know how it is with Brandy. I keep seeing myself—" She couldn't finish.

"Don't care too much," Connie warned. "You don't want to fall back into the Black Hole either."

Mickey was stunned into silence. Had she allowed herself to become involved to that point?

"One of these days we'll talk about it," Connie promised. "Bye. I've got catch-up work waiting for me at home." She started to roll up the window, then stopped and stuck her head out again. "Think about it," she said, and backed out the driveway.

Mickey watched her until the car disappeared around the corner, then, shivering, turned to go back into the house. Today had opened a lot of old wounds, and she wanted to put it behind her. From nowhere, she felt a strange need to see Cameron Scott, of all people, to talk to him, only for a minute....

How ridiculous. Annoyed with herself, she shook her head to clear it. She must really be tired.

Halfway up the walk, she glanced up at Brandy's bedroom and was surprised to see her at the window. Summoning a smile, she waved. After a moment's hesitation, Brandy answered with a wave and, finally, a small, tentative smile of her own.

CHAPTER NINE

"Wow!" M.C.'s voice came from the bottom of the stairs.

Mickey flushed with pleasure. He was watching her descend, and she could see the pride shining in his eyes. As always, she was glad she'd pleased him. As always, she didn't know how to respond to the compliment. She'd splurged on the dress, a simple violet-blue silk, telling herself that the open house tonight was so important that she needed to look her very best. That she also wanted to look her best for Cameron Scott, who had promised to drop by tonight, she refused to admit at all.

She took the last step. "Thanks." The stiffness she heard in her voice reminded her to give M.C. a smile.

"Some classy dame, I'd say," he said. "Where'd you get the dress?"

She named the store. The dress had cost too much, but for once she'd bought it anyway. "I figured I'd better look my best."

"You do." Pride lingered in his voice.

"Thanks." This time it was easier to say. In spite of herself, she felt the nerves just beneath her skin. Tonight had to go well. It simply had to. It marked Harbor House's official West Village debut, given jointly by the staff, executive board and advisory board for benefactors, the press, city officials, other important guests. And neighbors. Important anytime, but especially now. Prophetically, she hoped, she'd chosen the week after Valentine Day to hold it. Maybe a little brotherly love would carry over.

She glanced around her. The old house fairly sparkled. Hardwood floors shone with wax, furniture gleamed with polish. Flowers donated by one of the advisory board members graced the tops of the tables and the first steps of the stairway. They had all pitched in to make the house look its best, and it did. The rest was up to them.

"Who's coming?" M.C. asked.

"We've had a few regrets, but not many. All the executive board is coming and most of the advisory board will be here, too, except the Gordons, the Dunagans and the Dowells. Have you heard from any of the neighbors?"

"Some of 'em 'll be here, some of 'em won't." He licked his thumb and polished an imaginary spot on the stair rail. "We sent invitations to everybody in West Village. I delivered Miss Cunningham's personally, but I'm not sure she'll make it. She's unbent a little since we moved in, but it still rankles her that we did it without her permission."

Mickey smiled. "I'm sure you'll bring her around."

M.C. returned the smile with a grin of his own. "Just give me a little time." In the two months since they'd moved in, M.C. had continued to work at meeting the neighbors, making calls, building relationships. Now, maybe his groundwork would begin to pay off.

The girls were all downstairs by now, dressed in their finest, dancing with nerves and excitement, ready to show off the house. Four new faces had joined them since the completion of the upstairs bedrooms in January. Four young souls, each with her own set of problems, her own unfulfilled potential, her own particular battle to fight. Mickey knew that, to one degree or another, she could help each girl. She was grateful that she was going to have the chance to try.

One by one, the new girls seemed to be settling in. Tonight they were mingling with the others, running to finish last-minute errands, already feeling enough at home to pitch in. Automatically, she ran a diagnostic eye over each one as they passed. Rachel Johnson, her stolid front masking her fears. Mona Rodriguez, fiery, beautiful, her black eyes flashing defiance at the world. Tammy Harris, who hid her true self behind bravado and a cutting wit. Missy Williams, young, vulnerable like Lisa, trying desperately to find her way in a world not of her making. Mickey was proud of her original four girls—each, in her own way, had reached out to the new ones. Which in itself was a sign of progress. And in spite of the expected reluctance to trust, she could see the first tentative bonds being formed among them. Even Brandy had made a few friendly overtures, especially toward little Missy.

Mickey noticed that Brandy had taken pains with her appearance tonight. She was wearing a simple dress of a soft peach color that brought her fair skin alive and complemented her hazel eyes. The incident at school two weeks ago hadn't seemed to damage her new, fragile self-esteem. Maybe, Mickey thought, it was because she and Connie had stood behind her. As she knew, sometimes one vote of confidence could turn around a child's life.

Tammy Harris rushed past, carrying a cheese tray toward the living room. Joni followed with another tray stacked high with cups. Mickey smiled and shook her head. Tammy and Joni were already making a team she wasn't sure the world was ready for.

"Joni," she called, "put the cups by the punch bowl on the dining room table, please." The new table was Mickey's private delight. One of the advisory board members had donated it after she'd remodeled her own dining room. It fit the spacious length of Harbor House's dining room as if it had been made for it. Tonight a massive flower arrangement and a tempting array of goodies graced its polished surface.

"Okay, Mickey." Joni, who never did anything at less than full speed, rounded the corner into the dining room, tilting the tray of cups at a dangerous angle. Mickey closed her eyes. When she opened them, Joni had successfully negotiated the curve and was setting the glasses on the table next to the punch bowl.

She released her pent-up breath and glanced at her watch, then at M.C. "It's time," she said unnecessarily, and braced herself. This aspect of her job was the one she dreaded the most. Public relations. Selling what she did to the public in exchange for money and support. A vital part of their operation, but she didn't think she was any good at it. Whenever possible, she left the job to M.C., who was not only a natural, but enjoyed it. Sometimes, though, she couldn't dodge it. Like tonight.

The doorbell rang. "M.C.?" Mickey hissed. He was beside her as she opened the door.

A good thing. Martha Jenkins stood in the doorway. Or Mrs. Porter Jenkins IV, as she was known in Houston society. Mrs. Jenkins, who served as chairman of Harbor House's advisory board, was married to the sole heir of one of Houston's largest family fortunes. Tonight she had her wizened, silent little husband in tow. She had a particular soft spot for M.C., which was fortunate, because as a result, she had donated many of Harbor House's extras.

"Come in, Mrs. Jenkins." M.C. took her hand and kissed it.

Oh, please, Mickey thought, then shrugged to herself. Whatever worked.

Mrs. Jenkins cruised into the room like a schooner under full sail. "Mr. Mulvaney." Her smile was actually coy.

"May I say how beautiful you're looking tonight?" M.C. let his eyes linger soulfully on her face.

If only I can keep from laughing, Mickey thought.

"You remember my daughter Mickey, the director here?" M.C. gestured toward her.

"Certainly." Mrs. Jenkins shook Mickey's hand, but the glance she spared her was cursory. She didn't even bother to introduce her husband.

"Hello, Mr. Jenkins," Mickey said, feeling a little sorry for him. "Welcome to Harbor House."

"Thank you, Ms. Mulvaney." Mr. Jenkins gave her a timid smile.

"Come with me, Mrs. Jenkins," M.C. said with the courtliest of gestures, "and I'll give you the grand tour I've been promising you. If you'll allow me...."

Mrs. Jenkins sailed off majestically, M.C. at her side like an attendant tugboat. After hesitating a moment, as if he wasn't sure exactly what to do, the abandoned Mr. Jenkins followed them, trailing along in his wife's ample wake. Mickey was left to answer the front door alone, but if M.C. could take care of Mrs. Jenkins, she'd do it gladly.

More guests began arriving—a crew from one of Houston's television stations, a couple of reporters from the *Chronicle,* a city councilman, board members, neighbors. Mickey was pleased at the turnout. The neighbors approached them with varying degrees of friendliness or reserve, but none was outright hostile. The hostile ones had probably stayed home. M.C. had made great progress, but she knew from past experience that there was always a residue of ill will and suspicion, no matter how small. She noticed that, after they'd taken a tour of the house and met the girls, most of the neighbors were more cordial than they'd been when they first arrived.

Speaking of neighbors, where was Cameron Scott? Since that disturbing night just before Christmas, when the boundaries of their relationship had subtly altered, he hadn't asked her out again, keeping her torn between disappointment and relief. But he'd been calling or dropping by fairly regularly. He always kept the conversation light, bantering. Sometimes he would touch her shoulder or take her arm, but strictly on a friendly basis. She'd had to admit that she enjoyed it. That she wanted more, she refused to acknowledge.

A good hour into the reception, Mickey realized she'd been glancing with increasing frequency toward the front door. She caught herself wondering if he was going to show up at all. Or if he did, whether he would be alone. And was furious with herself for caring.

Another knock sounded at the door, and she opened it to four new guests. Cameron Scott was one of them.

He didn't speak at first, just looked steadily at her. In his eyes, those clear gray eyes that mirrored his every thought, she read stunned admiration. For her.

He was wearing a suit again, she thought hazily. Charcoal this time, with a crisp white shirt and a power tie that was bright red with a charcoal-and-red paisley print. Everything perfect—except for one unruly lock of hair, which had escaped to fall over his forehead. She could hardly resist the urge to brush it back. The man was more attractive than the law should allow.

She finally tore her gaze from his and remembered her manners. "Hello, Cameron. Glad you could join us." *Too damned glad.*

"Hello, Mickey." His voice was husky. He cleared his throat. "You're beautiful." He still hadn't taken his eyes off her. She felt her body warm.

"Thanks. Won't you come in?" As much to cover her own confusion as for manners' sake, she turned to greet the other guests with him. A tall man stood beside him, accompanied by a woman of medium height with a sweet, pretty face. With them was a thin, erect elderly woman with an impeccably coiffed chignon and very direct eyes. Something about the man looked familiar.... Suddenly she realized with certainty who he had to be.

"Mickey," Cameron said, "I'd like you to meet my parents, Marie and Cameron Scott."

As introductions were made, Mickey studied the couple with a curiosity she'd have preferred to deny. Cameron's father was the thinner, older mold from which his son was cast, right down to the gray eyes. They were kindly, but she had the feeling that, like those of his son, they never missed a thing. Cameron's mother radiated a warm elegance that Mickey knew she'd been born with. She suppressed a little tweak of envy.

"...And this is Miss Cunningham, the president of the West Village Homeowners' Association," Cameron was saying.

Instantly, Mickey came to attention. So this was the renowned Miss Cunningham.

"Miss Mulvaney." Miss Cunningham graciously inclined her head.

"Miss Cunningham, we're so happy you could join us tonight." Mickey took the woman's thin hand, feeling like a subject in front of her queen. Was she expected to curtsy? She stifled a giggle.

"Thank you. It's a pleasure to be here." But Miss Cunningham remained unsmiling, and her shrewd eyes were absorbing every minute detail. Mickey got the distinct impression that Miss Cunningham was here on business—the business of examining every square inch of Harbor House and its operation. Mickey didn't think she'd ever met anyone more formidable in her life.

She glanced covertly around. No one nearby but Brandy, who was always shy with people she didn't know, most of the time even with those she did. Where was M.C. when she needed him? Still romancing Mrs. Jenkins?

As if by magic, he appeared at her elbow. "Miss Cunningham! I'm delighted you could make it." He took her hand and, without the slightest hesitation, lifted it lightly, ever so briefly to his lips.

Mickey froze. It had worked with Mrs. Jenkins. But Miss Cunningham? *She's going to rap his knuckles,* Mickey thought in terror, *or turn him into a toad or something.*

But to her utter amazement, Miss Cunningham's stern mouth relaxed into a small, prim smile. "Don't try to cozen me, young man," she said. "I'm on to your tricks."

Mickey shook her head in wonder. Even *she* underestimated M.C. sometimes. Closing her mouth, she turned and introduced him to Cameron's parents.

"Good to see you, Cameron," M.C. said cordially, extending his hand.

"M.C." Cameron shook the proffered hand, but something in his voice made Mickey glance at him. He wasn't smiling. *Odd.* She looked at M.C., but he hadn't appeared to notice. She decided she must be imagining things.

M.C. drew Brandy forward. "Miss Cunningham, this is Brandy Williford. I showed you some of her artwork, remember?"

"Ah, yes. Miss Williford." Miss Cunningham extended her hand every bit as regally as she had to anyone else, but her smile actually warmed, and Mickey could have sworn that the sharp old eyes softened a little.

"Nice to meet you, ma'am." Brandy's head was still bowed, but her manners, which had improved vastly since she'd come to Harbor House, were more than acceptable.

"You have real talent, young lady," Miss Cunningham said. "I enjoyed seeing your work very much."

"Thank you, ma'am." Brandy almost met her eyes.

"Someday you must come to visit me," she said kindly. "I've some art you would be interested to see."

Mickey darted a questioning look at M.C. The twinkle in his eyes merely increased a few megawatts. So this was more of his doing. Why had she even wondered?

"Yes, ma'am," Brandy mumbled. "Thank you, ma'am." By this time her cheeks were bright red.

"Miss Cunningham, I promised you a tour of the house," M.C. put in. "Brandy, why don't you come along with us?" Still talking, he guided them both toward the interior.

Finding herself alone with Cameron and his parents, Mickey smiled uncertainly, not quite knowing what to say.

She needn't have worried.

"Cameron's spoken very highly of you, Mickey," Marie Scott said. "May I call you that?" She smiled, and Mickey felt as though she were basking in a sudden ray of summer sunshine.

"Of course. That's very—I mean, thank you," she stammered, catching Cameron's grin from the corner of her eye.

"Marie and I have been looking forward to seeing what you've done here," Cameron's father said. In a gesture as unconscious as it was loving, he reached up to put his arm around his wife's shoulders. It hit Mickey with the force of a physical blow that here, in all its glory, was that mythical fairy-tale oddity—a warm, loving, *normal* family unit. As rare as a spotted elephant. But her cynicism dissolved into an awful yearning. This family was dangerous. They made her want things she couldn't put a name to.

"Edward Brock is a friend of mine," Cameron's father went on. "I've been in and out of this house for years. From what I can see so far, it looks better than it ever has." He smiled at her. Cameron's smile.

"Thank you, Mr. Scott." Hopelessly charmed, she smiled back at him without reserve. "Would you like to see the rest of the house?" She turned to Joni, standing nearby. "This is Joni Jefferson, one of our girls. She'll be happy to give you a tour."

"Hi, Joni," Marie Scott said. "It's nice to meet you."

"Hi," Joni said. "I give the best tours. Nice to meet you," she added belatedly, glancing at Mickey.

"Nice to meet you, too, young lady." Cameron's father hid a smile. "If you give the best tours, we got here just in time. Lead on."

"Follow me," Joni instructed. She struck out at a smart pace, the Scotts behind her.

"That's dangerous," Cameron said. He put his hand under her elbow.

"What is?" She tried not to think about how right his touch felt there.

"Your smile." His hand lingered on her arm, moved in a light caress. "Especially when you're wearing that dress. My father has heart trouble. No telling what it did to him."

"Don't be silly." Unable to help herself, she smiled again.

"The dress matches your eyes."

"That's what the salesperson said." Whatever her earlier doubts, at this minute she was glad she'd bought it.

"She was right. Are you going to stay here tonight?"

"I'm going home." Her pulse quickened. "Why?"

"Do you have your car?"

"No. I rode with M.C."

"I'll take the folks and Miss Cunningham home when they're ready to go. Then I'll come back and pick you up."

She hesitated. Her pulse was pounding in earnest. "I'd better not," she said. "I've got to supervise the cleanup."

"I'll wait," he said promptly.

Frantically she cast around for another excuse. "It'll be late."

"I'll help."

She burst out laughing and gave up. She'd wanted to, anyway. "All right. I hope you're good at washing dishes."

"No dishwasher?"

"Sure, lots of them. Me included."

At his look, she relented. "We don't have one yet. We've budgeted it for next month."

"Cameron?" The voice came from the doorway. Mickey looked up to see a slight, dark young man standing at the threshold of the still-open door.

"Keith." Cameron's eyes lit with pleasure. "Glad you could make it." Putting a hand to the small of Mickey's back, he steered her toward the door. His hand felt good there. Right. "Mickey, this is Keith Rhodes, your neighbor one street over and mine across the street. He and his wife, Penny, are good friends of mine."

Mickey shook hands. "Thanks for coming, Keith." Lisa had been telling her about the Rhodeses, and she'd asked permission several times lately to visit them in the afternoons after school. She'd talked especially about Keith, but hadn't said anything about his wife except that she was "real classy."

Mickey studied him. His handsome face was open, honest, and he radiated a vitality so strong you could feel it. She liked him instantly. "One of our girls, Lisa Parigi, tells me she's been visiting you," she said. "I hope it's all right."

"Of course," he said. "I . . . we enjoy having her."

"Mr. Rhodes!" Lisa's voice came from behind them. Her face was animated and there was joy in her eyes.

"Hi, Lisa." Keith held out his arms to her. To Mickey's utter astonishment, she ran right into them.

"I'm so glad you came." She gave him an exuberant hug. "Where's Mrs. Rhodes?"

There was the merest hesitation before he answered. "She . . . isn't feeling well tonight. Sore throat."

Mickey made a mental note. *So Mrs. Rhodes doesn't like us.*

"That's too bad," Cameron said. "I'd really hoped she could make it."

"Maybe next time," Keith said, but his tone sounded unconvincing.

Mickey smiled. "You're both welcome anytime."

"Come on, Mr. Rhodes. I want to show you the house." Lisa took his hand and, laughing, towed him away.

Cameron touched Mickey's shoulder. "I'll go see what my bunch is doing."

Mickey nodded and turned to greet three new guests.

Thirty minutes later Cameron was back, shepherding his parents and Miss Cunningham toward the door.

"Thank you, Mickey, for a lovely evening," Marie Scott said.

"You obviously run a very efficient operation here," Cameron's father added. His handshake was warm, firm. "I'd like to commend you for it."

"Thank you, sir." She had the feeling that, coming from him, the words were high praise indeed.

"You seem to be doing a good job here, Miss Mulvaney," Miss Cunningham said. "I've been impressed with what I've seen . . . so far."

"I appreciate your saying so, Miss Cunningham. We intend to be the best neighbors possible." Mickey tried to put all the conviction she felt into her voice.

"Indeed," Miss Cunningham said obscurely. She inclined her head and made her stately way toward the door.

"Great party, Mickey," Cameron said. "You're making it hard for the opposition."

"I hope so," Mickey said sweetly.

He looked wounded. "You sure know how to hurt a fellow."

She laughed at him, feeling ridiculously happy.

He caught her hand, ever so briefly. "I'll be back in a minute," he added in a voice so low that she didn't think anyone could possibly have heard.

She glanced up to find M.C.'s knowing eyes on them both.

THE OPEN HOUSE was winding down. As Mickey helped the girls and the extra staff carry empty dishes to the kitchen, she cautioned herself against too much optimism. She'd learned long ago that it was a dangerous drug. Nobody knew better than she that Harbor House was still on trial. This neighborhood had been as tight-knit as any family for too long, and one incident could set Harbor House back well behind the starting point. Still, tonight had been an obvious success. She indulged herself in a moment of pride.

"Hell of a party, sweetheart," M.C. said.

"I thought it went very well." She shot him a glance. "You're outrageous, you know."

The blandest of looks crossed his face. "Beg pardon?"

"Miss Cunningham. Not to mention Mrs. Jenkins."

"Oh, that." M.C. grinned. "Mrs. Jenkins is an incurable romantic. She just needs a little attention. I give her the attention, Harbor House gets the benefit, and there's no harm done. As for Miss Cunningham..." He sobered and gave her a long, direct look. "You know, you might not believe it, and for all I know she might not, either, but I've really gotten fond of the old girl. I'm not trying to con her. At least," he amended conscientiously, examining his fingernails, "not into doing anything that wouldn't be for everyone's good, including her own."

"I stand corrected," Mickey said, feeling a little chagrined. *I'm too suspicious. Even of M.C.*

"Ready to go?" he asked.

"I, ah, Cameron's coming back to get me. He's going to take me home." She couldn't quite meet M.C.'s eyes, but she knew they were on her all the same. She felt her face redden.

But he let her off the hook. "Okay, honey. Think I'll head out then." His voice was devoid of any inflection.

A few minutes later, Cameron came walking back through the front door. "Did I wait long enough, or do I roll up my sleeves?"

"You waited long enough. Just a minute, I'll get my jacket." As she dived into the coat closet, she wondered uneasily if she was taking a step she'd never be able to retrace. Or if she even cared.

CAMERON FOLLOWED HER into her apartment. She hadn't expected him to do otherwise.

"Checking for serial killers again?" she asked around the tightness in her throat. Irrelevantly, she noticed he'd taken off his glasses.

"Never hurts." The amusement in his voice beckoned her. "As long as the cat's asleep..."

This time, when he pulled her to him, the alarm bells were fainter, quickly drowned out by her accelerating pulse.

He took her face between his hands, and the simple gesture splintered her defenses. He held her gaze as he slid his fingers into her hair. His eyes were half in shadow, but she could still see the desire in them.

"Mickey..." His voice was husky. His fingers tightened in her hair. She tried to protest, just once. Then the hammering of her heartbeat drove away coherent thought.

By the time his lips took hers, she was conscious only of his mouth and his warm, hard body so close against her. Always before, he had been gentle, patient. The patience was still there, but she knew by instinct that it was very thin. Underneath it, she sensed an undercurrent of something powerful.

His mouth left hers to trace the line of her jaw, leaving her gasping. Her arms went round him of their own accord, her hands moving on the hard muscles of his shoulders and back.

Then his hands began to move, whispering against the silk-clad length of her body, arousing a kaleidoscope of shimmering new sensations in her. He briefly held her waist, then, inch by inch, slipped his hands around her rib cage until they cradled her breasts. She gasped. She seemed to stop breathing entirely.

He drank in her taste, her scent, the feel of her breasts. Huge waves of need crashed into him, driving away the last of his control. He wanted her. Now. Here, on the carpet of her apartment, if need be.

His hands were at the zipper of her dress when he stopped himself. He could take her now. He knew it. All the barriers were gone, swept away on the tide of their need. But it wouldn't be right, not for her. He knew that, too, with a certainty he couldn't explain. She was willing for the moment, but she would only hate him later. And even more than he desired her, he wanted her to care for him.

Lost in a haze of unbridled feeling, Mickey felt Cameron's powerful body shudder, then go still. He caught her hands and held them against his chest, rested his forehead against hers until their breathing had quieted. Then, carefully, deliberately, he let her go.

Trying to clear both her head and her vision, she looked up into his face.

"Lord, that was the hardest thing I ever did," he confessed, his voice uneven. A tiny, rueful grin softened his features, and his hand brushed her hair away from her face.

She could do nothing but stare at him. Without a backward glance, she would have made love with him.

She started to speak, but he laid a finger against her lips. "There's something between us, Mickey. Are you going to deny it?" An old fear welled up inside her. But seeing the desire in his eyes, she couldn't help wanting him.

"No," she said baldly. "I can't deny it."

She sensed rather than saw the tension go out of him. She tried to go on, but really didn't know what she wanted to say, except that suddenly she was as afraid as she'd ever been in her life. "I can't get involved. My work—" Her voice trailed off and she looked at the floor. An excuse like that was so lame it was an insult. The silence stretched.

It was he who finally broke it. "No good, Mickey." Now his voice held a tinge of amusement. "Everybody works hard. Even I do."

She looked up. "I'm sorry," she said miserably. "I'm not trying to be difficult."

"Just comes naturally, is that it?" She caught the flash of white teeth as he grinned.

She gave him back a reluctant smile. "Thanks a lot." Then she sobered. "I don't know. It's just that this—" she stumbled over the words "—it's not for me. I can't afford..." Her throat blocked.

"Can't afford what?" He wasn't going to let up on her.

To let anyone hurt me? Betray me? She had no answer. Again the conflicting emotions welled up in her throat, threatening to choke her. She pushed them down, grasped desperately at anger.

"I can't afford any complications right now," she finished with a snap. "I don't need them. Or want them." She turned from him and started to walk away.

He caught her arm and turned her around, none too gently. "What we have together isn't a bad thing, Mickey. It can be wonderful. What are you afraid of?"

"I...don't know." What *was* she afraid of? She tried to face the question squarely, but it was like trying to find a distant star—it could be glimpsed from the corner of an eye, but viewed directly, it disappeared. She couldn't answer. She only felt, as deeply as she'd ever felt anything, that to give in to her need for him would leave her defenseless.

His gaze never wavered. She let her own play over his face. Sculpted features, wide brow, strong, firm mouth—it was a face to trust. To love? *No,* her mind screamed. Love wasn't for her. The risks were too great.

What if...? The thought snaked insidiously into her brain. Maybe, as he'd said, they could take the moment's joy and not worry about the consequences. What if she simply let go, gave in, allowed herself to enjoy? What harm could it do? Maybe, just this once...

"You don't have to be afraid." He spoke deliberately, as if to a frightened child. "I'll never hurt you." She heard the promise in his words.

"That's ridiculous," she said. "I'm not afraid of anything." And almost believed it.

He was still watching her. "Tell you what," he said. "I have to go over to Bolivar Peninsula to check on the family beach house a week from next Friday. Do you have plans?"

"I'll...have to see." What a laugh. She never had those kind of plans.

"We can go to Galveston. Make a day of it."

She said nothing, feeling as though she were about to step off a twenty-foot diving tower, not knowing if there was water below.

He pulled her to him once more for a quick kiss that became a lingering one. Once, twice, he pulled away, then came back to her mouth like a thirsty man. When he finally broke away, they were both breathing hard.

"If I don't go now, I won't," he muttered. "I'll call you next week." A last quick, hard kiss and he was gone.

Afterward, she paced the floor of her small apartment for a long time, fighting hard for the old control, the containment, the objectivity. Wandering restlessly by a small table, she picked up a framed picture of herself and her mother, an informal snapshot taken in one of their infrequent happy moments. It was one of the few personal items in her apartment. Her life hadn't exactly been crowded with the stuff of happy memories.

She looked at her mother's face. Although the older woman had been smiling when the picture was taken, lines of weakness and unhappiness marred her beautiful features. Her mother had been the child, she herself the caregiver from the time she could walk until her mother's death. Never had her mother been there for her, stood up for her, defended her. Never. With time and therapy, she'd worked through the old anger. Now, she just felt a sort of emptiness. She wished she could feel more. She set the picture down.

Scenes from her childhood flashed in a crazy collage through her consciousness. The bad times…plenty of *them*. The good times. There *had* been a few good times, after all. The beach, the fairs… Cotton candy. When she was a child she'd loved the cotton candy at the fairs, knowing how too much gave her a stomachache but unable to resist it. It seemed so harmless. Cotton candy had no substance. One instant of indescribable sweetness, then it would dissolve into nothing on her tongue.

There was substance to Cameron Scott. Value. Durability. But that part of him was not for her, only the sweetness of having him for the moment. Right now he wanted her, but for permanence, he would choose someone from his own world. Still, she could savor one vanishing instant of pleasure with him. Even though she knew without a doubt that, sooner or later, pain would eventually follow.

The real question was: would it be worth it?

CHAPTER TEN

PENNY RHODES CLOSED the book of fabric samples she'd
been thumbing through and glanced at her watch. Nearly
five o'clock. Just enough time to sit down for a quick cup
of coffee before Keith came home. She'd been restless lately,
dissatisfied with everything—her work, her clients, herself.
Telling herself she was working too hard, she'd sworn to
take more time to relax.

She took her coffee into the living room and had just settled into one of the matched Georgian wing chairs when the
doorbell rang. Her lips tightening in annoyance, she set the
cup and saucer down on the glass top of the coffee table and
went to answer the door.

As she opened it, a gust of early March wind pushed
against it, nearly jerking it from her hands. Lisa Parigi stood
on the top step, tendrils of dark hair blowing about her face,
her kitten in her arms. She'd been over several times in the
past few weeks. Each time she'd come, she'd brought her
kitten with her, for her to visit too, she'd explained.

"Hello, Mrs. Rhodes." Lisa's voice was soft as always,
her manners perfect. Not what Penny would have expected
from the product of a halfway house. But then again, you
never could tell. As she well knew.

"Lisa." Penny felt the pull of the girl's eyes, dark pools
that struck old chords, made her remember things she didn't

want to remember. Lisa never failed to awaken the old feelings, the ones Penny had so neatly tucked away.

"Am I interrupting you?" It was always the first question Lisa asked.

"No," Penny said reluctantly. "I was just sitting down with a cup of coffee to wait for Keith to come home. Would you like something to drink?"

Lisa opted for apple juice. Looking like someone's old-fashioned porcelain doll, she sat quietly on the chintz-upholstered sofa and drank her juice while the kitten napped in her lap. Spotting a bronze inkstand on the coffee table, she reached out tentative fingers to touch it, then looked a question at Penny.

"It's new," Penny said.

"It's beautiful." Lisa's fingers moved carefully over the chased ornamentation.

"I'm glad you like it." On Lisa's first visit, she had openly admired the house and yard. Every time she came back, she pored over each new object with awestruck fascination, as if she were amazed the world could hold such beauty. To her own surprise, Penny had actually begun to enjoy showing her things. The girl herself was such a thing of beauty, always obedient, sensitive to every nuance of their moods. But she was so shy, so contained that Penny never knew what she was really thinking.

"I'm sorry you couldn't come to the open house," Lisa said. "Mr. Rhodes said you didn't feel well."

"I'm sorry too, Lisa. I . . . had a sore throat." Which was a lie. Keith had wanted her to go, but at that point she would rather have been dragged out and shot. She'd flatly refused. They'd had sharp words and he'd gone on alone. She'd sat at home, curled into a ball of misery, and watched television until she'd been too tired to think anymore.

Since that night their lives had gone on as usual, but they'd both tacitly avoided the subject of the party and of Harbor House. Penny had known from the beginning that it would mean trouble. It was proving true already. And the trouble was between her and Keith.

"I'll take you over sometime," Lisa promised.

"We'll see," Penny said. The unease gnawed at her. She didn't want to hurt Lisa's feelings, but she wasn't ready to go to Harbor House. Not yet, anyway.

The back door slammed. "Penny?"

Keith. "In here," she called, relieved. Keith teased the girl, bantered with her, told her stories, talked nonsense with her as if she were his own....

"Hi, hon." When Keith entered the room, he revitalized Penny, as always. She saw Lisa's face light like a Christmas tree.

He bent to kiss Penny, then spotted Lisa. "Well, what do you know? How's my girl?"

"Fine. I brought Half-pint to see you again." Lisa returned his hug with interest, waking the kitten and almost spilling her juice. Penny felt a peculiar little twinge. Keith had loved her enough to marry her in spite of the fact that she couldn't have children, but she knew he'd wanted them. The old grief welled up in her. And the other feelings, too, hovering like vicious ghosts at the edge of her consciousness.

Within seconds, Keith was teasing the kitten with a bit of thread and drawing Lisa out, making her talk of everyday things—school, her chores, her clothes, how the kitten was growing. Penny stayed quiet, observing them together. She found herself watching Lisa's face, listening to her.

In a few minutes Lisa rose to go, taking her empty glass to the kitchen. She never stayed long. "Thanks for the apple juice," she said. "I'll come back soon. If it's okay, that is," she added.

"Of course it is," Keith said. "Come back anytime."

"Yes," Penny echoed. "Anytime."

Keith shot her a look of surprise, but she was more surprised at herself than he was.

After Lisa had gone, they met each other's eyes. Keith's face held a peculiar expression that Penny suspected was mirrored in her own.

"Did you mean that, Pen?"

"Yes." And realized she did.

"I'm glad," he said. "She's—" He paused. "She's a sweet girl."

"Yes," Penny said again. "She is."

THIS IS GETTING to be a habit, M.C. thought as he rang Miss Cunningham's doorbell. At least this time he'd been invited. He and Brandy, who was standing beside him right now, feeling every bit as nervous, he'd be willing to bet, as he'd felt the last time he was here.

He heard the brisk footsteps on the other side of the door. Brandy ducked her head even lower, if possible, and seemed to shrink inside herself. He just had time to touch her arm in reassurance before the door opened.

"Miss Williford, Mr. Mulvaney. Come in." It was the warmest greeting he'd received from Miss Cunningham yet. He flattered himself that it wasn't all because of Brandy.

They followed their hostess into the parlor. She had tea laid out, silver service and all. *Tea,* for the Lord's sake. It was a first for him. He wouldn't bother to bet it was a first for Brandy, too; nobody would take him up on it.

Miss Cunningham poured, just as he'd seen in a dozen old movies. They were getting the full treatment, he noticed.

Sugar cubes that she dispensed with delicate tongs, tiny, delicious sandwiches, wafer-thin lemon slices, each with a single whole clove garnishing the center. He searched his brain for any scraps of teatime etiquette he'd ever heard. He thought about the bit with crooking the little finger, but decided it was probably a joke. He wasn't going to try it, anyway.

He glanced at Brandy, dressed neatly and becomingly in a cotton skirt and blouse. She looked scared, ill at ease. But the girl had an innate class, a dignity about her that was beginning to emerge more and more as the days went by. He was convinced that, eventually, if they could keep her on track, she'd be all right.

"Now then, Miss Williford." Miss Cunningham set down her cup and saucer and touched the monogrammed linen napkin to her lips. "May I call you Brandy?"

Brandy's mouth dropped open and she actually looked Miss Cunningham full in the face. *It's a cinch no one's ever asked her that before,* M.C. thought. He'd bet she'd been called plenty of other things, but he didn't think anyone had asked her permission about those, either.

"Yes, ma'am," Brandy finally managed.

"Good." Miss Cunningham laid down her napkin. "Now, then. I want you to tell me about your artwork...."

A half hour later, M.C. was shaking his head in silent amazement. Steadily and kindly, Miss Cunningham had drawn Brandy out until the girl was talking more than he'd ever heard her.

"I've done several kinds of things," Brandy was saying. Her eyes held a spark of interest, and for once she wasn't self-conscious, cowed or belligerent. She was totally absorbed in what they were talking about.

Miss Cunningham indicated the drawing of the stag, sitting in the easel on the desktop. "Have you tried pen and ink? My niece did this when she was about your age."

Brandy stared appreciatively. "That's a really great job. I can't draw that good."

"That *well,* Brandy," Miss Cunningham corrected, but her voice was gentle.

"That well," Brandy amended. "I tried pen and ink, and it's sort of fun, but I like colors the best."

"I saw from your work that you have a wonderful sense of color," Miss Cunningham said. "You also have a good eye for form and proportion. I have some other things I want to show you." She picked up a book from the table in front of them. "Tell me, do you like the French Impressionists?"

"Oh, yes, ma'am. The colors are so pretty." Brandy was as near to being truly excited as M.C. had ever seen her.

"This book is a collection of Claude Monet's work...." Old and young, the two heads bent over the book together.

All at once, M.C. realized something. He was seeing the other side of Jessamine Cunningham, the dedicated, compassionate teacher, mother to none and therefore to all, the caretaker who, underneath the stern, disciplined exterior, truly loved the children she taught, coaxed and bullied into being everything they could possibly be. He watched and listened in quiet pleasure.

At the end of the visit, Miss Cunningham urged them to come back again.

"Thank you, ma'am," Brandy said. "I'd like to come back."

Miss Cunningham's eyes softened, and her smile held the beginnings of real affection. "I'll be looking forward to it. Good day, Brandy. Mr. Mulvaney."

As M.C. passed the little drawing on the desk, he allowed himself one more pat on the back.

M.C. TURNED into Harbor House's driveway. "Well, Brandy, what did you think?" he asked as he turned off the ignition.

"I thought it was really interesting." Traces of excitement lingered in her voice. "She has a lot of good stuff."

"She does at that. Would you like to go back again sometime?"

"Yes, sir. I had a good time."

"She's quite a lady. You won't meet many like her."

Brandy was quiet a second. "No, sir," she said slowly, "I don't guess I will." As she was getting out of the car, she turned back to him. "She's a nice lady," she said, a thoughtful expression on her face.

As he watched her go into the house, M.C. chuckled to himself. Some might not agree with Brandy's assessment of Miss Cunningham, but he certainly would. If he wasn't mistaken, which he rarely was, Miss Cunningham had given Brandy another little boost up the ladder today.

And what was good for Brandy was good for Mickey.

Oh, he'd do his best for Brandy because he cared about her, too, but Mickey's welfare was what mattered most to him in the world. If necessary, he'd lie down in front of an oncoming freight train for her. Of course, he'd find an easier way. Too messy.

He thought about Brandy again, and Mickey. He saw what was going on, all right; Mickey was allowing herself to get too involved in the girl's problems. It was the first time he'd seen it happen. Mickey was always compassionate and caring with the girls—it was one of the things that made her so good at her job. But until now, she'd always managed to keep her balance. Until now, he'd never seen anyone breach that wall she'd built around herself. Including him, he reflected without bitterness. God knew he'd tried often enough, hard enough. He knew Mickey was fond of him—loved him, if you would—but she couldn't quite let herself go and trust him.

It hurt when she shut him out. He could tell she realized it, but she couldn't seem to help it. Maybe someday...

He saw something else, too. She was falling for young Scott, and the feeling appeared to be mutual. Basically he approved. He liked the boy. He wasn't so sure Scott liked him, though—the last couple of times, he'd been pretty cold. Why, M.C. wasn't sure. But he knew his daughter. She was scared to death of her own feelings, particularly where men were concerned. He'd bet his last greenback that she was fighting Scott for all she was worth, and Scott was blaming him for whatever he had, or hadn't, done.

A wave of the old helpless anger washed over him. He knew why Mickey was afraid of her feelings. He hadn't done anything to her, but someone had. And he hadn't been around to keep it from happening.

When he'd decided to straighten out his life, he'd resolved to make what amends he could. He'd started with a little detective work. Then came the talk with Mickey's mother, the one he should have had about twenty years before.... During the talk, he'd found out the rest of it. All of it. Trouble was, it had been too late. The damage had already been done. He wasn't a killing man. Even so, he'd have hunted the son of a bitch down and shot him if he hadn't already been dead. He'd found that out, too. All he could do was try to make it up to Mickey the best way he could.

Slowly he got out of the car, scratching his chin in thought. Yep, he reflected, he approved of Cameron Scott, even if the boy didn't like him. He'd fix that later. For now, he'd leave him and Mickey alone, just wait a little, watch a little. He was good at that. Then, when the time came, maybe he could help things along.

He was good at that, too.

MICKEY CAUGHT HERSELF. Standing idle, for heaven's sake, staring out the tall window into the yard, watching the early-spring sunshine strew bright patches of light across the greening grass, looking for signs of buds on the trees. Spring was her favorite time of year. It meant new beginnings. It hadn't yet come out in full force, but the buds were definitely there. She could see them swelling on the bare branches, against the blue of the sky....

She muttered something under her breath. Why was she lollygagging in front of a window, looking for spring buds, when paperwork lay three feet high on the desk behind her and a million things still remained to be done to the house? The attic rooms were almost ready for the new occupants. But she wasn't.

She forced herself to sit down at her desk, began to work. And ended by staring blankly at the stacks of papers, remembering, rehashing, trying to make some sense out of the night of the open house, nearly two weeks ago now. That crazy night when she'd stood dumb—in more ways than one, she reflected—and allowed Cameron Scott to assume she was going to Galveston with him. Reason had come back with the dawn of the next day, and she'd wondered if she'd lost her mind. Since then, her emotions had been in such a turmoil that she'd hardly been able to concentrate on anything. Like now.

She had to break the date. She'd put off calling him as long as she could, but now Friday was only a couple of days away. Finally, a little while ago, she'd worked up her courage and dialed his office number. He hadn't been in. Feeling as foolish as a teenage girl, she'd left her number with his secretary.

When a knock sounded at the door, she jumped. But it was only Lisa Parigi who came in, looking as if she'd just seen the circus drive into town. "Mickey? Mr. and Mrs. Rhodes are here. Can you come and talk to them a minute, please?"

"Sure." Mickey rose. She remembered Keith Rhodes from the night of the open house—a pleasant man. She also remembered that, for what had sounded like a manufactured reason, Mrs. Rhodes hadn't come.

"They want to ask you something." Lisa was practically jumping up and down with excitement.

"Hang on a minute, Lisa. I'm coming." She laid a restraining hand on her shoulder. "Calm down a little. You're going to make yourself sick." She followed Lisa to the front of the house, barely able to keep up with her.

Keith Rhodes was standing in the entrance hall with a young woman around Mickey's age. She was petite, model-thin, expensively dressed, with the unconsciously assured carriage of a natural aristocrat.

"Hello, Ms. Mulvaney." Keith gave her his engaging smile. "This is my wife, Penny."

"I'm glad to meet you, Mrs.—" Mickey met Penny Rhodes's artfully accented eyes, and the expression in them stopped her cold. *Fear.* Stark, raw, unadulterated fear. It was concealed, but with her practiced eye, Mickey saw it plainly. In fact, the sheer force of it made her catch her breath. "—Rhodes." She covered her lapse as smoothly as possible, hoping no one had noticed.

When she took the woman's hand, it was clammy. She pressed it, trying to telegraph reassurance to her. Whatever was wrong, it was nothing minor. "Welcome to Harbor House," she said gently. "We missed you at the open house and were hoping you could come by to see us later."

"Thank you." Nothing else. The voice was beautifully modulated, but the tone was strained, and she spoke through stiff lips.

Unobtrusively, Keith Rhodes slipped a hand around his wife's waist. "We've come to ask a favor of you, Ms. Mulvaney."

"Make it Mickey. What can I do for you?" Behind her, she felt the tension and excitement that emanated from every line of Lisa's slender body. What on earth was going on?

"Penny and I would like to take Lisa to Astroworld this weekend," he said. "We came by to get your permission."

As if it were the most natural thing in the world, Lisa went to stand by him. He put an arm around her shoulders and hugged her to him, and she looked up at him with adoration. There was no other word for it. "Please, Mickey?" she pleaded. "I've never been to Astroworld."

"Well, I —" Mickey was caught flat-footed. Out of nowhere, she found herself with an extremely difficult decision to make. Harbor House's policy was that the girls were allowed to earn their privileges. Lisa had already earned the right to go to Astroworld many times over, and she knew it. Mickey was as sure as she'd ever been of anything that Lisa was trustworthy, but there remained the fact that she didn't know the Rhodeses.

She looked at Keith, still standing with his arm around Lisa. M.C. always accused her of being too suspicious, and maybe she was. Yet here in front of her was a situation, superficially innocent, that could be the worst problem of all. Keith Rhodes seemed like a fine young man—pleasant, intelligent, successful—to all appearances the last person in the world to abuse or endanger a child. Instinct told her she could trust him. Hard-earned knowledge said that appearances were often false. She'd be damned if she'd put any of her girls in such a situation if there was the slightest doubt. And she wasn't reading anything from Keith Rhodes's wife but fear and anxiety, which was hardly a recommendation. No, she decided, she mustn't jeopardize Lisa's welfare for any reason, even if the picture looked rosy. And she wasn't at all sure about this one.

She had opened her mouth to decline politely when a knock sounded on the front door.

Leslie, on perennial lookout for her boyfriend, bounded to the door before any of them could move.

"Mickey, it's Cameron," she announced unnecessarily loudly.

Mickey winced. How like him to come in person instead of just returning her call. But she was glad to see him.

He walked in as if the place belonged to him. "Hi. Hope I'm not interrupting anything." Then he spotted Penny and Keith. "What are you two doing here?"

"I might ask the same of you, buddy." There was a knowing twinkle in Keith's eyes.

"I like the company," Cameron said without a blink. "How are you, Penny?"

"Fine, Cameron. It's good to see you." Mickey noticed that some of the blood had come back into Penny's face. Even so, Cameron was eyeing her narrowly.

"Giving Penny the grand tour?" he asked.

"Not exactly," Keith said, "although I'd like her to see the house before we go. We've come to ask permission to take Lisa to Astroworld with us."

"Please, Mickey," Lisa said again. The pleading in her face was hurting Mickey almost physically. She could hardly bear to tell her no, but she was going to have to.

Cameron must have seen it coming, because he looked directly at Mickey. "I think that's a wonderful idea."

"I...don't think so," Mickey said reluctantly. "We have rules—" From the corner of her eye, she saw Lisa's face fall.

"Let me vouch for Keith and Penny," Cameron said. "They're two of my closest friends, have been for a long time. I'd trust them with anything I had or with anyone I loved."

"Thank you, Cameron," Penny said, real pleasure on her face.

Mickey smiled faintly. "That's quite a recommendation, but I really think it's a little too soon. Maybe after we all get to know one another better—"

Cameron, Keith and Lisa all spoke at once, Cameron and Keith trying to reassure her, Lisa begging.

In the end it was Penny Rhodes, who had scarcely said a word throughout the whole visit, who settled it.

"Ms. Mulvaney." Everyone stopped talking and looked at her. "Let her come with us, please," she said. "We'll take good care of her. I promise you."

When Mickey met her gaze, a strange thing happened. In the depths of those clouded dark eyes, she saw something familiar. It was as if, somewhere along the way, the two women had shared something. The silence stretched as their eyes held in a subtle telepathy. *Shared struggle, shared agony...* It was as if she were reading the other woman's soul.

With a gut feeling as strong as any she'd ever had, Mickey realized that, whatever Penny Rhodes's problems were, she would see to it that Lisa was cared for.

"All right," she said finally, breaking the tense silence. "She can go."

The last of the sentence was almost drowned out by Lisa's whoop of joy. Mickey put away the last of her doubts and told herself that she was doing the right thing.

"We'll pick you up at nine o'clock Saturday morning, Lisa." Keith's smile was a mirror of Lisa's excitement.

"Thank you, Ms. Mulvaney," Penny said quietly. On her face was a strange little look of peace.

After the Rhodeses left and the ecstatic Lisa went to do the rest of her chores, Mickey turned to Cameron. "This is against my better judgment," she said. "I normally don't allow the girls to go anywhere with anyone I don't know well. Tell me what you know about these people."

"Keith and Penny are as solid as they come," he said. "Keith was a college friend of mine, and I met Penny when he married her. Incidentally, she comes from a very wealthy family in Dallas. Keith's a good lawyer, a hard worker. Penny's a little quiet, but she's quite a talented interior decorator." He laughed wryly. "I'm the one who talked them into moving to West Village. I'll have to admit they weren't very happy when your operation moved in, especially Penny. That's why I was so surprised to see her here."

"Lisa's apparently been doing some PR work on her own." She smiled. "How could anyone keep from loving Lisa?"

"Beats me." He smiled back, deepening the laugh lines around his eyes.

And how can anyone resist you? she thought. But she had to do it, while she still could.

"Cameron." She dropped her gaze. "About this Friday. I can't —" How unfair of him to show up in person, so she'd have to tell him to his face.

"Don't even think of canceling," he broke in, still grinning.

Guiltily, she met his eyes. "I'm snowed under," she said. "Friday's a workday. There's a meeting I really ought to—"

"They can do without you at the meeting, and the work will still be waiting for you when you get back."

She stood still, remembering. How she'd wanted him . . . The first steps down a long, frightening road. If she went with him, she'd be going too far down it to come back unhurt.

"Sorry." He folded his arms. "You're going with me. End of discussion." He was still grinning, but there was an implacability about him that told Mickey she was wasting her time. *Maybe she wanted to believe it, anyway.*

"All right," she said on a long breath. "I'll go."

CHAPTER ELEVEN

"Nope." Cameron plucked the sand dollar from Mickey's hand and put it back in the bin with the others. "It doesn't count unless you find them yourself."

"But what if we don't find any?" She peered into the adjacent bin, filled with large pink-throated conch shells.

"Trust me. We'll find them over on the peninsula."

She dug through a shallow basket filled with brightly striped shells. "How about this one?" She picked one up and waved it under his nose. "I'll bet you can't find one like this."

He caught her wrist and examined it. "You're right." He chuckled. "There aren't any of those around here. That one's courtesy of the Great Barrier Reef. Come on."

Hands on her shoulders, he guided her out of the shell shop onto the Strand, Galveston's old commercial artery, lately reconstituted as a tourists' mecca.

The old island wove its own particular spell, and Mickey had already succumbed. She had allowed herself this day, these hours, to suspend the real world and become an inhabitant of fairyland. With Prince Charming? A giggle rose in her throat.

A blustery March wind whistled between the old buildings. With hardly a thought, she leaned gratefully into the warm pressure of Cameron's fingers.

She couldn't remember ever having felt like this with a man. To be able to relax and enjoy were new sensations. She should feel anything but comfortable; she knew only too well the emotions he could arouse in her. A part of her remembered his veiled promise, but his smile, and the sunshine of the Galveston afternoon, glossed over the small fear with the iridescent colors of joy.

He turned her around to face him, molding her shoulders with his hands. "Can we eat now?" he asked plaintively. "I'm starved. Besides, we've got to make Bolivar soon or we're going to run out of daylight. If we don't hurry, you won't find any shells," he added, slanting a look at her.

"Bribery'll get you anywhere." Laughing, she met his glance. "Okay, let's eat."

He towed her past the shops along the Strand with their large windows that displayed everything from profane T-shirts to fine imported china. Distracted, she missed her footing on the sidewalk, uneven from years of settling into the shifting island sand. She stumbled and was hurtling out of control when a strong arm caught her and pulled her back to her feet.

He was grinning. "Just learning to walk?"

"I've been at it for several years now," she said with dignity.

"Another ten years or so, and maybe you'll get it down." Even as he was laughing with her, he realized that it had felt so natural just to reach out and catch her, as if catching her when she stumbled were something he would always be there to do. Somehow, she *fit* beside him. He didn't remember having felt that way with a woman in years. *Ever*?

Since this morning when he'd picked her up, there had been a suppressed excitement about her that was new, childlike in its freshness. All day long, bit by bit, she'd been letting her guard slip, exposing the tender, joyous side of her nature he'd always known was there.

He stole a glance at her. Her black hair was wind-tousled, the magnolia-fair cheeks bloomed with color, and her eyes blazed a glorious blue in the island sunlight. He could hardly keep his eyes off her. Or his hands. He couldn't seem to keep from touching her. As they walked, he kept his hand at her elbow.

Stopping at a tall brownstone building, they turned into a sandwich shop and headed for a small table in a corner. Mickey inhaled the warm, yeasty smell of fresh-baked croissants. It was past noon now, and she'd only eaten a piece of toast before they'd crossed the causeway from the mainland onto Galveston Island. She ordered generously, and by the time their food came, she was ravenous.

"The Strand is all new to me," she said around a bite of chicken salad croissant.

"I figured, when you said you hadn't been to Galveston since you were a little girl."

Her childhood memories of Galveston were of blue water and broad, curving beaches—the gulf side of the island. The Strand ran along the leeward side, facing Galveston Bay. Cameron had told her that the old street, known in its day as the Wall Street of the South, had been the center of nineteenth-century Galveston's commercial district. But after a mammoth turn-of-the-century storm had laid the city waste, Galveston's prominence had faded, and the Strand had deteriorated into a strip of industrial warehouses and rough bars. It was only in the past couple of decades that a group of citizens and enterprising businessmen had united to bring it back, this time as a tourist attraction. Venerable financial institutions and crumbling market buildings had gained new lives as trendy clothing shops and chic restaurants, and a busy air of festivity pervaded the whole scene.

"Is this where you got the idea for Village Walk?" she asked.

"Not exactly." He swallowed the last bite of his pastrami and Swiss. "This is a genuine historic district. Most of the buildings have historic plaques, and the financing is different. But I'll admit the Strand's success made it easier for me to decide to put in Village Walk."

"It's the same principle, isn't it? New uses for old buildings?"

"In that respect, yes. It's all adaptive reuse."

"Save the neighborhood, huh?" She planted her elbows on the table and narrowed her eyes. "Good idea. But you can't be too careful who you let in."

He burst out laughing. "I've learned that. In more ways than one." He leaned over, bringing his face so near that for one wrenching second she thought he might kiss her. But he only caught her chin in his hands, scanned her face a moment, then let her go. He took her hand and held it lightly, and there was something in his eyes she found herself not wanting to think about. "Mickey." His fingers tightened. "What am I going to do with you?"

Caught up in his gaze, she could only shake her head. Besides the inconsequential bantering, there hadn't been many words, *real* words, between them today. The thoughts were there, elusive as rainbows. *What are you thinking? What am I to you? What's happening between us?* But neither spoke them aloud.

Pulling herself back to reality, she put her napkin back on the table. "Thanks for lunch."

He looked with interest at her plate. Not a crumb of food remained. "Sorry you didn't enjoy it."

"Yeah." She grinned at him. "I hated every bite."

Laughing, he stood, pulling her up with him. "Let's go."

Where? Good question. She put on her jacket. Bolivar, he'd told her. To inspect his family's beach cabin and to look for shells. *And what else?* This journey could be longer than just simply crossing another stretch of water. But, trapped as she was in the magic of the day, she couldn't seem to make herself care.

Thirty minutes later they were driving onto one of the huge ferries that connected the east end of the island with Bolivar Peninsula, the low, narrow tongue of land just across the Galveston Ship Channel. Cameron pulled the Mustang into line and Mickey put down the window. The air was alive with sea gulls, hundreds of them, wheeling above the ship and filling the air with their mewing cries. Still more sat like statues on the massive pilings surrounding the ferry, staring solemnly out to sea.

The ship's horn gave an ear-shattering blast, making her jump. Then, with a shudder, the enormous vessel slowly began to glide away from the pilings. Cameron set the emergency brake and pulled a bag of corn chips from a grocery sack on the back seat. "Come on, before all the good spots are taken. We're going to feed the gulls."

They threaded their way between the rows of parked vehicles to the stern of the vessel. As it turned out, they could have taken their time. The ferry was only about half full, and what passengers there were apparently preferred the warmth of their cars to the chilly wind blowing across the deck. Their only competition consisted of three small children, all sharing the same large bag of chips. Cheeks windchapped, voices shrill with excitement, they cannoned around the deck, high on childhood's particular energy.

Their excitement was contagious, and when Cameron tore open the sack of chips, Mickey took the first handful.

It seemed as if every one of the gulls she had seen at the landing were flying in the ferry's wake. They hovered, wheeled and dived, their sharp-angled wings stark white against the bluebird sky. After the first chips were thrown to them they grew bolder, bullying one another for the best position. It was their game, too, and they played it well, swooping to catch most of the tidbits in midair. Mickey threw them as joyfully as the children. The gulls came so near she could see their sharp black eyes watching her, never missing a move, and she found herself with a strong urge to reach out and touch....

From nowhere, a memory surfaced like a bit of flotsam in her thoughts—herself as a small child, riding this ferry or one of its siblings, reaching for the birds high above her head. She had cried because she was too small, and someone had picked her up so she could see them better. Who? She couldn't remember.

"Watch this," Cameron called.

"Okay." As if she could help watching him anyway. He had taken off his glasses, and the wind had tousled his hair and brought the healthy color to his face. She thought fondly that he looked like a little boy about to show off a new trick. In faded jeans and windbreaker, he looked big, powerful. Beautiful. She smiled to herself, wondering what he would think of such an adjective applied to him. Probably laugh. Beyond presenting a polished, professional appearance in his business, he seemed to give no thought to his looks. But he had substance.... She tried to deny the need that welled up in her.

He held a chip high over his head. Instantly two gulls angled in closer and hung in the air just above him, eyeing the chip. For long seconds man and birds remained motionless against the sky, and Mickey was about to declare it a stand-off when, from out of nowhere, a third gull swooped in front of the first two and snatched the chip from Cameron's fingers, flying off with cries of triumph.

Amazed, Mickey tried the same trick, feeling the strange, not-really-painful pinch of the bird's beak as it took the chip.

"See?" he said. "It doesn't hurt, does it?"

She met his eyes. They were warm, laughing. "No," she said. "It doesn't hurt at all."

He stuffed the empty bag into the pocket of his wind-breaker and brushed the salt off his hands. "Let's go." He pointed behind them toward the bow of the ferry.

She looked around and saw that the ship was pulling into the landing. The children, still shouting and laughing, were running toward their car. She and Cameron reached his Mustang just as a deckhand began directing the vehicles to disembark. She looked back. The sea gulls were circling the landing or settling back onto the pilings, waiting for the ferry to head back to Galveston so they could replay their endless panhandling. Who had held her up to see them? A good memory...

Five minutes later they were on their way down the two-lane highway that ran the length of Bolivar Peninsula. "Why is your house over here?" she asked. "Galveston's closer to Houston."

"It belonged to my grandparents. They lived in Beau-mont, which is closer to Bolivar. My father got the house when they died." Casually, he threw an arm across the space between the bucket seats, his hand touching her shoulder. "We went there a lot when I was growing up. Normally my sister uses it just in the summer, but this year she decided to bring the kids during their spring break. I promised I'd make sure everything works before she comes over.''

His fingers were warm, even through the layers of her clothing. Happiness bubbled just under her consciousness like vintage champagne. To conquer the urge to scoot closer to him like a lovesick adolescent, she looked out the window. The terrain was flat, marshy prairie, bounded narrowly by Galveston Bay on one side and the Gulf of Mexico on the other. Most of the buildings she saw were older, smaller, more like fishing cabins than the trendy, multilevel houses she'd seen on Galveston Island. "Do you come here often?" she asked, just to hear the sound of his voice.

"Not really. I don't have much time to get away. I love the place. It's old, not very fancy, but we always had fun there. I want you to see it." He turned to smile at her, and she gave him back a smile as giddy as a schoolgirl's.

A few minutes later he was turning down a shell road toward the gulf side of the peninsula. At the end, tucked behind its protective sand dunes in a field of winter-dead grass, sat a beach house.

Just as he'd said, it was nothing fancy. More like a big box painted white, sitting high on enormous dark creosote-stained piers. As they drew closer, Mickey could see that the walls were mostly windows, and a deck ran around three sides. Beneath the house a swing hung from rusty chains, rocking in the wind. The place exuded an ageless charm, as if it had sprung naturally from the landscape a long time ago. It was utterly bewitching, and she fell headlong into hopeless enchantment.

Cameron pulled the Mustang into the yard and killed the engine. "Here we are." Mickey could hear the quiet happiness in his voice.

"Cameron, it's—" She groped for the word, couldn't find it. "Perfect." Inadequate, trite. But she saw her feelings mirrored in his eyes. Briefly, he covered her hand with his.

She met him in front of the car. He took her hand and they walked to the top of one of the barrier dunes protecting the land from the Gulf of Mexico.

Today, because of the stiff wind, the gulf was the opaque brown of a good gumbo. The air was salty, clean in her nostrils, and the crash of the surf and the cries of the gulls were a symphony in her ears. One lone vehicle, an ancient truck, was in sight, but it was a good half mile away. They were alone, suspended in time and space. Here, where land met sea, she could put the real world away. She felt like a stranger to herself. A curiously happy stranger whose inexplicable excitement kept threatening to boil over at the oddest moments.

A gust of wind whistled through the marsh grass on the top of the dune and whipped her hair in tendrils around her face. She shivered, drawing instinctively closer to Cameron. He put his arm around her.

She wasn't sure who turned first. He tilted her face to his, and their lips came together.

The kiss was gentle, undemanding. His lips were warm, a little salty from the sea air, and their touch on hers was light. It was a kiss of welcome, nothing more. But she felt desire stir within her.

He raised his head and pulled her against him. She buried her face against his windbreaker and breathed in the good clean smell of him. For a while they stood motionless, each lost in the other's warmth, in the feel of their bodies pressed together.

At last he relaxed his hold. "I guess," he said in tones of resignation, "we'd better find some shells."

Mickey gave a shaky laugh and pulled away, saying the first thing that came into her mind. "Last one down's a rotten oyster." She took off for the beach at top speed without looking back.

Before she had gone thirty feet he had passed her, running all the way to the tide line before he stopped.

"What were you saying?" By the time she reached him, he was already bending to pick something up.

"I think I said that slow and steady wins the race . . . or something along those lines."

"Then you get the prize." He extended his hand. In it was a perfect sea bean, small, brown, its narrow edge banded neatly in black.

"How did you find it so fast?" She was breathing hard, but he wasn't even winded.

"Talent." He pulled a small plastic bag from his pocket and put the sea bean into it. "Come on." He grabbed her hand. "Let's see what else we can find." Like a couple of truant kids, they set off down the beach.

While the sun sank lower, they walked, heads down, scouring the beaches, pushing aside clumps of seaweed and overturning pieces of driftwood in search of hidden treasure. Nearly every pile of debris held a sea bean, sometimes two. When the bag was filled he pulled another from his pocket, and they moved down close to the water, searching the wet sand for shells and sharks' teeth.

With a cry of pleasure, Mickey picked up an unbroken sand dollar, and as she slipped it into the bag, she shot him a grin. Delight, mixed with—what? Mischief, he realized, enthralled all over again. She'd looked like a kid who had just found an Easter egg. He wanted to make it happen for her again. And again...

Something at his feet caught his eye. With a whoop, he bent down and picked it up, then held it over his head and danced like a football player who had just made a touchdown.

"What is it?" she called, running toward him.

"A wentletrap," he said gleefully.

"A what?"

"A wentletrap." He opened his hand. A shell—tiny, perfectly formed, spiraling to a point like a Turkish turban—lay gleaming like alabaster on his palm. Mickey stared down at it in fresh wonder.

"I've only found one or two here before," he said. "You're a walking good-luck charm." He put the shell into her hand and closed her fingers around it. "What'd I tell you about finding shells over here?"

"I didn't find it," she said. His hands were warm around hers, and the heat traveled up her arms to settle somewhere deep in her midsection. "You did." When he let her go, she slipped the tiny shell into her pocket.

"I'll never tell." He glanced up. The sun was a hazy orange ball hanging low in the sky, and dry sand from the dunes blew like smoke across the beach. "It's getting late. Let's go up to the house."

He pulled her to him, and they walked together. Away from the water the sand was soft and dry, and their feet sank into it as they trudged across it, making for hard walking. He led her to a crude walkway of bleached-out driftwood boards leading between the sand dunes to the front of the house.

She looked at the house again. It sat so comfortably here, looking as much a part of the windswept landscape as one of the dunes. This house had seen good times. Years and years of them. And love. Every plank must be saturated by now. With a yearning so sharp it snagged her breath, she wanted to experience it for herself.

"We're going inside, aren't we?" She asked the question deliberately.

Cameron was turning on the water at the main connection, but at her words he straightened and looked at her a long moment. Then he smiled. "Sure. I have to check out everything in there, too." The smile held reassurance . . . and promise.

He pulled keys from his pocket and they walked up the weathered stairs to the deck. After he fiddled with the lock for a few seconds, the front door creaked open. He put a hand to her back and, with the feeling she was crossing more than one threshold, she stepped inside.

The interior air was chilly, damp, a little musty. Fading light filtered through the lowered bamboo blinds. Once her eyes became used to the dimness, she could see that the house was basically one big room. Beds with bright yellow rib-cord spreads lined the walls on either side. A living area held a worn sofa, wicker easy chairs, and a glass-topped coffee table. The kitchen was no more than stove, refrigerator, sink and a little counter space. An old potbellied stove sat squarely in the middle of the house, wood stacked neatly against it.

No, it wasn't fancy, but she already loved it. And it was going to tell her a lot about Cameron's family.

"I'll be right with you," he said, heading for the back of the house. "Why don't you have a look around?"

She did, thirsty to absorb the smallest detail.

In the living area, a low painted bookshelf held toys, a stack of jigsaw puzzles, paperbacks and a plastic box with playing cards in it. A shallow basket of sand dollars and a glass jar filled with sea beans sat on the large trestle table in the center of the room. Good times, love. They fairly filled the air.

On one wall hung a bulletin board, bristling with business cards and numbers of service people, restaurants, bait camps, other beach houses. She wandered over for a closer look. In one corner of the board was tacked a crayon drawing of a red stick figure holding an enormous purple fish. The caption, printed in blue crayon in awkward block letters, read, Uncle Cam.

Feeling as though she had found a treasure, Mickey murmured the words to herself like a mantra and looked around for the original fisherman.

He had checked the ceilings and windows for signs of leakage and was putting a match to the wood that was already laid inside the stove. He watched it catch, then, satisfied, stood and regarded her. "How do you like it?"

"I can hear a lot of voices from a long time ago," she said, smiling. "I think I can tell which one is yours."

The gladness shone in his eyes, and the moment was warm, quiet between them.

"What next?" she asked, half-afraid of the answer.

He pulled his gaze away. "I'm going to check the fridge."

He moved to the kitchen and began rummaging through the refrigerator. "Let's see," he muttered. "Ketchup, mustard, butter, pickles, cornmeal, shortening." He straightened. "Think we can whip up something with that?"

"Fried pickles?"

"Uh..." He pretended to consider. "Maybe we should just stop somewhere on the way home."

She laughed, heady with an eerie excitement she was finding increasingly hard to contain. "I hope you bring more food when you plan to stay."

"Oh, sure. There's a good grocery store down the road. And there's always the gulf. Fish, crabs, all that good stuff." He grinned suddenly, fondly. "When we were kids, my sister and I used to fish out front in the surf every day we were here. Mom cooked whatever we caught, no matter how small it was. We still tease her about having to cook some of it with a magnifying glass."

"She must have been patient." Mickey had walked over to the trestle table and was idly tracing its dents and scars with her fingers.

He looked a little surprised, as if he hadn't thought about it. "She was, I suppose. When I ask her about it now, she just says that's what mothers are for."

Mickey's hand stopped midway across the table. "That's the way it ought to be, anyway," she said, then despised herself for saying it.

"Yours?" She heard the change in his voice. She didn't look at him, just kept her eyes on the table, but she knew he was watching her.

"Mom had to work, always," she said briefly, ready to barricade herself against any more questions. "She...didn't have a lot of time."

"Even working mothers have time for their children." He moved nearer. "She loved you, didn't she?"

She was so stunned by the question that she had to take a moment to think, found she couldn't answer it. "Mom had a lot of problems," she said reluctantly. "A sad life, really. She wasn't good at showing how she felt."

He didn't say anything, just laid his hands on her shoulders. No pity, just caring. And where she couldn't have borne the pity, the simple gesture nearly undid her. A real family. A normal, close, loving family. She'd never allowed herself to imagine being a part of something like that. Now it tempted her unbearably. *Why not?* The words appeared in her mind like a candle flaring in darkness. Maybe, with him, it could happen. She wanted it so badly. *She wanted him . . .* The realization crashed into her mind with dizzying force.

"Mickey?" Cameron cleared his throat against a sudden huskiness. Every nerve was alive with urgency. He fought it. He knew that with her he had to go slowly, or she would fly away like a frightened bird. He wanted to nurture her, cherish her, but his body was telling him that it was going to be the hardest thing he'd ever done in his life.

His fingers tightened on her shoulders, and he made himself relax them. For a long time he'd known where he hoped they were going, but it was she who had to be sure. It was more important to him than anything he could remember.

"I want you," he said. "You know it." There needed to be honesty and understanding, full and complete, between them.

"Yes." The word was direct, her voice low, steady, but she was searching his face with an intensity he could almost feel on his skin.

He forced his voice level. "I have to know if it's right for you."

The moment hung crystalline between them. He saw her answer in her eyes.

With infinite care, he pulled her toward him and lowered his mouth to hers.

On a sigh, she whispered his name. His lips moved undemandingly, gently coaxing. A sweet heat began to bud inside her. Wanting, needing, she moved closer. Of their own accord, her hands slipped around his waist. Their bodies were only inches apart, near enough for her to feel his warmth.

He ended the kiss, but made no effort to bring her closer to him. He simply waited. When she could bear it no longer, she took a stumbling half step closer. Blindly, she lifted her face to his. Again his mouth found hers, this time not so gently. She felt the urgency, strong as an undertow, just under his control. She opened her lips to him.

He put his arms around her and, with the deepening of the kiss, one hand wandered downward to pull her intimately against him. They stood locked together, his mouth exploring, persuading, his breath rapid against her cheek. She could feel his heart beating, hard, against her own. The heat inside her began to course through her limbs.

Together, they walked toward one of the beds. When he drew the covers back, twin bolts of doubt and fear pierced the haze of her need, and she stopped. Instantly, he released her.

"Whoa," he said softly. He sat on the bed and drew her down beside him. "I thought we'd crossed that bridge. What is it?"

"Nothing." Her voice shook in spite of herself.

"Like hell," he said quietly. He was silent a moment, his gaze on her face. Then he reached to outline the curve of her jaw with his thumb. "I promised you once that I'd never hurt you. Remember?"

Wordlessly, she nodded.

He turned her face to his. "I meant it."

She searched the clear gray eyes. Saw the honesty, the fundamental decency she'd sensed about him since she first met him. Found there, too, the strength, the caring, shining like night beacons that promised her safe harbor. Whatever the future brought, she reminded herself, she would have today.

Still holding his gaze, she lifted a hand to his cheek. The tension drained from his face and he laughed pure relief. In that moment she realized just how much her trust had meant to him.

The sun was going down outside, but the fire in the old stove was roaring, throwing out a surprising amount of heat and sending flickering tongues of orange light through the cracks in its door to paint the room with moving shadows. She felt her skin grow warmer. He slipped her jacket from her shoulders and gathered her close. "Mickey?" His voice was a rough whisper. "Lie down with me." He brought her down beside him.

She closed her eyes and buried her face in his neck. *Today,* she promised herself. *Only for today.*

After a time his hands began to move over her, gentle enough at first, then gradually with more urgency. His hand slipped around to find her breast, and desire bloomed inside her with an insistence that would have frightened her if she hadn't been lost to everything but him. At his urging she untucked his flannel shirt and ran her hands over his shoulders and back, glorying in the knotted muscles, feeling his instant response.

With the greatest of care he undid her shirt, button by button. With gentle fingers he freed her breasts, and his sharp indrawn breath told her he thought her beautiful. The feel of his hands, his mouth on her made her shudder with pleasure, and when he moved his body over hers, she arched against him. The moments drew out to exquisite slowness, until she was drowning in pure sensation.

Only when he had moved away from her to remove his shirt and faded jeans, and when her own garments lay on the floor beside the bed, did a shadow of the old fear return. He saw it in her face, and in an instant he was lying beside her again, pulling the covers over them both.

Gently, carefully, he drew her to him and, loosely interlacing his fingers, enclosed her in the circle of his arms. He made no move to take her, just held her, and for a timeless moment they simply basked in the warmth of their bodies, safe in a haven light-years away from the rest of the world.

She realized he was moving his feet beneath the covers. "What are you doing?" she asked hazily, diverted.

"Just checking." He trapped her feet between his. "Your feet are like ice."

"Cold feet, warm heart." It hit her then that her apprehension was simply gone, had melted away like a summer fog in the sun. "Cameron?" She tried to keep her voice steady.

"Mmm?" His deep voice was an intimate caress, quickening her breathing again.

"Thank you," she said. *For knowing I was afraid, and for caring enough to make it all right for me,* she added silently.

His lazy grin just tilted the corners of his mouth. "For what—warming your feet?"

"You know what I'm talking about."

He raised up on one elbow and cocked a brow at her. "I'm not sure I want your gratitude."

She smiled at him. "Too bad. You've got it anyway." She hesitated, then reached to bring his head down to hers. "And more," she whispered against his lips, wondering in a far corner of her mind where she'd gotten the courage to say such a thing. "If you're interested."

She felt his quick intake of breath against her mouth. "If I'm..." His lips closed over hers.

He kissed her until he banished the last of the shadows and her senses were swimming with his nearness, his scent, the hard, muscular feel of his body. Their words came in tattered, whispered fragments.

"Cameron?"

"It's all right. I want to kiss you here. And here."

"It's so..." Dazed wonderment shone in her voice.

"Mickey. Touch me."

"Like this?"

His moan. "Yes. Let me show you..."

He allowed her to set the pace, never rushing her. Only by the tautness, the faint trembling of his limbs did he betray the extent of his need—and his self-control.

Step by slow, loving step they traveled the spiraling road. There was no fear now, no shadows except the ones dancing on the walls. There was only him. The way he was making her feel. Long, slow kisses. Strong arms holding her so close, but not close enough... His hands, finding, awakening, teaching, giving her back a part of herself she hadn't known existed.

The world closed in, narrowing to the bed where they lay. Outside, the wind moaned at the corners of the old house and the noise of the surf was a muffled roar in their ears, shutting out everything but them and their need for each other. Inside, firelight. Heat. The sharp tang of wood smoke, mingling with his scent. The heat of their bodies, the creak of the springs in the stillness as they moved together. His hands discovering her secrets. His lips on her body awakening her to sensations she'd never imagined until she moaned and strained against him. Her own gasps, echoed in his fragmented breathing. In this strange new world, passion was made infinitely sweeter for being cherished.

Her body was soon crying out for completion. As if she had spoken aloud, he lifted himself up and over her. He hesitated briefly, his face taut, the contours of his lean body bronzed by the firelight and the fading sun. Still reassuring her with his eyes, he slipped into her.

They moved as if they'd been together all their lives. Even at the height of his own passion he remembered her, and with hands and body brought her to the brink—of what? She didn't know. She felt a fleeting wonder that she—that any human being—could feel this way. When at last he took her over the edge, she cried out with joyous surprise.

Seconds later, through the haze of her own ecstasy, she heard her name, torn from his lips. Then he fell against her, spent, still holding her tightly.

FOR LONG MINUTES he lay unable to move, joined with her body and soul. The light from the dying fire bathed the whole room in a faint red glow.

He lifted his head and looked at her. She lay curled beside him, her long lashes fringed darkly against her cheeks. He thought she was sleeping, but her eyes opened to meet his gaze.

He held his breath, then let it out slowly with a relief so great it made him dizzy. The trust was still there, shining intact from her eyes. Seeing it as they made love had been the most moving experience of his life. If it hadn't been there now, he couldn't have borne it. He winnowed his fingers through the glossy black hair at her temple and was rewarded with a tentative smile. Drained as he was, he had to admonish himself sternly not to begin things all over again.

He had exercised a self-control that he hadn't known he possessed. He'd been determined that, as physical barriers came down, no emotional ones would rise in their place, that each act of loving would be for her not an invasion but a joining. He'd had his reward. She'd given herself to him entirely. More than he could ever have imagined. Her feelings ran deeper for having been trapped inside her for so long. That fundamental innocence he'd sensed in her had blossomed, with his teaching, into something beautiful. He would have walked barefoot through molten lava to see her face in those last moments. Today he had caught a glimpse of the real Mickey Mulvaney, and his own fulfillment had been the sweetest he'd ever known.

She stirred.

"Hello there." He spoke softly, to keep from shattering the spell.

"Cameron." She pronounced his name as if she'd never said it before. "I didn't..." Her voice trailed off, the bewildered joy still shining from her eyes.

"It was beautiful, Mickey," he whispered. "It was the most beautiful thing that's ever happened to me." *I love you*. The words sounded like perfectly pitched bells in his mind. He heard them without real surprise. But he knew he couldn't say them to her. Not yet. He knew instinctively that there was still one part of her that remained behind lock and key.

She said his name again. This time, it was she who reached for him.

This time, it was she who gave him back his own, she who learned from his murmured words, his body's responses, his ragged gasps, what pleased him. His control frayed, then blew away, borne on the winds of his need.

On a groan, he buried himself in her.

AS THEY DROVE IN on Interstate 45, nighttime Houston was a wide-screen panorama of light before them. As if by tacit consent, they hadn't spoken much. Mickey reached inside her pocket to touch the tiny wentletrap, in awe of what they had shared. She thought longingly of the small dark haven of the beach house only two hours behind them and wondered at what she'd experienced. She hadn't dreamed life could hold such wonders.

She looked over at Cameron, silhouetted against the light, and, remembering, wanted to hold him again. As if she'd said his name, he turned to her and she saw her desire reflected in his eyes. He lifted her hand and raised it briefly to his lips. The single contact immersed her in remembered sensation.

As they merged with incoming traffic downtown, her stomach reminded her that they had forgotten to eat. Just as well. Without the intrusion of the real world, their illusion had lasted that much longer. She didn't yet want to return to the world of unpleasant realities, hard decisions. She knew that what they'd shared would be subjected to both, might survive neither. But she wanted to cling to these moments, to hold them to her heart as long as she could.

But with the small hunger pang, reality began to nudge her. *Harbor House*. She'd hardly thought of it all day. She felt a stab of guilt. Normally Harbor House was the center of all her waking thoughts and many of her dreams, with everything else occupying the sidelines. Now, it seemed, there was a new focus for her thoughts—and her dreams.

They were approaching the exit for her apartment, and Cameron put on his signal light to change lanes.

"No," she said reluctantly. She did have responsibilities, after all. "Stay on. I want to go by Harbor House."

"What for?" He frowned, but clicked off the signal and stayed on the freeway. "You asked somebody to cover for you, didn't you?"

"Yes. Ruth covered the day shift, and Sue's coming on at eleven."

"They're competent, aren't they?"

Mickey sighed. "Of course. Besides, M.C.'s always around."

"What's he doing? Making up for lost time?" Cameron heard the edge in his own voice and warned himself to be careful. After all, he had no proof that M.C. had deserted her; it was just that two and two generally did make four.

"What's that supposed to mean?"

He heard the defensiveness in her voice and grimaced. Why in hell had he opened his mouth? "Nothing," he hastened to say. "I don't know M.C.'s story, or yours, for that matter." He was quiet a moment, his hands gripping the wheel. "But I'll tell you this," he added because he couldn't help himself—she was suddenly the most important thing in the world to him. "If someone's hurt you, I care. A lot."

His words should have been a comfort. Instead Mickey felt a tiny chill of betrayal, as if he'd turned on her just when she was beginning to trust him. He was asking too much too soon. Besides, even if she tried to explain, he would never understand. She didn't herself, really. She'd never asked M.C. about those missing years, and he'd never brought them up. But one thing was certain: she couldn't let Cameron, or anyone, attack the one anchor in her life. "It's over now," she said shortly. "That's all that counts."

As usual, he knew when to back off. "Okay, okay. Forget it." He swung the car off the freeway onto the Shepherd Drive exit. "But someday..." He didn't finish.

The remainder of the ride, which luckily wasn't long, passed in silence. Even though she realized the barrier between them was of her own construction, she felt bereft after the closeness of the day. She'd hoped...

To cover the silence she looked out the window, watching for the elegant Victorian streetlights of Village Walk.

Three more blocks and they were there, surrounded on both sides by beautifully restored shops and restaurants and impeccable landscaping.

As they pulled up in front of Harbor House, Mickey saw a lone figure sitting motionless in the porch swing, barely illuminated by the corner streetlight.

Almost before Cameron stopped the car, she was out of it and running up the walk. She already knew who it was. Just as she knew something was terribly wrong.

The figure sitting so still in the dim light was Brandy Williford.

CHAPTER TWELVE

"BRANDY."

Mickey could read the misery in the angle of the girl's head, the set of her shoulders. When Brandy raised her head, Mickey could see the tear marks on her cheeks. But it was the expression in her eyes that cut Mickey as deeply as any knife. "What happened?" She forced her voice to stay level. Behind her, she heard Cameron coming up the steps to stand beside her on the porch.

Brandy stirred, as if waking from an uneasy sleep. "They found something in my locker."

No, Brandy. "What was it?" she asked, dreading the answer, already knowing it.

Brandy ducked her head and stared at her feet.

"Brandy?"

"A joint." The word fell into the charged silence.

Knowing it was coming didn't keep it from hitting Mickey like a blow to the stomach. Beside her, she felt Cameron stiffen. She struggled to prevent her own agony from showing; if she couldn't keep herself under control, she couldn't help Brandy.

Taking a deep breath, she knelt in front of her and laid a gentle hand on her shoulder. She could feel the stiffness, the tension in the knotted muscles. "Tell me what happened, Brandy. It's important that you tell me exactly."

"It wasn't mine." The words were strangled. "I didn't put it there."

"I didn't ask you that," she said quickly. "I just want to know what happened, so we'll know what to do. Tell me."

"During fifth period, an office assistant came to get me and told me Old Lady Lawrence wanted to see me. She'd gotten some note that said there was a joint in my locker. The custodian cut the lock, and they found it. I don't know how it got in there." Brandy spoke haltingly, as though she were having trouble finding enough breath to form the words. "It was Kelly, I know it was."

"Do you keep your locker locked?"

"Sure. But I have to open it between classes, to get more books."

"Think, Brandy. Do you remember a time you had it open, when someone could have put the joint inside?"

"I don't know." She was silent a moment. "Wait a minute. Today at noon, I was putting up my books to go eat lunch. One of Kelly's friends pushed me. I didn't push her back or say anything to her, so she left. But my locker was open. I remember, because I closed it after she was gone."

Another friend of Kelly's could have slipped it into the locker then, Mickey thought. She'd been afraid of something like this happening all along; she'd just hoped Kelly wouldn't play this kind of hardball. But it seemed she had. "What happened then?"

"I told Old Lady Lawrence I didn't do it, that someone must have planted it there. She said she'd find out what happened, but I know she didn't believe me." Brandy's face was closed, her eyes full of a dull bitterness. She was drifting beyond Mickey's reach. Mickey could see her going. The Black Hole . . .

"You don't know that, Brandy," she said, desperate to bring her back. "I'll talk to Mrs. Lawrence first thing Monday morning."

"It won't do any good," Brandy said. "She hasn't kicked me out of school yet because of the investigation, but she's already pulled me out of the art contest. School rules or something. She didn't believe me," she repeated woodenly. "I know she didn't."

Out of the art contest. Mickey stood up very slowly, feeling her own hope drain away. Brandy might not yet have been suspended, but if Mrs. Lawrence had taken Brandy out of the art contest, she might just as well have pitched her into the Dumpster. All the months of nurturing, careful planning, inch-by-inch progress, gone in a moment because of one girl's petty revenge.

"Brandy, think back," she implored. She had to try to reach her, at least. In her urgency, she gripped Brandy's shoulder. "We've got to have proof. Can you remember anything else? Was anyone else around, maybe one of Kelly's friends?"

"Mickey—" Cameron's warning came from just behind her. She ignored it.

"I already told you everything I remember." Now there was hostility in Brandy's voice. "What do you need proof for? It's not going to do any good. I already told you, she doesn't believe me." She got up from the chair, not meeting Mickey's eyes. "You don't, either." Her voice was flat, dead.

"Of course I do, Brandy." She felt the panic rising, fought to keep it down. "You know better than that. We're going to have to work this out. It's just that—"

Suddenly she was talking to empty air. Brandy had turned and was walking back into the house. She slammed the door.

Mickey stood still, cursing herself.

"Mickey." She felt Cameron's touch, light, comforting, on her shoulder. How she needed it.

"I handled it wrong." She could hear the pain in her own voice. "I knew better. I just handled it wrong." The first rule she'd learned in this profession was never to become so involved that you lost your objectivity or your composure. She'd just done both.

Briefly, his fingers tightened. "You pushed her too hard."

"Yes." She shook her head, furious at herself. "I should have told her to go in and get some rest, that we'd talk in the morning. Mainly, I shouldn't have lost my cool."

"Mickey—" He hesitated, took his hand from her shoulder, put both his hands in his pockets. "Are you sure she's telling the truth?"

Mickey could do nothing but stare at him. "Of course I'm sure."

"She might be lying." There was an edge to his voice.

"No." She felt her defenses going up. They'd been down all day. Boy, had they been down. "I know she's telling the truth. There's a girl trying to frame her. I've got to make Brandy understand that she can't just give up. She's got to fight."

"It seems to me that Brandy's got to want to fight."

Mickey's temper was fraying rapidly. "I'm supposed to help her do that," she snapped. "Now, if you'll excuse me, I have to check with the night manager about something."

"I'll wait." Just underneath, his voice carried tension, and an undercurrent of anger.

Sue, the night manager on duty, was in her usual spot in Mickey's office. Quickly, Mickey told her what had happened. "I'm not so sure I shouldn't stay here tonight," she added, undecided.

"Don't worry," Sue said. "I'll check her during the night and call you right away if there's a problem."

"Okay," Mickey said reluctantly. "Thanks, Sue. I don't think she'd do anything foolish, at least I hope not. But I'd appreciate it if you'd listen for her."

"Sure, Mickey." Sue was one of the best managers they had. If something went wrong, she'd know about it instantly. Mickey tried to lay her worries to rest and decided to go home.

Neither she nor Cameron said anything during the drive back to her apartment. The day that had been spent in such a magical world had ended with a crashing reentry into the real one, and Mickey was having trouble regaining her footing. Cameron drove with both hands gripping the steering wheel, his face a mask. She'd had no excuse to take out her distress on him, she thought guiltily.

At her door, she searched his face. His jaw was set, and she could see the anger at the back of his eyes. No wonder. She'd snapped his head off. "Cameron, I'm sorry."

"Sorry?" The anger vanished in the face of thunderstruck amazement. "For what?"

Because there are differences between us that will always be there, she answered him silently. *Because you don't understand what I'm doing, or why. Because I need you so much, and I know I can't have you.* She'd been foolish to think otherwise. The incident with Brandy had reminded her in a way she wasn't likely to forget.

"For being angry with you tonight," she said instead. "There was no excuse for it." She was conscious of a dreadful yearning to turn back the clock to early that morning when the world had been beautiful, when they'd set out together full of an uncomplicated joy for their own kind of adventure. Today, simply being in his company, sharing time and laughter with him, had been a pleasure so sharp it made her catch her breath to remember it. The memory of their lovemaking was unbearably sweet, made more poignant because she knew that someday, maybe tomorrow, she wouldn't have him any longer. Through it all, one thing was constant in her thoughts: he wasn't for her. Not ever for her. Tonight had merely served as a reminder.

"Mickey, for God's sake—" He grabbed her shoulders and shook her, not hard, but with a suppressed violence. "There's nothing to apologize for." He dropped his hands, turned away from her. "I don't like to see you hurt, that's all."

She stared at his profile, involuntarily tracing its clear-cut lines with her eyes. "What happened tonight was part of my job."

He swung back around to face her. "Don't try to fool me, Mickey, or yourself. I saw you. You were hurting as much as Brandy was. Do you hurt like that for all your girls?"

Do I? Her mind skittered away from the answer. "I'm afraid for Brandy. She's still so fragile. And when some little—" She stopped because once more she could feel the rage, the frustration welling up inside her.

"Mickey." He caught her shoulders again. This time his grip hurt. "Don't do this to yourself."

"My emotions are my problem, Cameron," she said stubbornly. "I'll deal with them. I always have."

"Ms. Independence again." His hands stayed on her shoulders. "Mickey, I care about you. I—" He stopped, thought better of whatever he'd been about to say.

"I appreciate your concern, Cameron," she said stubbornly, "but I have to do my job, even when it's unpleasant."

"'I appreciate your concern,'" he mimicked, his mouth twisting. "Mickey." Another shake. "Didn't today mean anything to you?"

Today? Mean anything to her? What a laugh. She shut her eyes against the wave of need. When she opened them, those gray eyes were spearing her soul. "Yes. Today—" She managed a shaky laugh. "Today meant something to me."

She fought the need, but it was too great. *Just once more. Let me have him just one more time.* She let her gaze play over his features—the wide brow, the high cheekbones, the generous, expressive mouth. The gulf between them was wide, maybe even wider than she'd thought. If only she didn't care so much for him. But, crazily, she had to recapture today's enchantment. Tonight. Now, while she still could. She'd hurt tomorrow. She'd never been able to resist cotton candy. . . .

"Cameron?" She covered the few steps that separated them and took his lean, tanned face between her hands. "Stay with me tonight."

She saw the stunned surprise leap in his eyes, his nostrils flare with his quick intake of breath. "Mickey. . ."

She laid her fingertips on his lips to stop the words and brought his head down to hers.

By the time he took her mouth with his, neither of them could think at all.

IT WASN'T until the next day, when she was blocking out the insistent thoughts and images by spending Saturday afternoon cleaning her apartment, that she finally admitted to herself that she was in love with him.

She'd never really loved any man before. She thought of the dead-end, rebellion-spawned relationships of her troubled youth and knew them for what they were. In the face of this new emotion, she felt raw, vulnerable, tender, a child of shadows feeling the warmth of the sun for the first time. And very clearly, she saw the pain ahead.

They had wakened together very early that morning, had made love again, quickly, urgently. Then he'd gone, with the promise to call her later. Since then, she'd tried without much success to put him out of her mind.

Just before the 7:00 a.m. shift change, she'd called Sue. Yes, Sue had assured her, everything was fine. Brandy was still in her room, presumably asleep, and was due at work at the ice cream parlor at ten o'clock. Sue would tell Jo, the manager who would come on at the next shift change, to keep an eye on her.

Mickey had checked in again several more times during the morning. Lisa, in a high state of excitement, had left with the Rhodeses to go to Astroworld, and Brandy had gone to work as scheduled. Mickey had finally begun to breathe a little easier. Maybe she'd overreacted. Maybe she'd been buying trouble. . . .

She pushed the vacuum hard across the carpet, as if it could sweep up all the complications in her life. She'd help Brandy lick this yet, she resolved for the fortieth time. Monday morning she'd go talk to Elaine Lawrence, and they'd get to the bottom of this one way or another. She would—

She almost didn't hear the phone over the hum of the vacuum cleaner. She shut it off quickly and sprinted for the kitchen.

"Mickey? Jo here."

Even before she said anything, Mickey felt her palms go clammy.

"Brandy didn't come home from work today," Jo said. "She was due in an hour ago. We called the ice cream parlor, and they said she'd left right on time. We waited a little while, then checked her route home. She wasn't down for permission to go anywhere else, so we thought we'd better tell you."

Mickey stood perfectly still, afloat in that peculiar numbness that fills the seconds after disaster before feeling kicks in. Then in a crashing wave, the pain hit her.

"Thanks, Jo," she managed. "I'll be right over."

THE PHONE RANG, shattering Cameron's reverie and yanking his wandering thoughts to attention.

He cursed. It hadn't been the easiest of days. It was never easy, he supposed, when something happened to change your whole way of looking at things. Or, he reflected, maybe the past twenty-four hours had just confirmed what he'd already known.

He'd left Mickey's apartment before sunrise, still dazed by all that had happened in the past twenty-four hours. *A lifetime's worth* ... He'd gone home to change. Then he'd had to hurry to make a Saturday morning meeting. Afterward he'd gone back to his office and tried to work awhile, but for all he accomplished, he might as well not have bothered. He'd finally given up and driven out to look at several of the renovations. They were going entirely too well; there was absolutely nothing for him to do. Still finding himself with the better part of a beautiful early spring afternoon to kill, he'd gone out and tried his best to annihilate several dozen golf balls at the driving range.

No good. He couldn't rid his memory of Mickey Mulvaney's image, the aroma of her skin, the taste of her mouth, the feel of her body against his. Above all, the way he had come to feel about her.

Face it, he told himself, *you're in for the long haul.* In the past hours he'd shared something with Mickey that he'd never dreamed could happen between a man and a woman. But in spite of her response to him, which he suspected had surprised her even more than it had him, he knew a barrier was still there, one that in all probability had never been breached by anyone. He intended to breach it, all right. He just didn't have a clue as to how to go about it.

The phone rang, and he jerked up the receiver. "Hello."

"Cameron."

In the first split second he didn't recognize the voice, because something was distorting the normal brisk, authoritative tone.

"Miss Cunningham? What's wrong?"

"It's Brandy Williford."

"Brandy?" he said blankly. "How do you know Brandy?"

"Mr. Mulvaney brought her over to visit me, to see some of my art books. But never mind about that." He realized then that Miss Cunningham was angry. There was a bite to her words that he recognized; he'd been on the receiving end more than once through the years. But there was something else, just beneath the anger....

"Is there a problem?" he asked.

"She robbed me."

"She *what?*" For a second, he couldn't even absorb the words.

"You heard me, Cameron. Brandy Williford robbed me. She stole money from me." The indignation swelled in Miss

Cunningham's voice, momentarily obscuring everything else. Normally, Cameron would have turned tail and run. Today he barely noticed. He was having enough trouble dealing with the bare facts of what she was telling him.

"Are you sure?" he asked stupidly.

"Of course I'm sure," she snapped. "Whyever would I be calling you if I weren't?"

It finally sank in. Then his own anger sliced through him, razor-sharp. *How dared Brandy Williford do this to Mickey? Ungrateful little...* "When?"

"A few hours ago. She came to visit me. She told me she'd just finished work and would like to see the art books again."

"Did she threaten you?"

"No. Apparently, she stole the money when I left the room to prepare tea. There was a little in the desk in the parlor—the dues for our Literary Study Club. I had prepared the deposit to take to the bank Monday morning and had set it in the drawer for convenience. She must have taken it while I was out of the room."

"How much?" He gripped the receiver and shook his head, still not really believing it. This whole thing had to be a bad dream.

"Several checks, and cash. Two hundred nineteen dollars and thirty-seven cents in cash." The numbers snapped out like little soldiers coming to attention.

Trust Miss Cunningham to know the exact amount. "How did she know it was there?"

"She couldn't have known. She must simply have looked into the drawer to see what she could take and found the money. I didn't even know until after she'd left, when I noticed the drawer standing slightly open. I've called the police," she added.

"Yes, of course," he said automatically. "I don't suppose you could do anything else." *Mickey*, he thought. *I've got to talk to Mickey.*

"Certainly not. I know my duty." There was a little silence. "I trusted her," she said. The anger in her voice had ebbed. Now he could hear the other note, the one he'd heard earlier but couldn't identify. *Hurt.*

"She has a great deal of artistic talent," Miss Cunningham went on. "I suppose I should have known...." For the first time since Cameron could remember, Miss Cunningham sounded less than completely sure of herself. She sounded defenseless. Old. It broke his heart.

"You couldn't possibly have known it was going to happen, Miss Cunningham," he said, desperate to comfort her. "She's a troubled child...." He trailed off lamely. How could he defend Brandy when he himself felt like murdering her for doing this?

"Yes. She's a troubled child. After all, she's from a halfway house." Now her voice was gaining strength, and he could hear the anger again, shoving the hurt aside. He felt relieved, even though he knew what was coming.

"I intend to pursue this, Cameron," she said. "And I want to remind you that, even though I have called the police, I consider this entire problem to be your responsibility. This is exactly the sort of thing I feared. As you will recall, I expressed my disapproval of the halfway house from the very beginning."

He started to protest, but she cut him off. "I realize, of course, that you couldn't have prevented it. But I expect you to do everything in your power to straighten out this situation, and to evict this institution from the neighborhood."

I wonder how the hell she expects me to do that? Cameron thought savagely as he hung up the phone. He'd tried everything he'd known to keep Harbor House out of the neighborhood in the first place, and he'd failed. He didn't know what else he was supposed to do. But then, small things like logic—and the law—apparently didn't make any difference to Miss Cunningham. Not this minute, anyway.

Right now he had to talk to Mickey. He picked up the phone, then hung it up again. He needed to see her, talk to her face-to-face, try to ease her feelings, protect her any way he could. He was afraid, really afraid of what this news might do to her, and he had to be there.

Before he could move, the phone rang again.

THREE-QUARTERS OF AN HOUR later he slammed down the receiver, wondering how the news had traveled so fast and what the hell *anyone* thought he could do about it. In the time since he'd heard the news, he'd had calls from two other neighbors and one of his investors. They'd all gotten wind of the incident and were demanding that he do something about it.

He stood, yanked off his glasses and threw them down on the desk. *What a mess.* And the devil of it was, he truly didn't know what to do about it.

He prowled restlessly from desk to window and back again, his footsteps sinking into the plush carpet. He looked around at his tastefully decorated office. He'd done well. He'd accomplished a great deal, still had a great deal more to accomplish.

For what?

The words bounced around in his mind like hard rubber balls. In the middle of the room, he stood stock-still. Without Mickey, he realized, this office, his growing professional reputation, his ambitions, his hopes, his dreams, weren't going to count for anything.

And he wanted her to stop hurting herself, even if it meant leaving her work. But convincing her to do it would be another matter. The only thing he knew for certain was that, to talk her into spending the rest of her life with him, he was in for the hardest, longest uphill climb of his life. It was going to take all his endurance, all his powers of persuasion and plain, ordinary, everyday patience.

Without so much as glancing behind him, he headed out the door.

CHAPTER THIRTEEN

BY THE TIME he reached Harbor House, it was nearly dark. Quickly, he parked the car and hurried up the front walk, feeling as winded as if he'd run the whole way.

The old house looked quiet. Normal. Maybe the situation wasn't as bad as it seemed. Maybe Miss Cunningham had been mistaken. Maybe, just maybe, Brandy would answer the door, and he would know that the whole thing had been a figment of someone's imagination. *Maybe pigs could fly . . . .*

Brandy didn't answer the door; Joni did. He could tell from his first glance at her that something was wrong. "Hi, Joni," he said in what he hoped was an everyday tone of voice. "Is Mickey here?"

"Yes, sir. C'mon in." The tension in the young face made him brace himself. "Brandy's gone," she volunteered spontaneously. Joni was nothing if not up-front, even with bad news.

"Gone?" he said blankly.

"She ran away. She's been missing since she got off work."

His stomach plummeted to his shoes. It figured. After taking the money, Brandy would hardly stick around. He spoke his first thought aloud. "Mickey?"

"She's in her office." Joni pointed. "Go on back."

He found Mickey at her desk, talking on the phone, obviously to the police.

"Thank you, Lieutenant," she finished. Her voice was perfectly level, but as she hung up the phone, Cameron could see that her fingers, where they gripped the receiver, were white. When she raised her eyes to his, he saw a blank, shuttered look in them that hid the tender, vital woman he'd glimpsed in the past two days as effectively as if she'd never existed.

"What happened?"

"Brandy didn't come home from work today. We're fairly sure she's run away." Her voice was still very even, but there was a quality about it that stirred the hairs at the nape of his neck. He'd thought he knew the extent of her toughness; now he saw a new dimension to it. The walls were up, and the barricades in place. Quite simply, she would *never* quit fighting if it involved one of her girls. And he knew already that, with Brandy, if she didn't bend, she'd break. He had to keep it from happening, find some way to reach her, to protect her. But his every instinct screamed at him to be careful.

"Where's M.C?" He meant it to sound like a casual question, but it didn't quite come out that way.

Mickey shot him a sharp glance. At least he'd gotten some kind of reaction from her. "M.C.'s gone to talk to Brandy's boss, over at the ice cream parlor." Her look dared him to say anything else.

"I see." He reminded himself again to be careful.

"It seems Brandy also stole some money from Miss Cunningham," Mickey went on in that same dead-even voice. "She's already reported it. The police told me."

"I know. She just called me."

"Oh?" Briefly, an edge of bitterness surfaced in Mickey's voice. "Was she concerned about the neighborhood?"

"You might say so," he said cautiously. "She was very angry, a little unreasonable. But there was something else, too. Apparently, she knew Brandy. She told me Brandy had been by to see her once or twice, to look at her art books, I think."

Mickey waved her hand impatiently. "I know. M.C. took her. I've already been over all that with the police."

"Actually," he said, watching her face, "Miss Cunningham sounded hurt."

Mickey heard him, he was sure, but he didn't think the words had registered. She stared back at him as if he were a total stranger. No, an enemy.

"Brandy's betrayed a lot of people," he said, forgetting his resolve and letting his anger swell until it obliterated his own pain. "It's hard for me to understand how she could do a thing like this to Miss Cunningham. Or to you, for that matter. You both were trying to help her."

That got a reaction. A big one. "Brandy didn't mean to betray anyone," Mickey said hotly. "She's been hurt so much that she tries to protect herself any way she can."

"At someone else's expense?" he shot back.

"You don't understand. When she was pulled from the art contest—" Mickey stopped, took a deep, tired breath, tried again. "Girls like Brandy think life's a losing proposition, because for them, that's what it's always been. Brandy was just beginning to learn that she could change her own life for the better. When this happened, it only confirmed what she's always believed, that she's not worth caring about. That's why she doesn't realize she's hurting anyone."

"You and M.C. both told me the first time we talked together that you didn't think there would be a problem with this sort of thing." He saw the anger flare in her eyes, and could have bitten out his tongue. He'd sounded accusing. Insensitive. He clenched his jaw, tried to push his own feelings aside; they were making him say things he shouldn't. But if he could have gotten his hands on Brandy Williford at that moment . . .

Mickey's eyes were still ablaze with anger, but she answered reasonably enough. "I told you we couldn't guarantee anything. I think I also reminded you that there are no guarantees anywhere. Even children of normal families get into trouble. Do you know the Gardner family, two streets over?"

"Yes."

"Three weeks ago, their oldest son was arrested for armed robbery. He'd gotten into the drug scene."

"I remember," he conceded reluctantly.

"Cameron . . ." For the first time he saw a little softening in her iron control. "I also told you that in this kind of work there's rarely a nice, neat ending. There's only hope for progress, for small steps in the right direction. If there are enough of those, there's a chance the girls can go on to lead normal lives. Brandy just took a big step backward, that's all. We have to find her, then start all over."

He jerked his hands from his pockets and spread them wide in a gesture of bewilderment. "But you might go through the same thing with her again."

Mickey shook her head. "You still don't understand, do you? I won't give up on her until I have to. Don't you care about what happens to her?"

"Of course I do." It was the truth. "But I care more about what this is doing to you." That was the truth, too. "It's hurting you."

She shrugged. "It's my—"

He struck his fist on the desktop. "If I hear that one more time, I'll..." He took a deep breath, forced himself to calmness. "You just said that Brandy doesn't know life can be anything but a bad deal. Well, I'm telling you to take a fresh look at your own life." He jabbed a finger at her. "Maybe you don't realize that it can be different for you, too."

For an instant, but only an instant, he saw the longing, the need leap behind her eyes. Then the wall was back in place, and she was looking at him as if he'd suddenly gone crazy. "Read my lips, Cameron." She spoke slowly and distinctly, as if to an idiot. "This *is* my life."

"Maybe it has been, but it doesn't have to be. You don't have to sacrifice yourself to save the rest of the world." Suddenly he felt as though she were speaking Greek, and he, Icelandic. He kept on talking, desperate to make her understand. "Your job is killing you, Mickey. Why don't you get out?"

It was only after the words had left his mouth that he realized they had been very foolish ones.

Helpless to take them back, he watched as her eyes darkened with shock and fury. "Haven't you learned anything about me?" she bit out. "About what we're trying to do here?"

"I can't stand to see you hurt," he repeated stubbornly.

"That's my problem, not yours."

"I want to make it my problem."

"No way." She rose hastily, knocking the chair backward. With a quick motion she righted it, then turned her back to him and stared out the window.

"Mickey?"

She didn't respond, didn't even move, just kept looking out the window, her back rigid, her head held stiffly.

"I love you."

There was a long moment of dead silence. Then she turned slowly to face him, her face bone-white in the light from her desk lamp. "What did you say?"

"You heard me." He cursed himself. The biggest blunder yet. He'd lost all objectivity about the whole situation. Or maybe just his head. But he couldn't take back the words, either. As a matter of fact, he decided, he didn't really want to. They could stand just for the record, if nothing else.

She found her voice at last. The blue eyes were unreadable, almost black. "You don't even know me."

"You don't think so?" He couldn't keep the challenge out of his voice.

"No." She cut the word off.

"I might know you better than you think." He took a step toward her. "What about you, Mickey? Do you know yourself?"

"Of course I do." Her words came a little too quickly.

"I want to marry you," he said. "I want to spend the rest of my life with you. Sometimes life can be beautiful. I'd like to show you."

She just stared at him. "I thought you said you knew me," she said finally. "Don't talk about how beautiful life can be when a child's whole existence is hanging by God knows what kind of thread."

"I care about Brandy," he repeated, the heat coming back into his voice in spite of his best efforts. "You've got to believe that. But I want to take care of you first."

Her chin lifted. "I don't need anyone to take care of me."

In for a penny, in for a pound, he thought, resigning himself. He might as well stumble on to the end of it. "Everyone needs someone, Mickey. Even you."

"No." Her face was still pale with shock and anger. "I never have."

"No?" *Damn her for being bullheaded.* He could feel his own temper getting away from him, God help him. "It seems to me that you could have used someone a long time ago. Like M.C.," he added before he could stop himself.

Her eyes blazed blue fire. "Get off M.C.'s back," she hissed. "He's done more for me than anyone else ever has. I've gotten along most of my life relying on myself." She jabbed a thumb at her chest. "I haven't needed anyone else. Not M.C., and certainly not you."

The words sliced at him like knives. As his temper drained painfully away, he cursed himself for his clumsiness, his bad timing. He'd resolved to handle things so much better.... He'd never been so acutely aware of how deeply he loved her. And because he'd made such a mess of trying to tell her, he was going to lose her.

Her own anger died out of her eyes, and she gave a tired little shrug. "You asked me if I knew myself." Her voice was almost a whisper. "I don't know anymore. But I do know this. I'm not for you."

He caught her arms. "I don't believe it."

She shrugged off his hands. "Leave me alone, Cameron. Leave all of us alone. Go back to your own world. We're not your kind."

"Mickey, that's ridiculous," he said desperately. "Trust me. Please."

"I learned a long time ago that there's only one person in the world I can trust," she said slowly. "Me. Now, if you'll excuse me, I have to make some calls."

She stared at him in pointed silence until he had no choice but to turn around and head for the door.

Just before he crossed the threshold, he turned back. "Let me tell you who you are, Mickey," he said. "You're someone I love. I'm sorry you can't trust me enough to believe it."

Quite gently, he closed the door behind him.

THE SIGN ABOVE THE DOOR was shaped like an enormous pair of eyeglasses, complete with staring eyes. It advertised adult literature and X-rated movies. Two teenage boys leaned against the wall beneath it, smoking and talking.

Brandy crossed to the other side of the street well before she reached them, but they saw her anyway. They stared at her insolently, suggestively. Then one of them said something, and they both laughed.

Brandy heard exactly what he'd said. She considered responding with an obscene gesture, the way she once would have, but thought better of it. No sense in attracting any more attention than she had to, especially from punks. She settled for ignoring them completely.

She looked around. Topless bars, pawnshops, cheap hotels, rooming houses—they were all familiar to her. What she'd forgotten was how dirty everything was, how ratty all the people looked. Not like at home . . . Harbor House, she corrected herself. Harbor House wasn't home.

She shrugged. The important thing was that she was out. Away from Harbor House, with all its stupid rules. If she kept out of trouble, no one would find her. Dallas was big, and it was a long way from Houston. She was sure she'd caught that ride out of town before anyone had missed her. Besides, nobody looked very hard for runaways. Not even people like Mickey.

Anger welled up inside her, at herself as much as anyone else. She should've known going straight wouldn't work, but she'd let herself be suckered in. She'd actually begun to trust Mickey and Connie, had believed all their lies about things going better if you cooperated. For once, she'd tried to play the game right, and look what it had gotten her. Disqualified from the contest and, by now, probably suspended from school. She was glad she hadn't stuck around to find out.

Kelly was probably still there, running her scummy little drug business, smiling that smug smile every time she thought of her. Brandy had learned one thing, at least; for her there would always be another Kelly, no matter where she went or what she did. Savagely, she kicked a can into the gutter. She'd love to get Kelly alone, just for a few minutes. Someday, she promised herself, she'd do just that.

In the meantime, since the Goody Two-shoes life wasn't for her, she'd have to go back to the old ways. Except for the dope. She never wanted any part of that again. It was a bad trip, made you dependent on other people. She'd make it on her own, and to hell with everyone else. It might be tough, but she could do it. She'd done it before.

She passed two hookers standing at the intersection, obviously waiting for customers. One stepped forward as if she might stop her, but after looking her up and down, shook her head. Brandy held her stare, obscurely pleased that they could tell from looking at her that she wasn't competition.

At least she wouldn't have to do anything like that. This time she had money. It was stuffed inside her bra, burning a hole in her skin. She'd never had so much money at one time before, and knowing it was there made her feel good. But she'd have to be careful about showing it, or it'd be gone in a second, and so would she. Her only chance in a place like this was to look as down-and-out as everybody else.

A bus roared by, blanketing her with warm air and diesel exhaust. After it passed, she scanned the signs across the street, looking for somewhere to stay. One place advertised rooms for a few dollars a night. Brandy's lip curled. She knew what went on there. But they probably had a few rooms where people could actually stay the night, and she was tired.

She stepped off the sidewalk into the littered street. M.C. kept everything really neat at Harbor House, she remembered, even the street in front.... She frowned. He was as bad as the rest. He never said anything, but he always knew what was going on with her. And he played on it. That was why he'd taken her to the old lady's house, because he knew she liked art. She almost laughed out loud, remembering teatime that day. Just for a second, she'd thought maybe she could belong in a place like that. But that was just another load of bull. Although the old lady had some pretty pictures, and she'd seemed really interested in Brandy's work... Well, that had ended for sure when she took the money. It never would've worked out anyway.

But M.C. had done her a favor, after all. If she hadn't met Miss Cunningham, she might be here in Dallas without a penny to her name. Unexpectedly, in her mind's eye, she saw the old lady, frail and erect, eyes alight as she discussed one of the pictures. Brandy wasn't prepared for the little stab of pain. Angrily, she willed it away.

The doorway under the Rooms For Rent sign was dark. In its dank, fetid recess a man sprawled next to the wall, eyes closed, finishing the last of a bottle. He didn't notice Brandy as she mounted the narrow staircase. In the dirty little reception room she signed a false name and handed the toothless old man a five-dollar bill she'd retrieved from her bra on the way up.

Five minutes later she was sitting on a lumpy mattress looking at the wall, bare except for its pattern of cracks and stains. Nothing like her room at Harbor House, which glowed in the soft colors she herself had chosen. Tonight Leslie had it all to herself. It was almost midnight. If she were at Harbor House, they would have long since turned out the lights.

She wondered what Leslie was doing. Sometimes they would lie across the beds and talk about things. Now Leslie was probably mooning all by herself over her dumb boyfriend. Brandy couldn't see it. He was just a kid from school, but the way Leslie went on about him, you'd think he was a movie star. And she didn't even seem to mind being teased about it.

Leslie was okay. Brandy had finally decided that. In fact, right now, she almost missed her. But not enough to go back.

There *was* no going back.

CAMERON THREW his keys down on his dresser, pulled his wallet out of his pocket and flung it after the keys. It skidded across the dresser top and teetered precariously on the edge, but he didn't bother to move it.

After he'd left Harbor House, after the shattering scene with Mickey, he'd gone straight to the police department. But the officer there wasn't hopeful. Kids like that ran away all the time, he'd said. They'd do their best, but it was unlikely they'd find her, anytime soon, at least.

Fine, Cameron thought. Just fine. Except they were talking about a human being. A child. His earlier anger had faded, leaving only worry. He was tired. Exhausted. But he made no move to undress, just stood staring at his reflection in the mirror, fragments of the scene with Mickey bombarding his mind like pieces of shrapnel. He cursed himself for a fool. He'd blundered through it with all the finesse of an ox in a cornfield. But she'd been so angry.... And what had she meant by that last shot, the one about not being his kind? He didn't know.

There were a lot of things he didn't know, including whether he could ever patch things up between them. Or whether, at this point, he was too hurt and too damn mad to try.

He sat down on the edge of the bed and buried his head in his hands. Unbidden, other images began to surface in his mind, merging, separating, coming together again like colors and shapes in a kaleidoscope. *Mickey* ... Her impossibly blue eyes blazing defiance, the next moment softening with love as she dealt with one of her girls. Night-black hair swinging free against the perfect curve of her jaw, then tucked carelessly behind an ear with a nail-bitten finger. White skin, heating under his hands and lips, as the firelight played tag with the shadows on the walls ... For a precious time, the sapphire eyes had looked into his with a trust that was complete. That was destroyed now. For good?

He shook his head to clear away the unwanted images. He didn't understand what had happened between them, and he was too shell-shocked right now to try. In the meantime, he sure as hell couldn't sit still and do nothing.

He raised his head. For starters, he was going to find Brandy. He could do that, at least. Thinking about what could happen to her made him go cold all over. And if anything did happen to her, he didn't want to think about what it would do to Mickey.

He was no pro; the police would have a far better shot at finding her than he did. Even M.C. had a better chance than he did. He smiled humorlessly to himself. M.C. probably had an even better chance than the police. But Cameron couldn't just sit around twiddling his thumbs. He'd never been able to do that. Even if he didn't have official credentials, he was as stubborn as a bulldog. It was the way he got things done.

He began to concentrate, to think the situation through. Slowly, methodically, in his usual manner.

After he left the police station, he'd gone by the ice cream parlor where Brandy worked. The girl there had told him a couple of things.... He sifted them through his memory. Brandy had brought a small backpack to work, the kind kids carried their books in. She'd obviously made her plans by then. She'd asked for her paycheck, and she wasn't due to be paid until Monday. The manager had turned her down. That was why she'd robbed Miss Cunningham.

He tried to put himself inside Brandy's mind. Where would a kid like her go? She could have relatives in Hoboken, for all he knew. A new wave of frustration hit him as he realized how little he had to go on. Well, he could only try. He had to do that much.

He kept turning the situation over and over in his mind. Brandy was a city kid. Most likely she'd head for another one. Besides, a big city was the best place to lose yourself. But which one? Austin? Nope. Too many college kids, not big enough. San Antonio? Maybe. Dallas? Absently, he drummed his fist on the quilted bedspread. *Dallas*. Bright lights, dark corners. Crowds. A hundred places to hide. Even the name beckoned. All the kids had grown up with "Dallas" on TV. He had no way of knowing, of course, but he'd bet a hundred bucks a kid like Brandy would head for Dallas.

He made his decision. Maybe M.C. and Mickey couldn't afford private investigators, but he could. He'd make some calls first thing in the morning, get his friends to put him in touch with good private investigators in Dallas. He'd cover San Antonio as well, just to make sure. And if they didn't find her in either place, he'd keep looking until he found her somewhere.

Rising, he stripped, went into the bathroom and stepped into the hottest shower he could stand.

CHAPTER FOURTEEN

"I TALKED to Cameron yesterday," Penny said. She poured coffee into the Limoges china cup, added cream and sugar and handed it to Keith. Then she poured herself a cup, leaving out the cream. "No one's heard anything from the Williford girl."

"I was afraid of that." Keith leaned back against the cushions of the deck chair and took a sip of the steaming coffee.

Penny rested her chin on one hand and gazed absently at her backyard, a fairyland of azalea, bridal wreath and wisteria blossoms in the bright sunshine of the perfect spring morning. She had worked hard to achieve just this effect. Normally, she derived a great deal of satisfaction from it, but right now she was too preoccupied to enjoy it.

"It seems to me the police should have found her by now," she said.

He shrugged. "The runaway list is a mile long, and no one even knows whether she left town or not." He laid his napkin in his lap. "It's not that hard to disappear if you're a kid on the run."

Tell me about it. Unpleasant memories pulled at her like briars. "It was a terrible thing to do," she said aloud. "Robbing Miss Cunningham after she'd gone out of her way to help her. It just proves what I said all along."

Keith grimaced. "Some kids just can't be helped. What worries me is that Lisa was around someone like that."

"Brandy was bad news all the way around." Penny picked up a croissant. When she realized her hands were shaking, she put it down. "I'm sure Lisa didn't have much to do with her."

"She was my friend." The voice made both of them jump.

"Lisa!" Keith's voice was a little too hearty. "I didn't know you were here."

She was standing at the edge of the deck, her dark eyes enormous, looking accusingly at them both. Penny's heart turned over. It was obvious she'd heard them talking.

"Sit down and have some breakfast." Keith indicated the platter on the table.

"No, thanks. I've already eaten." She sat down, but perched stiffly on the edge of her chair. For once she hadn't brought the cat. She was dressed neatly in a navy skirt and a white blouse with a lace collar. "I just came to see you before I went to church."

"Where's Half-pint?" Penny asked, hoping to divert the conversation.

"Asleep on the back steps. Mr. and Mrs. Rhodes..." She stopped as if gathering her courage, and clasped her hands in her lap. "What you think about Brandy and me is wrong."

"We weren't implying you were like Brandy," Keith hastened to reassure her. "We know you're not. Anyway, it's nothing you need to worry about."

"Yes, it is. I can't let you think I'm better than Brandy when I'm not." Her voice, still soft, was fierce in its intensity. "The thing is, I *am* like Brandy."

At their simultaneous protests, she shook her head. "The only difference is, she knows how to fight. I was always afraid of fighting, so I learned to get along." She smiled, a wise, weary little smile that broke Penny's heart. "I even wanted to be like her until she got into so much trouble." Lisa's expression sobered. "But it's not like she's bad and I'm good. All of us at Harbor House have been through the same stuff."

Penny looked at Lisa's fingers, twisting and untwisting, and felt her own insides doing the same thing.

"I better tell you about me," Lisa said. "Then maybe you'll understand better about her."

For the next ten minutes she talked, while they listened in shocked silence. Her voice kept its childlike quality and her words were simple, matter-of-fact, but her lustrous dark eyes were dull with remembered pain, like those of a beaten animal.

Gradually a frightening picture emerged, a world of damaged souls and hopeless lives, a world so fractured that Lisa was eventually sent to various foster homes. She had experienced not only grinding poverty but criminal neglect. Hearing it chilled Penny to the bone.

From what Lisa left unsaid, they were able to fill in the rest. Never wanted, never loved, in a desperate effort to be accepted somewhere, anywhere, Lisa had drifted into the drug scene even before adolescence. After she'd finally been caught and put through drug rehab she'd been drug free, but she was still as rootless, as adrift as before. It was only when she came to Harbor House that, for the first time, she'd begun to feel she'd found a home.

"Brandy feels that way, too, whether she'll admit it or not," Lisa finished. "That was why it was so hard on her when she got kicked out of the contest. I know she shouldn't have taken the money, but she's not really a thief. She's had a worse time than I've had."

As if that were possible, Penny thought, her own pain for Lisa so acute it was stopping her breathing. She glanced at Keith. He'd listened without interrupting, but his eyes were hard, his jaw set, and his hands were clenched on the arms of his chair so hard that the knuckles had turned white.

Silence fell, then stretched taut. Lisa stood. To Penny she seemed taller somehow, and she wore a dignity that should have rested on older shoulders. Yet never had she seemed so achingly vulnerable. "I'd better be going," she said. "Thanks for everything." Before either Penny or Keith could move to stop her, she was gone.

Penny sat very still, awash in the horror of what she'd just heard. She knew it was true. And it was all too familiar. Too much . . . "Oh, God." She covered her face with her hands.

"Pen?" She heard Keith stand, then felt him kneel beside her. His arms went around her, and she buried her face in his shoulder. He held her for long moments as the terrible sobs shook her, never saying a word, just rocking her gently.

After what seemed an hour, the storm of weeping quieted. He handed her his handkerchief and she dried her eyes. His dark eyes searched hers. "It's time to talk, isn't it?" he asked quietly.

"Yes." It was long past time. Oddly, she felt an enormous relief uncurl within her.

"I've known for a while there were things you weren't telling me. I didn't want to push you, but I'd like to know."

"I didn't want the halfway house," she began hesitantly, "but it wasn't because of the devaluation of the property or trouble in the neighborhood or any of the things I said. It was because the girls reminded me of myself when I was their age.''

"Oh?" But Keith didn't really seem surprised.

"I'm not very... close to my parents. You know that."

He nodded, his mouth tightening.

"With them," she went on, "I always felt in the way. Other people raised me—maids, baby-sitters, whoever happened to be available. My parents salved their consciences by giving me things. I had everything any child could want. Except love."

"I know," he said gently. She saw the pain in his eyes.

"I was always a behavior problem. By the time I was in high school, I was desperate for acceptance. Sure enough, I found it—with kids who were into drugs. They took me right in."

"Happens to a lot of kids," Keith interjected quietly. "Like Lisa." He still didn't seem surprised.

"Like Lisa." Penny tried to laugh, but the sound caught in her throat. "Only I didn't have it as hard as she did. At least I was never poor or physically neglected." She made herself go on. "The worst thing was, I got pregnant."

"You *what?*"

"That's right, Keith. I got pregnant." She said each word deliberately, so he would be sure to understand. "He was a kid in my class who paid some attention to me. I was only sixteen. Both sets of parents wanted me to have an abortion at some expensive private clinic that would take care of it very discreetly. But I wanted my baby. At least it would have been something that I could love." She drew a long, jerky breath. "So I ran away." She clenched her hands in her lap. "I know what it's like."

"My God," Keith whispered. His face was chalk white.

"By the time they found me," she said dully, "it was too late for an abortion. So they sent me to another discreet, exclusive place." She stared unseeingly at her resplendent backyard. The bees hummed lazily as they feasted on wisteria blossoms, and the birds sang in the trees. "I had my child, but I never saw her," she said. "The only thing I ever knew about her was that she was a little girl. My little girl. She'd be thirteen now. In my mind, I've never stopped looking for her. Every time I see a girl that age, I wonder."

"Oh, baby—" Now Keith's voice held a world of pain.

"I don't know exactly what went wrong, but afterward, they told me I couldn't have any more children." Her mouth twisted. "My mother said that children weren't a big thing, that I was lucky, really."

He muttered something under his breath that she didn't quite catch.

"Through the whole thing," she went on, "my parents' biggest concern was to keep it quiet." Her hands were aching from being clenched so tightly. She opened them, studying the marks her polished nails had made in the palms.

"All these years I thought I was fine. Then when I heard about the halfway house coming in and thought of all those unhappy kids right on the next street, it brought it all back to me. I couldn't stand it." She closed her eyes. "It was wrong not to tell you, Keith. I'm sorry. I just couldn't do it, that's all." Now he knew. She felt curiously cleansed. He might not want her anymore, but at least she didn't have to live with her secrets.

He stirred, as if after a physical blow. "I guess I'm not as smart as I thought I was. I'd guessed some of it, but never this. Why didn't you tell me?"

"I was afraid you'd stop loving me."

There was a long silence. "You should have known better," he said finally, his voice uneven. He pulled her against him.

Tears stung her eyelids, but this time they were tears of healing.

"That's why you were so set against adopting children," he said.

She nodded. "All I could think of was that I'd make as big a mess of rearing children as my parents had." She drew a breath that wasn't yet steady. "I thought if I could make a perfect life for you, it would compensate for... the empty spots. But you always wanted children, and even though you tried to hide it, I knew it." She sat up straight and blew her nose. Her face must be a mess, but she couldn't bring herself to care. "You know, Keith," she said slowly, "I never realized it before, but we're a lot like my parents."

"How's that?" There was a note in his voice that said he wasn't pleased with the comparison.

"Living in a fantasy world, putting all our stock in... things. As much as I hated the way they were—"

"Hold it." He didn't raise his voice, but Penny stopped. "We haven't misplaced all our priorities. You're forgetting how we feel about each other."

It was true. In her self-recrimination, she had almost lost sight of it. She thought about it. "I guess that makes up for a lot of mistakes?"

He chuckled and took her hand. "I guess it does." He kissed the tip of her nose. "Pen..." He hesitated a long moment. "How would you feel about adopting a child now?"

"I don't know," she said tentatively. "I'm not sure I know how to be a mother. I suppose love can make a difference...."

He met her gaze, and she saw hope flare in his eyes.

TWO WEEKS TOMORROW. Mickey shoved several stacks of
papers into her briefcase and glanced at her watch. Almost
time to go home. She was dead tired, never so glad to see a
Friday afternoon. She wasn't sleeping well, had no appetite
to speak of. In the days since Brandy's disappearance her
world had turned upside down, and she hadn't yet been able
to right it. And she hadn't heard from Cameron Scott.

She opened the desk drawer and glanced down into the
corner where she'd hidden the wentletrap. It glowed pearl-
escent in the dimness, almost with a light of its own. Seeing
it brought her both pain and comfort. She missed Cameron
more than she could ever have believed possible. Missed his
spontaneous laugh, his clear vision, his quick way of putting things into perspective. His solidity. His just being
there. What they'd shared together. She hadn't dreamed....

She touched the shell with the tip of a finger, then gently
closed the drawer. No matter how much she missed him, she
reminded herself, the gulf between them was too wide. She
didn't belong with a man who had just proved all too well
that he had absolutely no idea, no *real* idea, of what her
world or her values were all about. Just as he didn't belong
with someone like her.

He deserves better....

The words rose in her mind from nowhere. He deserved
someone who could meet his needs, she told herself hastily,
someone who would complement his life-style. But being
sensible didn't help the raw pain in her heart.

She set down the briefcase and took a last sip of coffee
from the mug on her desk. *Face it,* she ordered herself. *Life
hurts.* She'd been dealt bad licks before, but she'd gotten
over them. She'd get over this one. Right now she needed to

stop spending energy on mooning over Cameron Scott and focus all her resources on finding Brandy.

In the two weeks she'd been gone, there had been no word. None at all. At first Mickey had held out hope that she would come home or at least call to let them know she was all right, but there had been nothing. The waiting was killing her.

She swallowed coffee she didn't even taste and set down the cup. She couldn't afford to give in to her emotions about either Brandy or Cameron.

Several days after Brandy's disappearance, she'd done the honorable thing and called Miss Cunningham, apologizing for the incident and offering to pay back the stolen money from her own pocket.

"Certainly not, young woman," Miss Cunningham had returned frostily. "I don't need the money. It's the principle of the thing. She betrayed my trust. 'How sharper than a serpent's tooth is a thankless child,'" she'd quoted in awful accents. She'd reminded Mickey once again that she'd been unalterably opposed to Harbor House from the beginning. But then she'd unbent enough to ask if there had been any word on Brandy. Mickey hadn't missed the wistfulness in her voice.

Mickey's gaze fell on Rooney, napping comfortably in the out box. Half-pint, Lisa's kitten, had hopped up to join him, and had curled herself into the circle of the old cat's body. Both were fast asleep, in a tangle of yellow and black-and-white fur. When the kitten had come to Harbor House to live, she'd expected Rooney to swallow him in one gulp. Instead, he'd tolerated her for a while, then had developed a real affection for her. The kitten adored the battle-scarred old veteran and lost no opportunity to keep him company. The odd couple, she reflected, amused in spite of herself.

Maybe she and Cameron should take lessons. Except they weren't going to have the chance....

When a knock sounded at the door, she looked up in annoyance. It faded quickly when she saw who was standing in the doorway. "Connie. Come in."

"Hi." Connie looked her usual fresh, competent self. "I just dropped by to check in."

"Thanks," Mickey said with real gratitude. "I can use a friendly face."

"Anytime." Connie made herself comfortable in the chair across from Mickey's desk. "What's the word?"

"None." Mickey sighed wearily. "Mrs. Lawrence at the school is investigating, and I talked to the police again this morning. They have an APB out on Brandy and are making the usual inquiries, but nothing's turned up so far."

"You're looking a little thin, Mickey. How are you?" It wasn't an idle question. There was no fooling Connie; if you lied to her, she knew it before the words left your mouth.

"Dropping seven pounds never hurt anyone, especially me." Mickey shrugged. "I'm okay. I don't have a choice, do I?"

"No," Connie said thoughtfully, "I don't suppose you do. A lot of people would lie down and drum their heels on the carpet, but frankly, I can't see you doing that."

Mickey smiled. "Hysterics are a waste of time and energy."

"Hysterics might ruin that incredible face of yours. Mickey..." For the first time since she'd known her, Connie sounded a little hesitant.

"Go on," Mickey said. "Let me have it."

"I'm worried about you. I know you're bummed out about Brandy, but is that all?"

"What else?" Mickey tried to keep her voice noncommittal. Was Connie on to the thing with Cameron? You never knew what she was going to pick up.

"Nothing, I suppose," Connie said. "It's just a feeling I've got. I may be stepping out of line, but since I'm a friend, I'm offering my services as a professional." She grinned. "Free. How's that for a deal?"

Touched, Mickey had to smile. "A generous deal." She looked down at her hands, clenched together on the desktop. "Look, Connie, I'm not stupid. I've had therapy myself, and years of training. The whole bit. I know all the reasons, all the pat answers. I know I've involved myself too much with Brandy. It's just that…" To her horror, her voice wavered.

"It's just that what we know doesn't always have anything to do with what we feel," Connie finished gently.

Mickey took a deep, shaky breath. "I couldn't have said it better."

"You're not supposed to," Connie said. "That's *my* job."

"Right." Mickey managed a brief grin. "Anyway, I can't seem to shake it. I've felt Brandy's pain, her confusion, her isolation, every bit of it." She swallowed. "It's as if I'm living it all over again."

"Did you have the same problems?"

"Every one." Mickey closed her eyes.

"Do you want to talk about it?"

"I…maybe I'd better." Talking about it always brought it all back, but she'd learned a long time ago that if there was a problem, it was better to bring it out into the open. If she had to go through it all again, she would. For Brandy's sake—and her own.

"All right," Connie said. "I'm listening."

For the next half hour Mickey talked. And, as she went into the painful details of her miserable childhood and turbulent youth, she came to realize as never before how eerily parallel Brandy's case was with her own.

Connie summed it up neatly. "Trouble in school, trouble with relationships, trouble with the law, trouble at home."

"Afraid so." Mickey was worrying a pencil between her fingers.

"Let's talk about the last one," Connie said. "I've found it usually comes first, anyway."

Mickey kept staring at the pencil, but her fingers stilled. She felt a light sweat break out on her forehead. "Oh, just the usual. Mom always telling me I was no good, my stepfather—" She stopped.

"Go on. What about him?"

Mickey's mouth had gone dry. "He drank. When he was drunk, I had to step lively or he'd nail me a good one." How light, how flippant the words sounded. How different from what had really happened. . . .

"Is that all?"

"I—" She'd been over this before, all of it. It had been dug out years before, examined, worked through. She hadn't thought there could be anything left. But it still took every ounce of resolve she could muster to talk about it.

"Go on, Mickey." Connie's voice was quiet, like water over smooth stones. "Tell me about it."

Mickey opened her mouth to speak. Then, for an instant, just an instant, the resolve slipped and the years spun away. She was a frightened child again, lost in the moments of frozen terror when her stepfather would come in drunk and she would try to hide. When he would find her, hit her. Or worse. *Where are you, baby? Daddy just wants a hug. . . .*

Between her fingers, the pencil snapped in two.

"Mickey?" Connie's voice had dropped almost to a whisper.

She became aware that she was staring at the broken pieces of the pencil in her hands. "You can write the script," she said past the knot that had tied itself in her vocal cords. "You already know it. We both deal with it all the time."

"Afraid so." *I'm so sorry.* Connie didn't actually say the words, but Mickey heard them in her voice.

She cleared her throat, trying to regain control. "It was a textbook case. Mom knew he belted me occasionally, but she didn't know about the other. Of course, I was too scared to tell at first. Then, when I worked up the courage, she didn't believe me, partly because she didn't want to."

"Of course," Connie murmured. "They never do. Don't bite your nails," she reminded her.

"Right." Mickey recalled herself and dropped her hand to the desk. "After Mom finally believed me," she went on, "she divorced him. A couple of years later he was shot and killed in a barroom fight." Her mouth twisted. "Mom never quite got over the whole thing. She got sick not too long afterward."

"How about you?"

Mickey spun the broken pieces of pencil on the desktop. "I finally forgave Mom for not standing up for me, but it was one of the hardest things I ever did." She tossed the pencil down. "I still can't understand her. I feel more maternal toward my Harbor House girls than my own mother did toward me. If she had really loved me, how could she have stood by and let it happen?"

"Your mother didn't intend for it to happen," Connie said. "She was a victim of her own weakness."

"I know," Mickey said. "I just need reminding sometimes, that's all."

"In your case, you learned from your own bitter experience. You didn't want anyone else to have to go through it." Connie smiled. "Hard on you, but good for Harbor House."

Mickey considered. "That's a good way to look at it."

Connie wasn't through yet. "And M.C.? Where was he all that time?"

"Who knows?" Even after all this time, she still felt a twinge of the old bitterness. "He was at sea most of the time by then, I think, but he simply never came around. From the time I was about three, I never saw him until he waltzed back into my life about four years ago. I don't know why, and it's something I've never asked him." Restlessly, she drummed her fingers on the desk. "I suppose it doesn't matter, anyway."

"Maybe. And you?"

Mickey shrugged. "What's to tell? They dragged it all out of me, and I worked through it years ago." She tried to sound clinical, objective, but the words were choking her.

"Did you?" The question hung in the stillness between them.

"Of course I did." She pulled a hand through her hair and shook her head to clear it.

"You know what happens as well as I do," Connie went on. "Sexually abused children may try a lot of relationships in later life, may even be promiscuous at some point, but often they can't form genuine intimacies because their trust has been destroyed. That's what happened to Brandy." She leaned forward in her chair. "Mickey...is that what's happened to you?"

Mickey examined her bitten nails. "I don't know what you mean."

"I'm talking about Cameron Scott."

Mickey jumped, and her gaze flew to Connie's face. "What about him?"

"You're a very attractive woman, Mickey. A knockout, really. But you hardly date at all, and you always drop the ones who are brave enough to come around more than two or three times."

"So? I haven't had time—"

"People make time for what they want to do. You liked Cameron Scott. I saw it. He liked you, too. A lot. Where is he? Did you drop him, too?"

Mickey didn't say the expletive, but she thought it. It was one thing to put herself through talking about her childhood, however painful; it was another to rub salt into a wound that was still so fresh it hadn't quit bleeding. "We...had a disagreement," she said shortly.

"What kind of a disagreement?"

"He wanted to run my life for me." *This is none of your damn business,* she wanted to say. She knew Connie was only trying to help, but she had a strong feeling that, whatever this was, she didn't want to face it.

"How?" Connie persisted.

Momentarily, Mickey's control went. "Give me a break, Connie," she snapped.

"Hang on," Connie said gently. "I think this is important. How did Cameron want to run your life?"

Mickey took a deep breath and willed herself back to calmness. "He wanted me to give up my work because he wanted to protect me," she said. "From my own profession, for crying out loud. Then he had the gall to ask me to marry him."

Connie's lips twitched. "That's real gall."

Mickey jerked a thumb. "I told him where to get off."

"I can imagine. Does he love you?"

"He said so." Mickey shrugged restlessly. "He thinks so, anyway."

Connie was quiet a minute, thoughtful. "Tell me something, Mickey," she said finally. "Be as honest as you can. Do you love him?"

Mickey just stared at her.

"Mickey?"

"I . . . yes." She felt as though the word had forced itself out of her mouth of its own volition. Knowing she loved Cameron Scott was one thing, saying it out loud was another.

Connie smiled. "Okay, we've settled that. Mickey—" she steepled her hands "—you tell me you're in love with a man you've just said is trying to run your life. Call me silly, but there's something wrong here. I think you're focusing on a petty quarrel to avoid the main problem. Just a minute." She put up a hand to forestall Mickey's interruption. "I think you're still carrying around some old baggage from somewhere. Now—" she set her hand firmly on the desktop "—we're going to find out what it is."

"It just wouldn't work between Cameron and me, that's all." *Inane, juvenile, ridiculous . . .* An adolescent's answer. But for the life of her, Mickey could think of nothing else to say.

"Why wouldn't it?"

Let it go, Connie, Mickey wanted to beg. But she knew she had to see this one through. "Cameron needs someone from his own world."

"Don't you think that's his decision to make?"

"He doesn't need someone like me." The blood was starting to pound in Mickey's ears, and she was getting the beginnings of a vicious headache.

Connie was watching her like a cat at a mousehole. "What do you mean, someone like you?"

"There are things he doesn't know about me." To avoid Connie's gaze, she rose and walked to the window.

"Like what?"

"I just told you."

"So what?" Connie shrugged. "It's who you are now that's important. Wake up, Mickey, and smell the coffee. Haven't you said the same thing to at least a hundred of your girls by now?"

Mickey gestured impatiently. "Sure, but—"

"Are you telling me you don't really believe it?"

"Of course I do." She tried to marshal her scattered thoughts. She felt as if there were two different people inside her, and she couldn't seem to pull them together. She tried again. "It's just that Cameron doesn't know what I've been through, what's happened to me. What I did...what was done to me." She had to stop a moment before she went on. "I don't believe in selling anyone damaged goods if they don't know it...."

Her voice trailed off into nothing. She met Connie's eyes, and for a moment they simply stared at each other.

"Well, well, well." Connie sat back in her chair. "The smoking howitzer." She drew a long breath, then exhaled slowly. "Did you have any idea you think you're damaged goods?"

CHAPTER FIFTEEN

"I GUESS I DIDN'T." Mickey felt as if her voice was coming from a long way away.

"You traded the bad relationships for no relationships at all," Connie mused. "You're superfunctional in every other way, but your trust and self-esteem were damaged a long time ago, and they've never been entirely mended." The words were direct, but her voice held infinite sympathy. "There's one little corner of you that still believes you're not good enough for an honest relationship with a good man. As you just pointed out, both of us work with it every day."

Mickey toyed with the mug. The remaining coffee was stone-cold by now. "I thought I'd worked it all out." She tilted the mug and watched the brown liquid swirl back and forth.

"Take time to sort it out," Connie said quietly. "When you do, I believe you'll find some new answers for yourself. In the meantime do me a favor."

"What's that?" Mickey was still dazed.

"Start at the beginning."

"What do you mean?"

"Go talk to M.C."

Mickey was appalled at the intensity of the panic that sluiced through her. "I'm . . . not sure I can."

"You can't heal a deep wound with a Band-Aid. You know that. You've got to talk to him. For your own sake, and for his." Connie started to leave, then turned back.

"And for everyone else's," she added. "Cameron Scott is a fine man, Mickey. Be sure you don't turn him down for the wrong reasons."

"I'll think about it. Connie?"

"Hmm?"

"Thanks."

"Anytime. For a friend." A brief smile, and she was gone. Mickey was left to stare at the empty doorway.

"Cameron, line one," Vicky said over the intercom. He tried to squelch the surge of hope. "Mr. Jacobs," Vicky finished.

Oh, hell. Cameron yanked up the phone and jabbed savagely at the line-one button. "Hello, Mort." He tried to keep the irritation out of his voice. For two weeks now, his private investigators had been working to find Brandy Williford in San Antonio and Dallas. He'd checked both offices this morning. Nothing. Early days yet, of course, and they might be way off the mark. But his frustration, his sheer helplessness were killing him.

And for two weeks, he'd been fielding calls like this one from Village Walk investors, complaining about the theft and wanting him to take some sort of action—what, they weren't sure. He'd talked to Mort Jacobs on the subject at least twice in the past two days.

He sat and steamed as he listened to Jacobs recite his litany of complaints. More of the same. Trouble was, he thought impatiently, Mort had no insight into the other side of the situation. None at all. "I'll do what I can, Mort," he promised as soon as he could get a word in edgewise.

After he'd hung up, he buzzed Vicky on the intercom. "Vicky?" he snapped. "Hold my calls."

"Okay, Cameron." He clicked off, but not before he heard her say, "My, we're testy."

Yes, dammit, we *were* testy. He slammed a file down on his desk. He'd never been so completely stymied in his life. He knew without being told how frantic Mickey must be about Brandy. The first week or so he hadn't been able to get past his own hurt, his anger, but lately he'd been picking up the phone a dozen times a day to call her, to reassure her, just to talk to her. And then he'd put it down again. He wasn't at all sure she would even talk to him. He honestly didn't know what to do.

Since that last night he'd seen her, he'd been kicking himself at least once an hour. He'd tried to put her out of his mind, forget the whole thing and start his life all over again. No good. She was as firmly entrenched in his heart and soul, as much a part of him as his own name.

He admitted to himself that he didn't come close to understanding her. She was one of the most complex human beings, one of the most independent souls, he'd ever encountered. And completely involved in her work. If he could ever talk her into marrying him, he'd be marrying her work, too.

With surprise, he realized that he was willing to do just that.

He gave a half laugh, thinking of how much she'd taught him. She'd opened up a whole new world for him, made him see things through new eyes. Before he'd run into her—headlong, he reflected ruefully—he'd considered himself a compassionate man. In the abstract, he'd always felt sorry for those less fortunate, had donated generously to causes. He'd practiced the same kind of compassion as a lot of people he knew—the ones who'd never seen anything beyond their BMWs and their backyard barbecue pits.

Like Mort Jacobs. Mort wasn't a bad man. In fact, he was really a good one. Mort wrote a lot of checks for charity, too. But he hadn't ever laughed at Joni's crazy antics, watched Leslie's pursuit of Eternal Love or met Lisa, with her eyes that tore at a body's soul. He hadn't cheered for Brandy's inches of progress. Hadn't grieved when she'd run away.

Like himself, before he'd met Mickey... Hell, he hadn't even known the meaning of compassion. She'd taught him that, with her hands-on caring, her willingness to dive into the ugliest depths of life and bring up something—or someone—beautiful. Whatever happened, she'd changed his life forever.

He let out a short, explosive breath and dragged his hand through his hair. What a hell of a mess.

When the idea occurred to him, he wondered briefly why he hadn't thought of it before. Even if Mickey never spoke to him again, even if he never found Brandy, there was something he could do. A little thing, really, but...

He felt a grin begin to tug at the corners of his mouth. Reaching for the Rolodex on his desk, he found Mort's number and dialed it. He had the feeling he was going to enjoy this.

"Mort?" he said when he'd gotten through the receptionist and a couple of secretaries, "Cameron Scott again. Yes, I know I just talked to you, but I've made a decision on the halfway house, and I thought I'd better tell you." He took a deep breath. "I'm going to leave it alone, Mort. Harbor House isn't going anywhere."

His grin grew to a silent chuckle as the voice on the other end rose at least ten decibels. This was even more fun than he'd thought it was going to be.

"It's not hurting anybody, Mort," he said. "They do a lot of good over there that no one knows about, and I think it's important for their operation to stay in West Village."

This time he had to hold the phone away from his ear. Mort sounded like Donald Duck.

"That's the way it's going to be, Mort," he said finally, stifling his laughter. "I'm staying the course. Village Walk and the neighborhood will just have to survive. It goes without saying that I'll be on hand to help any way I can, but from now on I'll be helping Harbor House, too." Mort would get used to the idea. He and the rest of the investors needed him for this project. They knew it, and he knew it. And he would see to it personally that everything worked out just fine.

"Just remember that kids can get into trouble in normal families, too," he added as a final reassurance. "There's never a guarantee that they won't. It doesn't mean that, just because they do, the neighborhood will go bad or a shopping center will go broke."

It wasn't until after he'd hung up that he realized he'd quoted Mickey Mulvaney almost verbatim.

He sat back in his chair, still grinning. Hell, who knew? He might end up as president of the Harbor House executive board. Then, at least, Mickey would have to talk to him. From here on out he was working for Harbor House. Not because of Mickey, he realized. For himself.

"MICKEY!"

She could see the pleasure and surprise on M.C.'s face. She rarely visited his apartment, although he lived upstairs and just down the hall from her.

"Come in, sweetheart." He opened the door.

"Thanks." She fought the urge to bolt, then stepped inside.

"What's up?" He closed the door behind her.

"M.C...." She tried to still her jangling nerves, slow her breathing. She wasn't afraid of much in life, but the idea of talking to M.C.—really talking to him—frightened her more than anything she could remember since she'd been a child. "Do you have a minute?" she asked.

She saw something change in his eyes. "All the time in the world," he said. "Want a cup of coffee?"

"Sounds good." She sat down on the living room sofa, hands balled in her lap, while he headed toward the kitchen. Looking around her, she reflected not for the first time that M.C. had the soul of an artist and the spirit of a pirate. Unlike the Spartan simplicity of her own living quarters, his contained a hodgepodge of mementos from his travels and objects that had simply caught his fancy. An elephant gun and a Polynesian wooden spear hung one atop the other over a doorway. A sari from Sri Lanka, undoubtedly a gift from one of his conquests, draped itself sinuously over the back of the couch, which she was sure was a relic of a flea market somewhere.

On top of an American country-pine table sat a photograph of her.

She stared at it. She remembered when it was taken—on a field trip to Astroworld with the girls a couple of years ago. She didn't like being photographed, but M.C. had called to her, catching her off guard, and snapped the picture.

The blue eyes of the girl in the picture stared back at her. She was smiling, her chin tilted at a confident angle. Who was she? Mickey didn't know anymore. It was what she'd come here to find out.

M.C. came back in with two mugs of coffee. "Black, right?"

"Right." Mickey rubbed her clammy palms on her slacks and reached for the coffee. She'd rather talk to a dozen rebellious teenagers. But she knew Connie was right; she was missing a part of herself.

He sat down opposite her. "What's on your mind, honey?"

"I need to—ask you some questions." She cupped the mug of hot coffee in her palms, drawing comfort from its heat.

He looked at her sharply, then grew very still. "I'm listening."

"Where were you?" The question, wrenching, agonizing, came from nowhere. It wasn't at all what she'd intended to say. Then, as if it had been the cork that held the rest inside, she couldn't seem to get the words out fast enough. "I know you and Mom were divorced, but at least you could have come around sometimes." She set the cup down on the table so hard that a few drops of coffee splashed out. "When you showed up, I didn't even remember what you looked like." Her voice cracked, but her eyes stayed dry. "Why weren't you around?"

There it was. The big one. The question she'd lived with all her life. Out on the table, as M.C. liked to say.

She saw his eyes glaze with pain, but in a second his mouth crooked into a half grin. "Fair question." He lowered his gaze to the mug in his hands. It made it easier that she didn't have to see his eyes.

"Tell me." Beneath the anger, she heard the pleading in her own voice, like a child crying in the night.

With a sigh, he sat back in his chair. "Valerie and I were very young when we married. Did she ever tell you anything about us?"

"She never mentioned your name," Mickey said. "It was always 'your father' this, or 'your father' that. 'Your father was a hopeless drunk,' she'd say. 'He never supported us, he's never given us anything.'"

"Not entirely true," M.C. said. "I made good money as a seaman, and before I left, it went to both of you. But she was right about the drinking. The worse things got between her and me, the more I drank."

"Why didn't you come back after you and she split?" Like a broken record, she could do nothing but repeat the question, over and over, until she had an answer.

He grimaced. "When I left, she told me that if she had anything to do with it, I'd never see you again. She tried to make sure I didn't."

Not good enough. M.C. was one of the most resourceful human beings Mickey had ever known. If he had wanted to see her, he'd have found a way. She stared stonily at him and waited.

"She had some good reasons for keeping me away." He made a self-mocking little gesture. "I was an irresponsible young punk, and when I wasn't shipping out, I was drinking way too much. When I was in port, I came to see you at first, but Valerie started hassling me every time I wanted to take you, even for a little while. She had full custody of you—I hadn't fought her over that. I figured that since I was at sea so much, you'd be better off with her. Maybe it was what I wanted to believe. Anyway, after a while—" he hesitated, and the next words came slowly, painfully. "—I just stopped trying."

Stopped trying. Suddenly the anger she'd lived with for so long that she hadn't even known it was there mushroomed inside her and exploded in a hot torrent of words. "You took the easy way out, didn't you?" Her voice was harsh, unrecognizable to her own ears. "You just left it all to Mother, knowing how weak she was, and didn't think about me at all. Well, if you'd really cared what happened to me, you would've come back sooner. By the time you decided to show up again, I'd been through all the bad stuff." She paused, breathing hard, some far corner of her appalled at her own words. But the anger was still flooding her whole being, blocking out rational thought.

M.C. didn't move, just sat watching her, and she could see the pain flaying him alive. "Spit it out, darlin'," was all he said. "It's been a long time coming."

"All those years I needed you, I never had you," she said, unable to stop herself. "When I finally got my life straight, I did it by myself. I learned I didn't really need anyone, and I learned that no matter what anyone did to me—" She stopped, realizing even through her blind, hurting fury that she was about to say too much.

For a minute there was dead silence. As quickly as it had erupted, her anger evaporated, leaving her drained. She stared down at her hands.

"Mickey." A peculiar note in M.C.'s voice made her look up. With a shock, she saw that the blue eyes had gone ice-cold. On his face was a terrible anger. Dimly, it occurred to her that it was the first time she'd ever seen him angry. Even through her own misery, she knew she never wanted to again.

"If I'd had any idea what that bastard was going to do to you," he said, "I swear in my own blood I'd have knocked the door down and gotten you out of there."

She went cold all over. He hadn't raised his voice, but his tone made the hair stir on the nape of her neck. "How did you know?" Her voice was a hoarse whisper.

"I didn't until about a year before I saw you again." His anger was ebbing, but suddenly he looked every day of his fifty-two years. "I got a letter from your mother."

Stunned into silence, she could only stare at him. She'd thought the past could hold no more surprises for her, but it seemed she was wrong. Again.

"Valerie wrote me about six months before she died," he said. "I think she knew by then she wasn't going to get well. I went to see her one day while you were at work."

If he'd announced he was running for President, she wouldn't have been as surprised. "I had no idea," she said lamely.

His gaze turned inward. "It's funny," he said, "but the talk I had with her that day was the only really good one she and I ever had. If we'd been able to communicate half that well before…" His voice was heavy with an old grief. "Well, what's done is done, and there's no sense wishing it was any different. Anyway, she apologized to me."

"Apologized? Mom?"

"Yes. For hating me so much that she made a big mistake. In trying to protect you from what she saw as one kind of abuse, she exposed you to another kind. A worse one." Carefully, he set his mug on the table. "Her biggest regret was that she hadn't believed you in time."

"By the time I told her, it had already been happening for several years," Mickey said dully. "It wasn't her fault."

A spark of the icy anger flared again behind M.C.'s eyes. "That bastard did us both a favor by getting himself killed. He saved me from having to serve a jail term for murder."

"He wasn't worth it," Mickey said with all the fervor she could muster. *He's angry on my account,* she thought in awe. *My father's angry on my account.*

"Anyway," he went on, "by the time Valerie's letter came, I'd already crawled out of the bottle and was on the road to straightening out my life. It reached me just in time, for all three of us." He paused. "There was a time I loved your mother, Mickey. For what it's worth, we parted friends."

"It's worth…a lot."

"I'd already made up my mind to find you," he added.

"Before you talked to Mom?" For some reason, it was important to her.

"Yep. I never quit loving you, sweetheart. Even all those years I'd lost myself. It was just that I never thought I'd be any good to you. Until I took hold of my own life, that is."

I love you. She wanted to say it, but couldn't, quite. "Mom used to tell me I was like you," she said instead. "That I had your blood." Her laugh sounded more like a sob. "She meant I was no good. I believed it, too, even after I was old enough to know better." *Like yesterday, for instance.* "When I was talking to Connie the other day, I found out I still thought I wasn't good enough."

M.C.'s eyes narrowed. "For what?"

"Just . . . no good." He was too damned acute.

He eyed her sharply for a long moment, opened his mouth to say something, then apparently changed his mind. "You're beautiful, you're bright, you're doing good in this world," he said finally. "What more can you ask?"

She managed a laugh. "That's what Connie said." She realized something. Needed to say it. "Do you know, M.C.? I'm proud to have your blood." She rose. "It's the best thing I've got."

She watched the emotions chase themselves across his mobile face. Pride, pain. Love. Slowly, he stood. "I failed with you, Mickey. I've lived with it every day of my life. I don't have all the answers, never pretended to. But maybe I've given you some you didn't have. The only thing I've ever known for sure is that I've loved you from the time you were born until this very minute."

He'd loved her. All those years she thought he hadn't cared. And her mother had loved her, too. Now she knew it for a certainty. Funny that, today, her father had given her both her parents' love.

"Your mother was proud of you, honey. She told me so."
M.C. flashed her a shadow of the old grin. "Almost as
proud as I am." He seemed to rouse himself. "Warm your
coffee?"

"No, thanks. I'd better go." Suddenly she felt shy. But
one question remained. "Why haven't you told me before?"

"You wouldn't have believed me, darlin'," he said simply. "I had to show you I was for real. You're the most important thing in the world to me, Mickey. I can't change
what happened, but I'm going to spend the rest of my life
trying to make it up to you. Can you try to forgive me?"

"I—" Unexpectedly, her throat clogged with tears. She
couldn't remember the last time she'd really cried. She
cleared her throat and tried again. "If you can forgive me,"
she managed. She saw her tears reflected in the eyes so like
her own and felt something crack inside her, begin to thaw.

"M.C.?"

"What, sweetheart?" His voice had thickened.

"I love you."

As naturally as waking in the morning, she crossed the
space between them and walked into his arms. His tears
mingled with her own.

It wasn't until she was unlocking the door to her own
apartment that she remembered who had held her up that
long-ago day on the ferry, to see the sea gulls.

Her father.

CAMERON LOOKED AROUND the nondescript office of
Luther Smith, Private Investigator. He wasn't even sure why
he was here, except that he'd had to be in Dallas today on
business anyway. A complete dead end in San Antonio so
far, as he'd expected. But he would keep trying. It was too
soon, he kept reminding himself, even if they were looking

in the right cities. He was a fool to think a runaway could be found in three weeks. Three months, more likely. Or three years. Or never . . . The thought snaked insidiously into his brain.

One of his Dallas contacts had recommended this particular PI. "A bit of a renegade," he'd said. "He uses some pretty unorthodox methods, but he's creative. A smart guy. He gets the right solutions, but he adds up the numbers differently than most people do."

So Cameron had engaged Mr. Luther Smith, giving him the few facts about Brandy he knew and a Sam Houston High School annual that he'd managed to get hold of, containing Brandy's picture. Beyond that, he'd had nothing else to tell the man. He couldn't very well have asked anyone at Harbor House for more background on Brandy. Besides, this was his own deal.

Smith had taken down the scraps of information. "Anything else, Mr. Scott?" he had asked. "Anything at all, no matter how unimportant you think it might be?"

"Not really." Suddenly he'd remembered about the art. Brandy's incredible talent . . . "Oh, yes," he'd added. "She paints and draws quite well." He hadn't really known why he'd even mentioned it.

"I'm afraid I can't offer you much hope, Mr. Scott, at least not right away," Smith had said. "These are always difficult cases, and you haven't given me much to go on. But I'll do the best I can."

Hoping now that the man's best was going to be good enough, Cameron stepped up to the desk and gave the secretary his name.

"Go right in, Mr. Scott," she said. "Mr. Smith's expecting you."

"Sit down, Mr. Scott." Smith, a mild-looking, balding man with round metal-framed glasses that didn't quite conceal the cold intelligence in his eyes, gestured him to his seat.

Cameron sat back, expecting to hear what he'd heard in San Antonio.

He was just that much more surprised when Smith leaned forward in his chair. "I've got a lead, Mr. Scott," he said. "A very strong lead." His bland, nondescript face never changed expression, but the eyes were sharp, intent. "Sometimes I just walk along the streets where these kids might be hanging out, and think about what I know about them, what they could be doing. Put things together, you might say. Late yesterday afternoon, I saw something. Followed it up this morning. Good thing you remembered to mention the art...."

BRANDY WASHED UP the paintbrushes and put the body paints away. She was actually pleased with herself in a weird sort of way. She'd gotten creative and painted a really neat picture of Captain Hook on Mimi's back, with the hook reaching around to... She pushed down the repugnance that rose like bile in her throat. She might have to fill in part-time as a dishwasher in this sleazy joint, but she was getting to paint part of the time, and at least she didn't have to go out and do what the girls did on stage. And most of them were nice to her—except Pearl and a couple of the others. But she could handle them.

On her way out she found the owner, a short, heavy man with a fringe of oily gray hair. He was sweeping the concrete floor. He stopped sweeping and looked at her without speaking.

She stood in front of him and planted her feet. "I worked ten hours today."

The man leaned on his broom, a nasty little smile on his face. She stood her ground, and after a minute he reached inside his pocket and pulled out a roll of bills. Peeling off three tens, he dangled them between two fingers.

"More than the job's worth." He grinned at her. His teeth were yellow, with brown stains. "You owe me."

Brandy swallowed the wave of anger and revulsion. "I doubt it. That's not even minimum wage." She took the bills and turned to go.

"Yeah? You gonna tell the IRS on me?" When Brandy didn't answer, he laughed. "I could show you how to make more money. A lot more," he called after her.

As the door closed behind her she heard him laugh again. The sound made her feel dirty all over. Sometimes it seemed like she'd been hearing that laugh all her life. It used to frighten her. Now it made her mad. She'd be damned if she'd let him touch her. She'd starve before she'd make money that way.

She'd have to be careful about how she refused him, though. After several days of roaming the streets of Dallas, asking door-to-door, she'd gotten a job at this strip joint, washing dishes and body-painting the strippers, only because she could paint. The owner had hired her on the spot, not even asking for identification, probably figuring her for a runaway. She was sure that suited him just fine. That way he could pay her in cash, whatever amount he chose to give her, and she wouldn't be able to cause him any trouble no matter what he tried.

She walked the few blocks to her room, glad it wasn't any farther. The streets were deserted, but that wasn't much comfort. People around here tended to lie low, then make their moves quick. If anything happened to her, no one would know. Or care. She shivered and walked faster.

Once in her room with the door locked, she stripped off her clothes and sat on the lumpy bed in her underwear. The air in the room was chilly and dank, so she turned out the light and climbed under the covers. But as tired as she was, she didn't feel sleepy. She felt lonely and miserable.

She lay on her back, staring up at the neon reflections on the ceiling. She wondered what they were doing at Harbor House. She'd wanted to get away from there in the worst way. The last thing she'd expected was to miss it.

It'd be fun to see Leslie again. Or Joni or even Lisa. They'd had their differences, but it had been almost like being in a real family. She wondered if anyone missed her.

They'd all be leaving Harbor House soon. She'd never see them again. Or M.C., or Mickey, or Connie.

She turned on her side, curling around the knot of misery in her stomach. She'd made her choice. When she'd left Harbor House, she'd hated them all. Particularly Mickey. Now she kept seeing her face. Mickey had been angry, for sure. Brandy thought she'd been angry at her about the joint, but maybe she hadn't been. After all, she'd said she believed her. Brandy kept forgetting that. Now it occurred to her for the first time that maybe Mickey had been angry *for* her.

She remembered the day Mickey and Connie had spoken up for her at school, the day the picture of Leslie had gotten torn. And how Mickey had always encouraged her in her artwork. She sat up in bed. What if she did go back? Would they let her in? Worth a try. Anything was better than this hellhole. Maybe she could convince Mickey that she'd follow the rules this time. And she would, dumb as they were. But she couldn't stand it here alone any longer, and Harbor House held the closest thing to friends she'd ever had.

With a physical shock, she remembered the money. Her hand went to her bra to touch it. She'd stolen it. That made her a thief. If the police wanted her, it wouldn't matter whether Mickey was willing to forgive her or not.

She sank onto the hard mattress. She couldn't go back. She couldn't go anywhere. She'd have to keep on living in this dingy room, try to hold this lousy job or another one just as bad. She'd really screwed up this time. If she had stayed at Harbor House, she would at least have had a decent place to live. The art contest didn't seem so important now. She bowed her head and let the waves of despair wash over her.

She remembered that Mickey had been the first to say that life wasn't fair, but she'd also told her, over and over again, that running away wasn't the answer, that you had to stick around and work things out. Brandy had always chosen to run away when things got rough. Now it looked as though she'd come to the end of the line. There was nowhere else to go.

She raised her head, trying to think through the fog of misery. If she went back and returned the money, maybe they could work something out with the police. If not, she'd just have to take her medicine. She would even apologize to Miss Cunningham. She'd never done anything like that before, but she guessed she was willing to give it a try. Besides, even if the old lady did talk like a schoolteacher, she'd been nice to her. She'd treated her like a real person instead of a punk.

Brandy reached into her bra for the money and counted it carefully. She hadn't spent much, and what she had, she could replace with what her boss had given her tonight. As soon as she'd gotten the job, she'd paid for her room and her food with her own earnings. She'd told herself she was saving the money for when she really needed it. Well, now she did. She needed to give it back. Maybe then she could go home.

She rose and, in the dim light from the single bulb suspended from the dingy ceiling, packed her few things into her backpack. First thing in the morning, she'd hitch a ride back to Houston.

She'd just crawled back into bed when the knock sounded. She nearly jumped through the ceiling. Whoever was on the other side of the door meant no good for her, that was for sure. She lay as still as she could, trying not to even breathe.

The knock came again, louder. She started to shake, and her breath began to rasp in her throat.

"Brandy?" It was a man's voice. "I know you're in there. Open the door."

The window. Could she reach it? She could try. Her room was on the second story, but maybe she could climb down some way or other.

She was poised to sprint for the window when it dawned on her that there was something familiar about the voice. She slipped from the bed and crept to the door, crouched like a wild animal for instant flight.

"Who is it?" Her whisper was hoarse with fear. She must be imagining things. The voice had almost sounded like...

"Cameron Scott."

Brandy's knees went so weak she almost couldn't get the door open.

CHAPTER SIXTEEN

WHEN THE FRONT DOORBELL rang, Mickey was in the kitchen. She'd slipped over to Harbor House early this Saturday morning to catch up on odds and ends, as much to keep her mind occupied as anything, and was pouring herself another cup of coffee. Three weeks, and still no word from Brandy. Or from Cameron. But how could she expect to hear from Cameron? she wanted to scream at herself. She'd told him effectively—and brutally—that she wanted no part of him or his world.

Reflecting that it was a strange hour for visitors, she set down the coffeepot and made her way to the front of the house.

To her amazement, she opened the door to Keith and Penny Rhodes. What in the world were they doing here? If she'd had to guess, she'd have thought that, after the trouble with Brandy, the Rhodeses wouldn't have darkened the door again.

"Hello." She shook hands. "Won't you come in?"

"Hello, Mickey," Keith Rhodes said. "Do you have a minute?"

"Of course." Mickey showed them into the living room. Maybe they were coming to complain about Brandy. Or Lisa. As they sat down, she stole a curious glance at them. They appeared a little nervous, maybe, but certainly not hostile.

"I'm sorry Lisa's not here," she said, fishing for information. "She went to play tennis with Leslie."

"We need to talk to you," Keith said. "I realize you're here a lot beyond your normal hours. Are we interrupting you?"

Mickey almost laughed. Lately she'd been here virtually every waking hour, mainly because her apartment seemed too lonely. "Not at all. I was revising meal schedules with the weekend manager, but we've just finished."

Penny and Keith exchanged a quick look. Almost, Mickey thought, as though they were telegraphing encouragement to each other. Mystified, she waited.

It was Penny who finally spoke. "It's about Lisa."

"Yes?" Here it came, whatever it was. Mickey braced herself.

Penny cleared her throat and twisted a sizable ring around and around on her finger. "It's our understanding that she doesn't really have any family."

"That's true." It wasn't what Mickey had expected. "Only distant kin, and they're not at all interested. No one's even bothered to keep up with her progress here."

"What's going to happen to her when she leaves here?" Keith asked, his dark eyes intent.

"I've begun preliminary paperwork to have her placed in a foster home, but that's not a permanent solution."

"No, it's not," Penny said. "Lisa needs a real home." There was something different about Penny, Mickey decided. The desperation she had sensed in her before seemed to have disappeared. Whatever demons had tormented her, she'd apparently laid them to rest.

"Of course Lisa needs a real home," Mickey said. "Unfortunately, girls who come to Harbor House don't often have that advantage."

"That's why we're here," Keith said.

Mickey held her breath, afraid even to move.

"Yes." Penny glanced at her husband. "We'd like to adopt her."

The magic words. The ones you always hoped to hear, but so seldom did. Mickey squelched the surge of joy that leaped inside her and reminded herself that it would be most unprofessional to cheer aloud. But she couldn't keep the smile from spreading all the way across her face. "That's wonderful," was all she could say. "Just wonderful."

"How do we go about it?" Keith asked.

Mickey made herself come back to earth. "There's a lot of red tape," she warned. "The adoption process is a tedious business and takes a lot of time and patience."

"I'm a lawyer."

"Shouldn't we ask Lisa how she feels about it?" The question came from Penny. "It's possible she won't want us."

Mickey looked into the other woman's eyes and saw the yearning in them. "You're right, of course," she said gently, "but I don't think you have a thing to worry about."

A few minutes later, Lisa came in, pink-cheeked and breathless from her tennis match. When she saw the Rhodeses, gladness warred with apprehension in her face. "Hi," she said hesitantly.

"Lisa," Mickey said. "Mr. and Mrs. Rhodes have something to ask you."

"Your time at Harbor House is almost up," Keith said. "We were wondering—" He stopped, looked at Penny. Yes, Mickey thought. It should come from her.

"—If you would like to make your home with us." Penny's words came so quietly it was a moment before Lisa absorbed them. Then her face paled and her eyes grew huge and black. For a moment she couldn't speak, just looked from Penny to Keith and back again.

When she found her voice, it was trembling. "For real?"

"For real," Penny said. "With all our hearts."

Lisa stood very still. Finally the words must have sunk in, because Mickey thought she'd never seen a face so transformed by joy. Lisa flew to Penny to hug her, then to Keith, then back to Penny. All three ended up in one happy, tearful heap, with Lisa in the middle. Lisa didn't say anything else for a while, probably because it was too difficult to talk around the grin that stretched from one ear to the other.

In the midst of the general happiness, Mickey sent up a small prayer of thanks.

THIS TIME it wasn't the doorbell, it was a knock.

It came at the back door, so softly Mickey almost didn't hear it. This was evidently going to be a day of interruptions. Just as well; she was having trouble concentrating. Besides, she could stand a few more interruptions like the last one. Laying down her pen, she went to the back door and opened it.

And found herself staring at Brandy Williford.

For a moment neither moved. "Brandy." Mickey thought she'd shouted it; it came out as a whisper. She fought back the tears that suddenly scalded her eyes. "Come in, please."

Brandy shifted awkwardly. "Is it okay? I mean—"

Mickey reached out and pulled her inside. "You don't have to ask."

From behind the doorjamb, another figure moved into Mickey's line of vision.

This time she couldn't say anything at all.

"Hello, Mickey." There were lines of fatigue around Cameron Scott's eyes and a day's stubble of beard on his face. His hair and his shirt actually looked a little rumpled. He looked wonderful.

"You brought her back," she said stupidly, unable to think of anything else to say.

"Yes," he said. "And no. I tracked her down last night, but by the time I found her, she was all packed and ready to leave for home. I just furnished the transportation."

"I'd already made up my mind to come back," Brandy added quickly. "I was going to hitch a ride this morning."

Mickey suppressed a shiver. "Where were you?"

"Dallas. I thought no one would find me there."

"We've had everyone looking for you, including M.C." She raised her eyes to Cameron's. "I didn't realize you were looking for her, too."

"I had to," he said simply. He half raised a hand, then dropped it. "You and Brandy have a lot to talk about. I'm going home for a shower. Then I've got some work to do. I've got some things to discuss with you, Mickey, but now's not the time." He turned. "Brandy." Briefly, he laid his hand on her shoulder. "I'm glad you're home."

"Thanks, Cameron."

"Yes, Cameron. Thanks." Mickey met his eyes. For the first time since she'd known him, they were unreadable.

With a curt nod, he turned and walked out the door.

No, she wanted to call after him. *Come back. I need you....* But she couldn't say it. She knew she'd ruined everything between them. Oh, he'd said he had things to discuss with her, but they were probably just details about Brandy.

With more strength than she'd known she possessed, she put him out of her mind. Brandy was home. She put an arm around the girl's shoulders. "Come in, honey."

Minutes later, they were sitting in the kitchen, Mickey with a cup of coffee, Brandy with a cola. A thousand questions hovered at Mickey's lips, but she knew better than to ask them. Brandy would volunteer the answers in her own good time—if ever. For now, the important thing was that she was home.

Brandy glanced over to the chair where Rooney was snoozing so soundly that he lay on his back, all four paws in the air. "Hello, Rooney," she said. "D'ja miss me?" The cat opened his one good eye, gave a cavernous yawn, then went back to sleep, still on his back, an errant fang hanging over his bottom lip.

"He's thrilled out of his gourd," Mickey said. "Can't you tell?"

"Yeah." For the first time, Brandy smiled. "How's M.C.?" The weary, too-wise expression left her eyes, and for a moment she was just a kid again, asking about a friend.

"Fine. He'll be a lot better when he knows you're home."

"How's Leslie? Is she still going with that dumb guy?"

Mickey smiled. "Still going strong."

"Joni?"

"As bad as ever."

"What about the new kids? Missy?" Brandy had always shown a special kindness to Missy.

"She's fine," Mickey said gently. "She's missed you. We've all missed you."

Brandy drained the last of her cola. "I guess I didn't know if you'd take me back or not."

Mickey smiled. "What did you think I'd do? Close the door in your face? Brandy..." She set her coffee on the table. "I told you when you first came here that we were here to help you. That hasn't changed."

"I'm in trouble." Brandy stared down at the ice in her glass. "I stole some money."

"I know. There are some problems that'll have to be worked out." *Like a major one with the law, for starters.* She sat back and looked at Brandy. Her clothes looked as if they had been slept in for several nights. She was pale, a little thinner, and there was a desperate look around her eyes. Mickey had seen it many times in the eyes of the kids from the streets. Physically, Brandy looked to be intact. Emotionally, it remained to be seen. "We'll just have to deal with them as they come," she said aloud.

"I wanted to get out of here," Brandy said. "I thought you and Connie had lied to me, telling me everything would be okay if I just went by the rules." She raised her eyes to Mickey's. "You said you believed me, about Kelly, and about the joint, I mean, but I guess I didn't think you really meant it."

"We meant it," Mickey said quietly. "By the way, Mrs. Lawrence called last week. One of Kelly's cronies, probably the one who pushed you at your locker, got mad at her and told on her. When they investigated, they found out all about her—the drug sales, everything."

"So they got her." A pleased smile curved Brandy's lips.

"Right. She's been expelled and you're in the clear."

Brandy digested the news a moment, as if a happy ending were more than she could comprehend. "At first I was glad I was out of here," she said slowly. "Then, when I got to Dallas, I couldn't find a decent job. The one I found wasn't so good." The hunted look flickered again in her eyes. "You and Connie always told me that running away didn't solve anything. You might not want me around anymore, but I came back anyway." The words had begun to spill rapidly from her lips. "If I get in trouble—" She shrugged. "That's the way it goes, I guess. I'll take what's coming to me." She reached inside her shirt and fished out a crumpled envelope. "I brought the money back. Best place to hide it," she confided.

"Miss Cunningham's money?" Mickey held her breath. This was better than she'd hoped for.

"Yeah. It's all here. I tore up the checks. I knew if I tried to cash them, they'd catch me for sure. I spent some of the cash at first, because I had to, but I worked until I made it up." She handed the envelope to Mickey.

"Keep it, Brandy," she said gently. "We'll go talk to Miss Cunningham in a few minutes, and you can give it back to her yourself."

Brandy nodded. "Mickey?" Slowly, she stood.

"Yes?"

"It was wrong of me to take the money from the old lady. From Miss Cunningham. I kept seeing her, sitting there, showing me the pictures...." Her eyes filled.

Mickey let out her breath on a long sigh. She didn't remember getting to her feet, but suddenly Brandy was in her arms, her head tight against her shoulder. Her own tears streamed down her cheeks in the wake of the gratitude that flooded her. In her business, major breakthroughs were as scarce as a butterfly's tears.

She held Brandy as the first sobs began to rack the girl's body.

"Miss Cunningham, I'm sorry I took the money," Brandy mumbled, staring at the Aubusson rug beneath her chair.

"As well you should be, young lady," Miss Cunningham said sternly. "It was wrong of you to steal it, then to run away like that. You hurt many people who believed in you."

"Yes, ma'am," Brandy said miserably.

"I trust you've learned your lesson. Now you'll simply have to take the consequences."

"Yes, ma'am." Brandy ducked her head lower and lower.

Mickey held her tongue in check. Miss Cunningham had every right to be angry. Anger often served as a camouflage for pain, and Cameron had said she, too, had been hurt by

Brandy's betrayal. *Cameron*... She wouldn't think about him. Not now.

"Here's the money," Brandy blurted. She held out the battered envelope. "Two-nineteen thirty-seven," she added conscientiously.

Miss Cunningham sat very still. "I beg your pardon?"

"The money." Brandy got up and carefully laid the envelope on Miss Cunningham's lap. "I brought it back to you."

If Miss Cunningham had been anyone else, her mouth would have dropped open. As it was, her face held a look of surprise that would have been comical to Mickey if her own throat hadn't been so tight with unshed tears.

"My dear child—" Miss Cunningham stopped in midsentence, and Mickey could see the glint of tears in the old eyes.

"Mickey always told me it was wrong to run away," Brandy said. "She said that if I'd stay and face things, everything would turn out all right. Well, I ran away, but I'm back now, and I'll make it up to everybody the best way I can."

Miss Cunningham's rare smile dawned. "My dear, I believe you've just done that very thing."

THAT AFTERNOON, M.C. stopped Mickey in Harbor House's hallway. "How'd it go?"

"Great. Brandy gave the money back and Miss Cunningham is going to drop the charges against her. She even gave her an art book, to start her own library."

"Monet, by chance?"

"As a matter of fact, it was. How did you know?"

"Just a lucky guess." He looked pleased with himself. "I saw Brandy. It's great to have her back."

Mickey smiled. "A miracle, you mean."

"No question about it." He sobered. "Young Scott worked a miracle for all of us. I'm grateful to him."

"So am I." She tried to keep everything but the gratitude out of her voice.

"Ah, Mickey?"

Something in his tone made her eyes sharpen. "What's up?"

"Oh, nothing." She eyed him suspiciously. His expression was at its blandest. "I was just thinking that I hadn't seen him around lately."

"He brought Brandy home this morning," she said, stalling.

"That's not what I mean and you know it."

"He's had no reason to come around."

"Just what I was thinking," he said promptly.

"What do you mean by that?"

"Don't snap my nose off." With a grin, he ran his fingers through his shock of white hair. "I thought you and he might have had something going, that's all."

"No. We...enjoyed each other's company for a while. Nothing else." She wondered if she were going to be struck down on the spot for such a whopper.

"I see." He shrugged. "Frankly, it didn't seem to be such a bad idea."

She looked down at the sheaf of papers in her hands to keep him from seeing what was in her eyes. "He's a nice guy. He's just not our kind."

"Not our kind?"

"No," she snapped, losing patience in spite of herself. "I've already been through all that with Connie."

"With Connie?" M.C.'s expression didn't change, but she could sense his concentration sharpening. *Careful, Mickey,* she cautioned herself. M.C. had never needed two and two to come up with four.

"I'm not going to go through it again." Her look dared him to say anything else.

"Okay, okay." He put up his hands. "Just curious, that's all."

"Fine. Remember, there's nothing to be curious about." She eyed him sternly a moment more, to make sure he got the message. Then she turned to go to her office.

But not before she saw the glint, shining far back in the depths of the jay-blue eyes.

CAMERON POPPED an ice-cold beer. When he finished it off, he promised himself, he was going straight to bed. In the past thirty-six hours he hadn't closed his eyes. The drive home from Dallas had been interminable, and he'd had to fight sleep the whole way.

Tomorrow, when he had his head on straight again, he was going to tackle the problem of Mickey Mulvaney. Seeing her again a few hours ago had only confirmed what he'd known already. Quite simply, he loved her too much to let her go.

He cursed when the doorbell rang. He didn't feel like talking to anybody, especially a door-to-door salesman. Reluctantly he set down the beer, went to the front door and opened it.

"Hello, son." M.C. Mulvaney stood on his front porch, looking as if he dropped by every afternoon.

Cameron stared. If M.C. had been the devil himself, he couldn't have been more surprised. *What the hell are you doing here,* he almost said, then stopped himself in time. "Come in, M.C.," he said finally, realizing he still sounded ungracious. But he wasn't glad to see him. Not one damn bit.

"Thanks," M.C. said promptly, stepping inside.

"Beer?" Cameron asked when they reached the den.

"No, thanks." M.C. waved a hand. "Never touch the stuff." He took a leather wing chair adjoining the sofa. "I know, I know." He grinned his pirate's grin. "The question you're dying to ask is, 'What the hell are you doing here?' "

His words hit the nail so precisely on the head that Cameron burst out laughing. "Okay, M.C.," he said when he was able, "I give up. What the hell *are* you doing here?"

The Cheshire-cat grin widened. "I'm so glad you asked."

"I have the feeling you were going to tell me anyway."

"Right," M.C. said without a blush. "First, I want to thank you for finding Brandy. I couldn't have done better myself." He waved a hand. "I had a few leads, of course. I would've found her eventually. But you beat me to the punch. Good job."

"Thanks." Reluctantly, Cameron smiled. He had to admire the sheer brass of the man. Besides, in the last words, he'd heard real gratitude. "Incidentally," he unbent enough to say, "you might like to know that I told my investors that, as far as I'm concerned, Harbor House is staying in Village Walk. I also told them to get off my back—and Mickey's." He smiled reminiscently. "They took it surprisingly well."

M.C. chuckled. "They should've, considering they need you for the project. That's good news, Cameron. Give 'em hell."

"I figure that now that Brandy's back, they'll settle down, and you and I can handle any neighborhood PR problems," Cameron added.

"No question about it. Now, about Mickey," he said without the slightest check.

The name sizzled in the air between them. Caught flat-footed, Cameron stiffened. He didn't want to discuss Mickey with anyone, especially her father.

M.C. caught the movement and fixed him with a knowing gaze. "You don't like me one little bit, son, and I think
I know why. It's time we had a talk." His eyes cooled then,
lending them a rare sternness. "First, I'll tell you to your
face that you have no right to sit in judgment on me or on a
situation you know nothing about."

Cameron felt the anger kindle inside him again. Holding
his temper, he met M.C.'s gaze squarely. "That may be true,
but it's obvious that somewhere along the way, Mickey got
some rough treatment. I'm not saying it came from you,
because she's too fond of you. But it happened, and from
what I can gather, you weren't around to prevent it."

He saw a shadow of pain flicker across M.C.'s face, but
the austere expression didn't relax. "You've got it. Be glad
you don't have to look in the mirror every morning at a man
who deserted his child." He jabbed a thumb into his own
chest. "Every day I have to live with the fact that if I'd been
around, I could have stopped it." In his voice was a bitter
sadness.

Cameron's anger faded as, with a shock, he saw that there
were tears in the older man's eyes. "What happened?" he
heard himself ask.

M.C. drew a long breath. "You need to know."

He told him. All of it. The whole sad, ugly story, with all
its sordid details. Cameron sat rooted to his chair in rapidly
growing horror. What he'd suspected was nothing compared to the truth. He thought his heart would break for
Mickey. *Mickey, his love* . . .

"I've had a hard time forgiving myself," M.C. finished.
"But as you may have noticed, I'm trying to make her life
easier. It's the least I can do. Now." His face cleared, and he
sat forward. "You're in love with my daughter, right?"

"I . . . yes." He was too stunned to lie.

"Thought so. Do you want to marry her?"

Cameron gestured helplessly. Ordinarily he'd have told anyone asking questions like these to go to hell. "Of course I do," he snapped, "but she turned me down flat."

M.C. leaned forward even farther. "Now, let me tell you something, son," he said conspiratorially. "She loves you. She may think she's mad at you, but the real reason she won't marry you is that, deep down, she thinks she's not good enough for you."

"What?" Cameron exploded. He stared at M.C. "That's the most ridiculous thing I've ever heard." But in his mind, he heard her words again. *Go back to your own world. We're not your kind.* At the time, he hadn't understood what she'd been talking about. Now...

"Sure it's ridiculous," M.C. said, "but deep down she believes it. I'm no psychologist, but I'd say it's because of what she went through as a kid."

Cameron sat back in his chair. "I had no idea." He shook his head. "None at all."

"Of course you didn't. She couldn't very well tell you what she hardly knew herself. That's why *I* told you," M.C. added magnanimously. "The important thing is, what are you going to do about it?"

Tiredly, Cameron massaged his jaw. "I haven't figured that one out yet."

"Let me give you some tips, son," M.C. said. "If you approach her just right..."

MICKEY GLANCED at the clock on the table. It was late and she was tired. But Brandy was back; that was all that counted.

She looked in the refrigerator. There wasn't a thing to eat in the whole apartment. She would just run down to the fast-food place and grab a cheeseburger. Then she would come home, go to bed and face tomorrow when it got here.

She picked up her pocketbook. "Be right back," she told Rooney, who had settled on the living room sofa for a nap. She opened the door of her apartment, and stepped out.

And collided, hard, with Cameron Scott.

He'd had his hand raised to ring the doorbell. Instead, he used it to steady her. She needed it. She was reeling from the impact and from shock. She could do nothing but stare at him.

"What are you doing here?" she finally managed. His jaw was set and his feet were planted rock-solid, and it looked as though it would take a bulldozer to move him. Or a Sherman tank.

"I need to talk to you, Mickey." There was an expression in his clear gray eyes that set her heart drumming in a hard, steady cadence against her ribs.

"It's late." She tore her gaze away from his face and glanced pointedly at her watch. Suddenly she was afraid, whether of him or of herself, she didn't know. What she did know was that talking to him could be very dangerous. "Tomorrow, maybe?"

"Now," he said. "Please."

When he put it that way...

Wordlessly, she stepped back and let him in.

He reached behind him and shut the door, thinking that she looked dead on her feet. Beneath her eyes were violet shadows and she was pale with fatigue. She looked thinner, too. He couldn't get enough of looking at her. He fought the urge to take her into his arms on the spot.

"I have to thank you for finding Brandy," she said, not quite meeting his eyes. "There's no telling what would've happened to her if you hadn't found her so quickly."

"That occurred to me, too," he said. *And had haunted his dreams.*

"How did you find her?"

"A wild guess, a good private eye and a hell of a lot of luck." Luck? he thought to himself. More like a miracle. He still wasn't sure how it had happened. "I figured she'd go to another big city, because it's easier to disappear there. To begin with, I hired investigators in San Antonio and Dallas. As it turned out, she was in Dallas, but it could just as well have been San Antonio. Or Austin or a dozen other cities."

"You hired a private investigator?"

"Yep. I knew I didn't have the expertise to find her on my own. The investigator in Dallas was my biggest stroke of luck. A smart guy." He smiled faintly. "By the way, I wasn't the only one looking for Brandy. My man ran into another investigator right off the bat."

"Another..."

"And guess who hired him."

M.C.? she thought dazedly. Of course not. He couldn't afford it any more than she could. A board member? "I have no idea," she said.

"Jessamine Cunningham."

"You've got to be kidding." Finally, Mickey managed to close her mouth. It seemed that Miss Cunningham had cared more than they'd known.

"Nope. My PI just happened to find Brandy first. Anyway, I'd told him she could paint, and on a wild hunch, he checked out a strip joint that used body paints on their strippers." He grimaced. "Brandy was there, painting pictures on the girls."

Mickey closed her eyes. "Oh, God."

"He followed her to her apartment," he went on, "then notified me. I found her there. You know the rest. I'd have kept looking for her, Mickey," he added. "As long as it took."

The look in her eyes told him she believed him. "I don't know how to thank you," she said again, lamely.

"For starters, you can listen to me." He rubbed his eyes, tried to focus his mind. He couldn't afford to bungle this one. "A week ago, I informed the other investors in the Village Walk project that, as far as I'm concerned, Harbor House stays here in West Village where it belongs, and that from now on, I'll be actively supporting it."

For a moment she said nothing, just kept her eyes on his face. "Why?"

"Because what you do here is so damned important. More so than neighborhoods or business deals or anything else you'd care to name. I never realized it before you showed me. I had a classic case of tunnel vision, I guess." He spread his hands, palms up. "Anyway, I thought you'd want to know."

He'd done it for the right reasons. Mickey breathed a silent prayer of thanks. "I'm glad," she said simply.

He gave her a mocking little bow. "Now. I owe you an apology."

She stared at him. "What in the world for?"

"For the other night."

To hide her expression, she turned to set her pocketbook on the table. "No." Under control again, she straightened and shook her head. "You don't owe me anything."

Something flared in his eyes. "Dammit, Mickey, it's not a question of owing you. There's something I need to say."

"Fair enough." She waited, afraid of herself.

He hesitated, groping for the right words. "I said everything wrong." He stopped, started again. "I said what I meant, but I didn't express myself very well."

Her hopes sank along with her heart. For a second, she'd thought… "What you said the other night just proved how different we are," she said. "I don't understand you. You

don't understand me." She gave a hopeless little shrug.
"Thanks for the apology."

His control went. "You don't understand a damned
thing," he snapped. "Do you remember what else I said?"

Did she remember? She wanted to laugh, but felt more
like crying. He'd said he loved her. She'd only replayed it in
her heart a thousand times.

"You're going to listen to me, and for a change, you're
going to understand what I'm saying," he said through his
teeth. "We have something priceless between us. If you'll
think about it for at least half a second, you'll know it as
well as I do."

She wanted to believe it. God, how she wanted to.
"Cameron," she said, trying to hang on to her own resolve, "you need someone who'll—" She stopped. She'd
been about to sell herself short again. She had a sudden
mental image of Connie, waggling a finger and saying,
"Tsk, tsk." She suppressed an insane desire to giggle.

"Someone who'll what?" His voice was getting louder.

"Someone who'll go with you to benefits and make
cocktail conversation," she said, trying not to think about
how ridiculous the words sounded. "Someone who'll im-
press your clients."

His expletive was short and harsh. "I was married to
someone like that. Cathy was good at impressing clients.
After she left me she married a millionaire, and she's probably impressing *his* clients now." He flung up a hand. "I
hope she's enjoying it." He was almost shouting now.
"That's not for me. Not since I met you, anyway."

He stopped, and they both stood staring at each other,
listening to the echoes of his words die into silence.
"Mickey, you're the only woman on the face of this earth I
want. You do more good than anyone I've ever met. You'll

never stop surprising me. And I'll never stop loving you. That's the one thing I got right the other night."

The cotton candy again . . . It had always tempted her so. No, she told herself, this wasn't cotton candy. She'd always known Cameron Scott's substance, his durability, his worth. She'd simply believed she didn't deserve him. *It's who you are now that's important,* Connie had said. *Are you telling me you don't really believe it?*

To keep her hopes from soaring too high, she tried once more. "You don't know me, Cameron. You don't know what my life has been like. I've racked up a lot of mileage, and you haven't been along for the ride."

"It doesn't matter," he said quickly.

"I need to tell you," she said. "I didn't exactly have a perfect childhood. Things happened to me that...left scars. I was abused, Cameron. In a lot of ways..." While she was holding his gaze, could watch his eyes change, she made herself tell him directly. And found in the telling that, quite simply, the pain was gone. In illuminating that last dark corner, it seemed she'd finally swept it clean. Maybe, after all, Connie had been right. Maybe there was a chance. . . .

His face came back into focus. His eyes hadn't changed, except to mirror his own pain.

"Mickey, listen to me and believe me." He spoke quietly, steadily. "I know all I need to know about you." He paused. "Everything."

She gave him the ghost of a grin. "I'm a terrible cook."

"We'll eat out every night."

"I'm a slob." Her grin grew. "And I bite my nails."

His voice was rising again. "Dammit, I'll hire a house-keeper, and you can chew your nails off for all I care."

"Rooney?"

He sighed. "You drive a hard bargain." He shot a malevolent glance at the snoring cat. "I'll take him."

She sobered. "My work . . . ?"

"Is as important to me as it is to you," he finished for her. "I blew things so badly the other night. All I could think of was to keep you from hurting. I still want to do that, but I can't do it by denying what you are, any more than you can deny what I am. Mickey, if I can't ease the hurt, I'd like to share it. I'd like to be there for the good times, too. Knowing you and the kids at Harbor House has taught me more in six months than I've learned in the rest of my life put together."

All she could do was look at him. She was so damned tempted. . . .

He caught her shoulders. "In your own immortal words, Mickey, read my lips." He spoke slowly and deliberately, as if to the village idiot. "I love you. Are you going to tell me you don't love me?"

She was silent. She couldn't lie to him, not with those gray eyes boring into her.

"Mickey?" He slid his hands down to take hers, and his grip tightened until it was a sweet pain.

"I love you." Her words came out in a rusty whisper.

She heard them with wonder. Funny, she'd never imagined she'd be saying them to anyone, and in the past few days she'd said them to the two most important people in her life.

High time, she decided, and walked into Cameron's arms.

EPILOGUE

THE SUPERINTENDENT'S VOICE sounded tinny over the loudspeaker. "Our last award tonight is the Helen Woodward Bell Art Scholarship, for achievement in the visual arts. And the winner is—" he paused dramatically "—Brandy Williford."

M.C. clapped, whistled and cheered as the auditorium full of graduating seniors and their assorted families and friends erupted into applause. The award furnished a full scholarship to a first-class art school. If Brandy succeeded, she could write her own ticket.

Brandy, looking suddenly grown-up in her cap and gown but awkward as always at being the center of attention, rose from the ordered rows of graduates and grinned sheepishly as she made her way to the stage.

She'd come so far in the past year, M.C. reflected, since she'd come back home, home to Harbor House and the people who could help her. The people who loved her. Young Scott had beaten him to the draw on that one. A bright young man, he admitted. He'd give him that.

He stole a glance down the row. Scott was there, of course, with Mickey. They wouldn't have missed this night on a bet. They were so happy together it did the old ticker good to see them. After almost a year of marriage, they were still so goofy about each other that it almost made you sick. Good thing he'd taken a hand in getting them together. Otherwise they both might still be wandering around miserable and not having the sense to do anything about it. He was hoping that someday soon they'd decide to make him a grandfather, before he was too old to enjoy his grandchildren. His hints were getting broader and broader, but no luck yet. He wished they'd get on the ball.

Not that he was getting old, of course. Far from it. He straightened his tie and ran a hand over his shock of white hair. He was still a young man.

Miss Cunningham was there, too, sitting beside Brandy, as straight-backed as ever but applauding as hard as anyone. Another one of his accomplishments. If he hadn't paved the way, she'd probably still be fighting Harbor House. She'd really taken Brandy under her wing, had provided her with much of the direction the girl had needed. On Brandy's other side sat her mother, a faded, shy little woman who never had much to say. After Brandy had left Harbor House she'd moved in with her, and they seemed to be dealing pretty well together. The most important thing was that Brandy seemed to have taken charge of her own life. Which was all they could hope for with any of the girls.

He looked down the row. At Missy, determined to be present at her idol's graduation. Brandy had been responsible for much of Missy's progress. At Joni, Leslie. They'd been gone from Harbor House for a while now, but both were doing fine. Rachel, Mona, Tammy. They'd moved on, too, but the bonds remained strong, which was lucky, because they didn't always.

He glanced over his shoulder at the row behind them, where Lisa was sitting with Keith and Penny Rhodes, happy as a clam at high tide. The adoption was due to go through soon, they'd told him. It was amazing what a little TLC could do.

As the school orchestra swung into the measured, familiar strains of "Pomp and Circumstance," M.C. sat back

with a sigh of satisfaction. Lucky he'd been around to fa-
cilitate things. Of course, Mickey, Cameron, Miss Cunningham, were all smart folks. They might have done just
as well without him.

But he doubted it.

HARLEQUIN SUPERROMANCE®

HARLEQUIN SUPERROMANCE NOVELS WANTS TO INTRODUCE YOU TO A DARING NEW CONCEPT IN ROMANCE...

WOMEN WHO DARE!
Bright, bold, beautiful...
Brave and caring, strong and passionate...
They're unique women who know their
own minds and will dare anything...
for love!

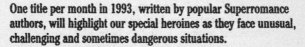

One title per month in 1993, written by popular Superromance authors, will highlight our special heroines as they face unusual, challenging and sometimes dangerous situations.

Discover why our hero is camera-shy next month with:
#545 SNAP JUDGEMENT by Sandra Canfield
Available in April wherever Harlequin Superromance
novels are sold.

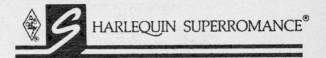

COMING NEXT MONTH

#542 WORTH THE WAIT • Risa Kirk
Jack Stanton's dream was to buy the Gallagher family ranch and make
Margaret Gallagher his wife. But Margaret had her own plans . . . and
they didn't include Jack or a life on a Kentucky horse farm. She
belonged in New York. So why was she having such difficulty leaving
the farm?

#543 BUILT TO LAST • Leigh Roberts
Mary Ellen Saunderson had put her romance with Ramsey MacIver
behind her until her eccentric aunt decided it was time for them to
rekindle the flame. What Aunt Alma didn't realize was that her
scheme had put her niece's life in danger. Ramsey had enemies who
would stop at nothing to harm him—even if it meant hurting
Mary Ellen.

#544 JOE'S MIRACLE • Helen Conrad
Though Carly Stevens had just returned home to California to take a
breather and make some decisions, for Joe Matthews, Carly's arrival
was a miracle. His kids were crazy about her, and so was he. But then
she began asking questions about her family's past, and Joe knew he
had to keep her from learning the truth . . . for all their sakes.

#545 SNAP JUDGEMENT • Sandra Canfield
Women Who Dare, Book 4
There was no way Kelly Cooper was going to be a willing hostage.
Will Stone would rue the day he had broken into her apartment to
enlist her aid in clearing his name. He said she owed him—her
photograph had implicated him. Deep down Kelly was sure Will was
innocent, so maybe she'd help him. But not before she taught him
some manners.

AVAILABLE NOW:

#538 HALFWAY HOME
Marie Beaumont

#540 FOR THE LOVE OF IVY
Barbara Kaye

#539 REMEMBER WHEN
Anne Laurence

#541 CRADLE OF DREAMS
Janice Kaiser

Where do you find hot Texas nights, smooth Texas charm and dangerously sexy cowboys?

COWBOYS AND CABERNET

Raise a glass—Texas style!

Tyler McKinney is out to prove a Texas ranch is the perfect place for a vineyard. Vintner Ruth Holden thinks Tyler is too stubborn, too impatient, too...Texas. And far too difficult to resist!

CRYSTAL CREEK reverberates with the exciting rhythm of Texas. Each story features the rugged individuals who live and love in the Lone Star State. And each one ends with the same invitation...

Y'ALL COME BACK...REAL SOON!

Don't miss *COWBOYS AND CABERNET* by Margot Dalton. Available in April wherever Harlequin books are sold.
